WATERMARK

ALSO BY THIS AUTHOR

Even if Your Heart Would Listen:
Losing My Daughter to Heroin

WATERMARK

The Broken Bell Series

ELISE SCHILLER

Published by SparkPress, a BookSparks imprint,
A division of SparkPoint Studio, LLC
Phoenix, Arizona, USA, 85007
www.gosparkpress.com

Published 2020
Printed in the United States of America
ISBN: 978-1-68463-036-3 (pbk)
ISBN: 978-1-68463-037-0 (e-bk)

Library of Congress Control Number: 2019917776

Book design by Stacey Aaronson

To the FISH Writing Group
With tremendous gratitude

PART ONE

chapter one

———

JEANNINE

Nannie Lou said it was normal to cry at weddings. In 1987, when Pic married Frank, the tears fell for months and flowed into years.

When the judge said Pic could have us back, and Angel and I would move with her and Frank and leave Nannie Lou's, Pic cried.

So did Angel, but as usual, she steadied herself quickly. She cornered Frank one afternoon just before the wedding and said, "Why do you want us to live with you? We like it here."

Frank was shocked, then furious, stammering under the icy gaze of a thirteen-year-old. "I don't care where you live," he said. "It's what your mother wants."

"Yeah, today," Angel said. "Get one thing straight. You might be marrying my mother, but you'll never be my father. Never."

"Who'd want to be your fucking father?" he whispered. "Trust me, if there was any way to leave you here, I fucking would."

That was about as good as it got between Frank and Angel. What followed were years of distrust, simmering hatred, and tears.

Early in the hot August mornings, Nannie Lou cried at the kitchen table as she talked to Pop.

"I'm attached to them now. Besides, I don't trust her with them, especially with this new baby coming. I don't know if she can take care of them and a baby. Ain't that a terrible thing to say about your own daughter?" she whimpered.

"Lou, we always knew this day might come," Pop said. "It's what we said we wanted. She's cured. She can take care of her own kids. That's the right way."

During the last days of the summer, I sat on the rug in the hallway outside my room while Uncle Jimmy and Angel talked and Angel cried and cried.

"I'll see you all the time," Uncle Jimmy said.

Angel had been sobbing so hard she had to take deep breaths in between words.

"You won't come over, not with Pic there," she said, and started crying again.

"I'll see you at swimming," he said. "I'll come and watch you practice. I'll come to your meets. You can come here. We can go places. Come here, Angel, come here. Please, stop crying."

And then, on another day, "You'll go to college and forget all about me," Angel wailed. "You'll probably marry stupid Franny instead of me."

"Forget Franny. You know I never see her anymore. Anyway, what are you talking about, marry! I'm seventeen and you're thirteen, for Christ's sake. And uncles can't marry nieces. I think it's against the law."

Anger and frustration seeped into Angel's voice. "That's so stupid. Who would make up a law like that!"

"But Angel, you know this is crazy anyway. My mother

would kill me if she knew about us. If Pop didn't kill me first."

Angel sniffed. "Just at first."

Uncle Jimmy sighed. "No, they'd never accept it."

Angel's voice grew calmer. "Yes they would, Jim. People can get used to anything, until it seems normal."

I expected Pic's wedding to be like the weddings I saw on television. But it wasn't. Pic got married by a judge in a hotel restaurant. She was wearing a short, hot pink dress and Frank didn't even have on a tie. We all sat in folding chairs—Nannie Lou and Pop, Aunt Christine and Uncle Tony, Uncle Jimmy, Albert, Angel, and me. A few ladies from Pic's rehab program were there, and so was Frank's mother. She cried.

Before school started, we were going to move into the new house Pic and Frank had rented in some neighborhood called Kensington. Angel and I were going to new schools again, and Angel was going to be repeating seventh grade.

The day before the move, Angel told me to start packing. Nannie Lou had bought us huge black duffel bags and Pop gave us boxes. I had a lot more stuff than when I arrived. Even with my clothes folded neatly I had to squeeze to get them all into the duffel bag.

I looked at all the things on our dresser and on our bookshelf and wondered what I could take. I decided to go through all the books I had read and put aside the ones I wanted so I could ask Nannie Lou about them. I wound up my snow globe and, listening to the skating song, I started to pick out my books.

Pop stood at the door, looking in. He came and sat on the bed.

"Ah, Sprite," he said.

He was wearing his Saturday clothes: old jeans and the T-shirt he wore to do chores. He bent his head into his hand so all I could see was his thinning gray hair.

I felt dizzy, and the edges of the room seemed to get dark.

I thought about all the pictures in the house that I'd been dusting all these months.

I thought about the cool basement and the smell of the laundry and the damp steam from the ironing.

I thought about waking up early in the morning in the new house, no Pop there.

My eyes filled up and spilled over.

chapter two

———

ALEX

I t was right after Christmas vacation of our senior year that we couldn't find Angel. We just didn't realize it for a few days.

Late on New Year's Day it began snowing and snowed over a foot, so our vacation lasted an extra day—happiness! On Tuesday the streets were so bad, you'd think our coach, CJ, would have closed the pool, but no, even though there was no school and the streets were still a mess. So we went back to practice with less than forty-eight hours of rest after swimming 100,000 yards in eight days and staying up late at a New Year's party. I was amazed that most people from the team made it—everybody, actually, except Angel and one lazy guy.

Until practice on Tuesday, I hadn't talked to anyone from the team since the party on Sunday night. I called Angel's house when I woke up on Monday but there was no answer. I was so tired that I wanted to sleep all day, but my mother made me get up and go to my grandmother's house before the snowstorm got bad to eat this lentil soup that's supposed to give you good luck for the coming year.

I ate a lot of soup because I wanted a lot of luck. I was

swimming flat. I was a second away from Junior National cuts in three or four events, but I hadn't made any drops in over a year. And this was it for those of us in the class of '93 who hadn't already signed with a school—it was recruiting time, and how we seniors swam in the next few months was going to have a lot to do with where we went to college.

So I ate those lentils.

Hell week was intense. I guess because we had done so well the summer before, we all had the sense that we had a big chance to prove something at the championships in April. We knew we had to get our yardage in over Christmas. So we trained three hours in the morning and three hours in the afternoon.

We weren't just building our endurance, we were building our teamwork. We helped each other out when it got really hard and it hurt. We made each other stay focused.

In between the morning and afternoon sessions we ate a meal that the parents provided, usually a lot of pasta and meat. Then we curled up in sleeping bags on the gym floor and slept. CJ made sure the boys were way down at one end and the girls way up on the other end.

I always slept in between Angel and Melanie, my two best friends. Angel fell asleep within thirty seconds of lying down. She usually slept on her side, face toward me, one arm up over her head in an arc, her sleeping bag only pulled up to her waist. The windows in the building were high above, where the walls met the ceiling, and covered with rusted grating to protect against stray basketballs from the inside and stray projectiles from the outside. The grey winter light turned the scar on Angel's cheek into strings of pearls.

Mel slept snuggled deep in her sleeping bag, so only the bun on the back of her head showed. Swimming all the time, we had learned to give up fussing with our hair. Angel kept hers short and spiky. Mel's hair was thick and kinky, so she just greased it and pulled it into a knot. It suited her, though. She had beautiful, high cheekbones, and the way she pulled her sleek hair away from her face made her look elegant.

My hair, meanwhile, was a swarm of light brown ringlets. When I started swimming, I struggled to get it all in a cap, so Mel decided one day that I should cut the back like a boy and keep the rest of it long. I thought it would be weird but I let her do it anyway, and it worked out pretty well: without the heavy mass in the back I could get the rest into my cap, and it actually looked good, too— people commented on it a lot.

Unlike Mel and Angel, it usually took me a while to get to sleep, and then I woke up tired before we even got back into the water. I guess it doesn't sound like any way to spend Christmas vacation, but it was one of the best weeks of my life.

Even in the past three years of college swimming, I've never felt like that.

Anyway, even though Angel and I would usually talk every day, on New Year's Day I didn't talk to her. When we got home from my grandmother's, I went straight to bed.

ON Tuesday when I got to the pool, Angel wasn't there. CJ came up and asked me where she was. He was pissed.

"Snow wouldn't stop her from seeing one of those knucklehead boyfriends she's got! Just because she made it every day last week, she thinks she can blow today off," he muttered, kicking the bleachers. "She must think she's some stud." And so on, banging the deck with the golf club he always carried around.

Angel's training habits were an ongoing sore point. It was actually a small miracle that Angel had made every practice during vacation, so I thought CJ should be pretty happy, but I wasn't about to say so.

I called Angel's house when I got home. Her mother wasn't too friendly, like always. *She's not here.* Click.

Like everyone else, Angel called her mother "Pic." When I first met Angel, when we were about twelve, I thought it must be some abbreviation of "ice pick"—like, "This woman has a personality like an ice pick." But no, it was a childhood nickname taken from her maiden name, Piccola. At first, I thought she was Angel's older sister from hell instead of her mother; no wonder, since she was only twenty-eight! My mother was forty-one!

After a while, I got used to her.

SCHOOL was open on Wednesday, but Angel wasn't there. No surprise. Angel cut school a lot, and after the party and all that swimming, and then the snow, I didn't really expect her to be there. On New Year's Eve, she'd danced for three hours straight after we'd swum to exhaustion all week, and then left the party for her own private party with Jamal.

On Tuesdays, Thursdays, and Fridays, the days we had morning practice, I drove to practice at 4:30 a.m. and my mother took the bus to school, but on Mondays and Wednesdays, we drove to school together. Actually, it sucked, because even on those days I couldn't sleep late because my mother always had something to do in her classroom.

That particular Wednesday, it was barely light when we left the house, and it was freezing. It had been a very cold winter so far. There had been freezing rain on Thanksgiving. Then it had snowed a lot just a few days before Christmas, and the snow hadn't melted much because it was so cold. And then we'd had the big storm on New Year's Day. I huddled up under the blanket my mom always kept in the car and watched the icy patterns on the window melt away.

We got to school an hour before homeroom. My mother went to her classroom and I went to the nurse's office and slept on the examining table until the bell for homeroom, when the nurse woke me up. Her name was Mrs. Spencer, which is what I had to call her inside school; outside, I called her Miss Lorraine. She and my mother were friends, so she didn't care if she came in and found me asleep there. She understood about the swimming. Besides, even then I knew I wanted to be a nurse, and I talked to her about it all the time, so she liked me.

I'd meant to go to Angel's homeroom before the bell, but I overslept. Our homerooms were far apart, since they did it alphabetically (her last name was Ferente, and mine was Williamson).

Alexandra Williamson. Not one announcer at one meet ever managed to say it right, because my name was so long that it didn't fit on to the entry forms and they ended up calling me Williams. Then CJ started called me Williams, after Esther Williams, some famous swimmer who was in the movies or something.

"Yo! Williams!" he'd say every day when I walked on deck.

And that's not even the whole thing. My mother gave me her maiden name for my middle name, making me Alexandra Wyremski Williamson.

At short recess, instead of getting a bagel like I usually did, I went looking for Angel, but I couldn't find her. I went to my mom's classroom and checked the absence list, and she was on it.

"What's the matter?" my mother asked me.

I told her, no Angel. A day out of school, okay, that happened with Angel. No practice the day before. Okay, that happened with Angel. But no phone call for three days, not since the New Year's Eve party? That was strange.

My mother called the office and had them track down Jamal, Angel's boyfriend. Well, Angel's sometimes boyfriend. They had been going out the previous summer, but then she'd started hanging out with her neighbor, this guy Ramon, but then during hell week she and Jamal had started it up again.

Jamal came slinking into my mother's room. He always wore such big clothes you couldn't tell what his body was like, but when you happened to put your hand on his arm, it felt like you were touching a cinder block. He was our fastest sprinter; in fact, he was one of the fastest 50 freestylers in high school in the country. He had signed early with Georgia.

He knew right away what we wanted. He was confused, too. "I been calling her," he said. "Her mother keeps answering."

That meant Jamal kept hanging up. Angel's mother did not like Angel's boyfriends.

My mother decided we would get Miss Lorraine to call. We went to her office and she put on the speakerphone.

"Mrs. Ferente . . ."

First mistake. Angel's mother wasn't ever married to Angel's father, and now she was married to someone else, and her name was Mrs. O'Neill, but Miss Lorraine didn't know that. Angel's mother didn't correct her, anyway.

"We're concerned because Angel isn't in school today."

"So she's out a day," Angel's mother said. "Don't other kids miss school?"

Miss Lorraine was gesturing wildly at my mother, trying to figure out what to say.

"She's missed a lot of time . . ." my mother mouthed to Miss Lorraine, who repeated it to Angel's mother.

"Angel's almost nineteen and she likes to think she can do whatever she wants." And she hung up.

Angel wasn't *almost* nineteen. She wasn't going to be nineteen until July, July 22 to be exact, the feast day of Mary Magdalene. Mary Angela Ferente. She was old to be a senior because she'd gotten held back in seventh grade.

"Okay," my mother said, sighing. "Well, at least she's not cutting. Her mother knows she's not here."

"She'll probably be at practice," I said.

"I'll come to the pool this afternoon," my mother said. "I want to speak with her. All she needs is to flunk something now."

MY mother did come to the pool. She was the secretary of the swim team parent committee, so she was at the pool a lot. She did all the computer work for our meet entries.

She was the only parent on the team besides Melanie's mother who knew how to use a computer.

Our pool was part of a decrepit recreation center that CJ had bought from the city. There were crumbling recreation centers all over Philly, and after a while the city government realized they'd do better selling the worst ones to non-profit organizations than trying to repair them all. So when the building went up for sale, CJ managed to convince some guys from his church to help him get a loan to buy it. His dream was to introduce inner-city kids to sports they didn't get to compete in—mainly swimming, golf, and tennis—and get them to college that way. It was called the Philadelphia Center for SportsStars, but sometimes, when we were fooling around, we called it the Nest, because one time when CJ was giving us one of his puzzling lectures, he used an analogy about how he was the parent bird and we were the baby birds and he was teaching us how to fly.

Angel didn't come to practice. CJ was steaming until my mother told him she was worried, and then he got worried. It wasn't hot on the pool deck but the sweat was rolling down his neck into his T-shirt. He was pacing up and down, swinging his golf club and watching us work out, and my mother was pacing up and down beside him. When I turned to breathe, I could see them.

I was thinking about Angel and wondering if maybe she would have run away for some reason. Well, she had a lot of reasons, because her mom had kind of gone off the deep end lately and she and her mom didn't get along well anyway, and her stepfather was basically a criminal, and her dad ignored her. And she was always juggling around a few boyfriends and some of them were pretty wacko. But where would she go that I wouldn't know about? And besides, she was being recruited by all kinds of schools. She was so fast they didn't care about her bad grades. She only had to stick it out until August, and then we'd be going to college.

One time in our freshman year she decided she couldn't live in her house anymore and she went to her dad's over in New Jersey and begged him to let her stay there. It was a few days before anybody knew where she was. Then it was a few more days before it didn't work out and she came home. I thought about that, and then I started thinking about the time she disappeared for three or four days and it turned out she went to New York with Ramon. CJ almost killed her because we were a few weeks out from our first meet of the season. Then she dropped out of sight for three days in the fall when she had an abortion, but I knew where she was that time because she was at my house.

I was so lost in thought I forgot where I was in the set and had to stop and ask CJ. He didn't even yell at me.

ON Thursday, the same thing happened. Angel was not in school, not at practice. I kept calling her house and getting no answer. They didn't have an answering machine. I wanted to call her father's house, but I didn't have the number. I tried to get his number from information but I must have had the wrong town because they didn't have a listing. I had been there once, but I couldn't quite remember where it was.

After practice on Thursday, my mother and CJ decided to talk to Aisha Greene's dad. He was a cop. He said he could drop by Angel's house.

Mr. Greene called my mother after he went there. He said Angel's mother told him she hadn't seen Angel since New Year's Eve. When he asked her why she hadn't called the police, she said she'd told Angel to stay home and babysit the younger kids and Angel had refused. So she'd told Angel that if she went out, not to come back, and she figured that's what Angel was doing. She said again, Angel's almost nineteen and God knows she's always had a mind of her own. But then she said she was getting worried and was getting ready to call the police when Mr. Greene showed up.

LATER that night, some detectives came to our house. They had already been to see Angel's mom. They wanted to know about the swim team party.

On New Year's Eve, we had a swim team party at Melanie Johnson's house. She's been one of my best friends my whole life. Her mother taught with my mother and I went to school with her from kindergarten on and my older sister, Vanessa, was in her older sister's class. Her family got us into swimming. Mrs. Johnson was president of the team.

Anyway, the Johnsons had the nicest house of everyone on the team, so we had the party there and everyone in the National Team training group was invited, even the youngest kids in our group, who were about fourteen. There was lots of food and they rented videos and we hung out in the recreation room, playing pool and dancing and watching movies. Of course, Melanie's parents were there, and some other parents, too, including my mother, who naturally had nothing to do on New Year's Eve except be around me. CJ and his wife came, and Andrew. Of course, there was no drinking, but we didn't really care. We were beat up from training so hard all week; I mean, we had a three-hour practice that very morning.

Angel and Jamal were all over each other all night. They left the party around twelve thirty or one, right before my mother and I went home, with another kid, Bryce, who had a car.

"And what about the younger sister?" one of the detectives asked.

"Angel has three sisters," I said.

"The fourteen-year-old."

"Jeannine."

"The mother says she doesn't talk."

I looked at my mom. "Well, she does talk," I said. "I've heard her talk plenty of times. She's real shy, though. She doesn't talk around strangers much. Or to adults. I mean, she can seem weird if you don't know her. Sometimes she might not talk to anyone but Angel for a while, like a couple of days or maybe a week."

"Well, she wouldn't talk to us," one of them said.

"Did you speak to Angel's stepfather?" my mother asked.

"He wasn't home."

I frowned at my mother. If Frank had anything to do with where Angel was, it would be something like he sold her to one of his sleazy friends.

"Does she have a good relationship with her stepfather?"

"Well, not really," I said.

The detective turned to my mother. "Do you know if there's ever been any incidents of abuse?"

My mother looked to me. I thought of the times Angel

had turned up at practice with a bruise on her face or her arm.

"I think he does occasionally hit her," I said. "They argue sometimes."

The detective nodded sternly and made notes.

"Have you checked with her real father?" my mother asked. "My daughter was thinking that Angel might be there."

"We have people over in Jersey checking on that now. What do you know about her boyfriend?"

"Which one?" my mother asked.

"There's more than one?"

"Alex," my mother prompted.

"Well, lately she was seeing this guy Ramon who lives across the street from her. I can't remember his last name. And there's Jamal Joyner from our team, who she was at the party with."

"And how well do you know Jamal?"

I shrugged. "Real well. I've known him for years. He goes to our school, too."

"Any trouble between them?"

"Well, yeah. They argue and break up and get back together. I don't think he would ever really hurt her, though."

"Did he ever hurt her before?"

"Well, once that I know about, but it was kind of an accident," I said.

My mother gasped audibly and I felt bad. I didn't want to tell them anything that might get Jamal in trouble. He really cared about Angel, despite that one incident that I had seen. And then they were having an argument and she was pulling away from him. It was an accident.

JAMAL told us the next day in school that the police came to his house late in the evening to question him. He told the police that Bryce dropped him and Angel at his house. They were there until three and then he walked Angel to the bus.

"The bus?" my mother said.

"I don't have a car." Jamal shrugged. "I wanted her to stay over, but she said she had to go home." He was slouching around, looking dazed.

"Mom, she takes the subway and the bus all the time," I said.

"Alex, it was three o'clock in the morning. Where was your mother, Jamal?"

"Out. It was New Year's Eve."

"So you and Angel were there alone?"

Jamal nodded. He was eighteen and six-foot-two, but right then he looked about twelve. My mother could have that effect on people.

"Have you talked this over with your mother?" my mom asked him.

"Kind of. She was there when the police came."

"Maybe you shouldn't talk to the police again without a lawyer," my mother said.

I looked at my mother like she was out of her mind. A lawyer? This was Jamal. And Angel. She was known to do any number of unusual things, and she had been taking care of herself for most of her life. I knew she was fine, off somewhere doing one of her Angel type things. Making Jamal upset. Punishing him for something he didn't even realize he did wrong. With Ramon, because she didn't want Jamal to think she was his, or with someone else she just met, not even thinking about Jamal. It was odd that she hadn't called me, but when she went to New York with Ramon, she hadn't called either. She just showed up at practice, let CJ yell at her for a while, and got in the pool like nothing had happened.

She had probably called Jeannine, though, and Jeannine hadn't talked to the detectives because she didn't want to tell them where Angel was. I decided I would call her after school and find out.

Then I started thinking about the letters and wondered if I should tell my mother about them.

The letters began arriving after a picture of Angel and three of our teammates appeared the summer before on the front page of the sports section in the *Philadelphia Inquirer.* The picture was black-and-white and grainy. The four of them—Angel, Aisha, Melanie, and Kim—were soaking wet and arm in arm, standing on the deck of the outside pool up in Lancaster. Angel was second from the left. Of course, they had on their team suits and caps, but still, Angel stood out. First of all, the other girls were smiling and making the "V" sign, but Angel's mouth was wide open, because when the picture was snapped she'd been screaming, "*Fucking A—We're number one!*" And secondly, she stood out because she was the only white girl in the picture.

The four of them had just set a record at the Middle Atlantic Championships—an unbelievable thing, really, for four girls from SportsStars. The other teams were shocked. It was funny how years before, when the team was relatively new and we weren't that good, everyone was friendly to us, at least outwardly, and parents made this big deal of

how great it was that "inner-city" kids were getting to
compete in swimming, but that went away when we started winning. It was bad enough that our boys were almost
all black and had been winning quite a few races for the
last couple years. I think people figured, well, black guys
are athletic, just look at basketball. But these girls? From
that ghetto pool where instead of lifting weights they lift
coffee cans filled with sand?

I enjoyed the reaction of those teams so much, I didn't
care that I wasn't on the relay.

The letters began arriving about a week after the picture was in the paper. Maybe it took the sender that long
to find Angel's home address. I was at her house the day
the first one was delivered. It was friendly enough: it
praised her success in the 100 butterfly and in the relay,
and talked about how great she looked in the picture. She
was a "tiger," the writer said.

"Shit, fan mail." Angel grinned. And she taped it to her
mirror.

MORNING practice comes really early when it's dark and
cold on winter mornings, but it's not so bad in the summer. That summer between our junior and senior year,
when the girls set the record and qualified for Junior Nationals, was the first summer I could drive. Since my
mother's a teacher, I got to use the car a lot in the summer. She would wake me up and then come back in five
minutes and wake me up again—*Alex, sweetie, come on, get
up.* I slept in my sweats, so all I had to do was brush my
teeth and put on my sneakers. My swim bag was always
packed the night before. As I was walking out the door, my

mother handed me two English muffins—one for me and one for Angel—and a water bottle filled with Gatorade, and I was good to go.

All that summer, I picked Melanie and Angel up for morning practice. Even though we were going to be seniors, Melanie was still sixteen and hadn't passed her driver's test yet. She lived around the corner, but it was out of my way to pick Angel up. I lived on one side of the pool and she lived on the other. For her to get there was a bus ride, the elevated train, and another bus ride, though, and the El didn't even start running until five.

Besides her stepfather's giant motorcycle, Angel's family owned a huge rusted something—one of those big Chevrolets or Buicks that car companies don't even make anymore. Usually no one drove it except her stepfather, and most of the time he didn't drive it either, because it didn't work. And Angel didn't have a license, although she claimed to know how to drive. So there was no way for her to get to practice on time unless I picked her up.

I'd pick Melanie up, and then we'd go get Angel. She would open the back door, throw her swim bag in the corner of the backseat, then throw herself in and, using the swim bag for a pillow, crash until we parked in front of the pool. She always ate her English muffin in the locker room, yelling at the roaches and mice to keep the fuck away from her food.

Melanie and Angel and I went to Robert Kennedy, one of the magnet schools for academically talented kids. There were not too many people like Angel at Kennedy, except for a few other kids from the swim team and the basketball team. Most of the kids at Kennedy were kids whose parents just didn't have quite enough money to send them to private school, but would have liked to. And most of the kids at Kennedy were good students, which Angel was not. Melanie and I did well—especially Melanie, she was about fifteenth in the class—but Angel was always almost flunking out.

The only reason she got into Kennedy was because of my mother, who had been teaching there forever and was friends with the principal. If she hadn't gone to Kennedy, Angel would have gone to her neighborhood high school— not a very good school, in fact kind of a scary school, and it didn't have a swim team. Not that our high school swim team was all that great—we were good because of CJ, and the Kennedy swim team benefited from having a bunch of us at school there. The high school coach didn't even make us practice with his team; we just showed up at meets and cleaned up. My mom helped get Angel into Kennedy because she thought it was better for Angel to get bad grades at Kennedy than bad grades at Kensington. Sometimes Angel tried, but she couldn't keep her mind on her schoolwork for very long.

But she was a great athlete, and a natural one. She didn't have to try very hard to do well, although, as CJ incessantly reminded her, everybody has a wall, and you have to actually work to make it over the wall. She was strong, even though she never lifted and rarely did the push-ups and other stuff CJ made us do. Why she chose swimming, I don't even know; it's so much more work than other sports, and it's just never-ending. You only get three or four weeks off all year. Not that Angel was always that consistent at training. She could be pretty lazy and she and CJ got in some big fights about it. But Angel could pull it out like no one I've ever seen. You'd think she

couldn't possibly be ready to race because she'd been
screwing around so much, and then she'd get up on the
block and get this look on her face. At that moment, she'd
be focused like a laser. "The Gunslinger," CJ called her one
time after she won a race.

Actually, Angel probably chose swimming for reasons
that had nothing to do with swimming. First, it got her out
of her neighborhood and away from her family all the time,
because we practiced all the time. Second, it was something her mother didn't know how to do and didn't want
Angel to do.

Angel said Pic had played softball very well before she
got pregnant with Angel. She was a catcher and, the year
before she got pregnant, the best hitter in the state. Her
team went on the following year to regional and state
championships, but of course by that time Angel was born
and Pic's softball days were over. Even though Pic's body
seemed sort of ruined and she smoked nonstop, you could
see that she might once have been athletic.

Anyway, Angel sometimes did things just to separate
herself from her mother, and choosing swimming, a sport
Pic couldn't relate to, might have been one of those things.
Or maybe it was just choosing sports altogether that got to
Pic—Angel being successful at something that Pic herself
had been forced to give up.

In the end, though, maybe it was just chance. One
summer, Angel and Jeannine were living with their
grandmother and their uncle was a lifeguard at the neighborhood recreation center pool. Angel went to day camp
there, and her uncle Jimmy got her swimming. When they
had the city-wide rec center swim meet, CJ saw Angel's
talent and came after her. CJ's hard to resist when he tells

you how special you are (which is usually followed by, "So why the hell aren't you working harder?"—but Angel couldn't have known that back then.)

Just like Angel, probably a lot of us chose swimming for reasons that didn't have a whole lot to do with swimming. I started because my sister Vanessa swam, and she started because her best friend, Melanie's older sister, swam. It was right around the time my father left for good, and I think the routine—the intense, demanding, treadmill of a routine—helped my mom get through it. She made friends, Vanessa made friends, I made friends.

And then there was CJ: crazy intense, too demanding, but always there. He was Dad to everyone on the team with no dad. And there were a lot of us.

Although SportsStars didn't quite work out the way CJ had first imagined it—there was baseball instead of tennis, and most of the kids who played golf weren't good enough for scholarships, and there were a whole lot of bad students in all three sports who needed lots of tutoring before they could even qualify for an athletic scholarship—after ten years, he was beginning to see some success. People from his church, which was also the Johnsons' church, were helping a lot with tutoring and homework and connecting to schools. Kids were starting to get into college.

CJ tried to do his best by us. He demanded to see everyone's report card and got with our parents if there was anything lower than a B. Anyone can get a B in anything, he said. It's just about doing the work. He tried to get us all to go to church. He lectured us on no sex and safe sex. He ranted about alcohol and drugs and threatened to smack us into next week if he ever caught us doing either. He tried to tell the boys how to treat women, especially their mothers, sisters, and fellow swimmers, and he tried to instill a little modesty in the girls. He quoted to us constantly from Martin Luther King, and sometimes from Malcolm X. He used stories from the Bible to try to teach us things.

Needless to say, Angel drove him absolutely crazy. All her report cards had Cs and Ds. She wore provocative clothes, slept around, and didn't care who knew it. She told CJ that she couldn't "do the Jesus thing" because God must be a jerk for letting so many bad things happen to so many good people.

But CJ stuck with her. He believed in her talent and was attracted to her spirit. When she came to the pool banged up, which happened from time to time, he tried to talk to her and tell her she didn't have to let her stepfather (or her boyfriends) hit her, that he could help her do something about it. When she was stressed out by her responsibilities at home, missing practices and meets, he offered to call her mother.

Angel always said no.

CJ's relationship to Pic started off rocky and stayed that way. CJ believed in parents being involved and expected them to bring their kids to practice, come to the swim meets, and work in the parent group, and he told them so straight up. Angel started swimming for Sports-Stars when she was living with her grandmother, and Pic felt no obligation to him, the team, or the activity, and she told him so the first time he called her to ask why she hadn't come to a championship meet.

Her unwillingness to support Angel moved CJ to support her that much more.

~

CJ had a nickname for everyone. I was Williams and Melanie was Ice, because, as CJ said, she was always "cool, calm, and collected." Michael Traylor was Wrench because when he turned sixteen his father bought him this junker and he was constantly fixing it. Rosalie Cruz was Salsa, because she was always bringing CJ spicy food that her mom made.

Jamal's nickname was Spark—or, when CJ was teasing him, Sparky. How he got that name is a story in itself. Jamal was always a bit temperamental, something unacceptable to CJ but forgiven because Jamal had put SportsStars on the swimming map. Sometimes he was sulky and withdrawn, sometimes angry and volatile, sometimes cocky and funny. It drove CJ nuts, especially since Jamal was so talented, the most outstanding swimmer CJ ever had on his team. He wanted Jamal to be engaged, responsive to coaching. CJ never gave up trying to get inside Jamal's head—he was constantly working on him.

One summer, a college swimmer who was doing an internship in Philly trained with us at the Nest. His college coach advised him to bypass some of the white suburban teams and come with us instead. We were a lot closer to his internship, and the coach also knew CJ and thought he was good and would be good for his athlete.

The guy's name was Colin. CJ gave him a lot of attention. For one thing, CJ didn't get a chance to coach college swimmers very often and this guy was really fast and had a great work ethic, too. So CJ moved someone out of Lane 1 and put Colin in there with Jamal and two other guys.

The college coach had given CJ a bunch of distance

workouts for Colin, since he swam the 500 free and the 400 IM. CJ often used those workouts for all of us, which made the sprinters, like Angel and Jamal, very unhappy campers. Colin could kick everyone's butt on those workouts. At practice, CJ usually had two or three stopwatches going at once, tracking what different people were doing on certain sets. While Colin was with us, CJ always had one watch on him. When someone finished a set well, CJ would take his golf club and swing it wide, grinning like he'd made a hole in one. Colin accounted for a lot of those swings that summer.

After a few weeks, it was obvious that Jamal didn't appreciate all the attention Colin was getting and didn't like having someone on the team who could challenge him for the top spot. This was what CJ wanted—he was trying to get Jamal to appreciate being coached, as well as prepare him for college, where he wouldn't be the top swimmer the day he got there. But it all backfired. One day near the end of a killer set, Colin accidentally jammed his elbow into Jamal's face as they were passing each other in the lane. Jamal stopped dead, grabbed Colin's shoulder, and, when Colin was upright, punched him straight in the jaw. Hard.

I thought CJ was going to *kill* Jamal. Here was a white college swimmer training with us on the recommendation of his coach, and what happens—he gets whammed by some black punk. That's the story that would go around swimming circles, and CJ knew it. He yelled at Jamal to get out of the water, but at first Jamal wouldn't come near the side of the pool.

"Son," CJ threatened, "if I have to come in there and get you, somebody better call 911."

When Jamal finally got near the wall, CJ grabbed him by his ear and twisted it so hard Jamal started screaming. CJ was old, at least fifty, but he was strong as a bull. He took Jamal into the locker room and shut the door, but we could still hear him hollering and slamming things around.

"We're having a testosterone moment," Melanie said, pulling herself out of the water and wrapping herself in a towel.

In the end, it all worked out okay. Forced by CJ, Jamal apologized to Colin, who proved he was a macho college man by taking the high road and acting like it was no big deal.

Meanwhile, CJ said to Jamal, "Boy, I guess I found the spark," and that was how Jamal got his nickname.

Angel was almost the only one without a nickname, because, CJ liked to joke, "We're waiting for her to live up to her real name."

Angel and Melanie were on the relay team that set the record. I was never good enough to be on their relay; I was always the fifth fastest freestyler, and I couldn't swim near Angel or Aisha's butterfly. So I was always on the B relay, unless one of the A relay girls was sick or hurt. It pissed me off for a long time because I worked as hard as Melanie and harder than Angel, but eventually I made my peace with it. You have to, or you can't keep going.

The girls set the record in July. That was a big deal, and it was in the newspaper, but what was a bigger deal if you were a swimmer was that both their relays qualified for Junior Nationals. Actually, not just the relay team but also both Angel and this other girl, Kim, made individual cuts.

Our boys had been to Juniors before, and a few had even gone to Seniors; the boys at SportsStars had always been better than the girls. That summer, about eight of the guys were going to Juniors, which was going to be in Orlando; that by itself was exciting—what fun, going to Orlando—but getting to swim in a national meet was a really big deal. And CJ was going to take me as insurance, in case one of the girls got sick or something. And also, I think he wanted my mom to go because he was worried about having to supervise the girls, especially Angel.

AFTER the girls qualified for Junior Nationals, Angel asked me to take her to her father's house. She was trying to figure out how to pay for her trip. The tickets had been bought and there was one for her. All week, she counted her money and obsessed about how she would pay for the trip. She had $127. She kept going over what she needed: $200 for her share of the hotel room and the vans CJ would rent, plus money for food and anything else that might come up. She recited the menus from places she was familiar with, like Friendly's and McDonald's, trying to figure out how much she would need for food.

Angel worked at a laundromat around the corner from her house. She did other people's laundry and kept the place clean, and refilled the vending machines with little packets of detergent and bleach. It was a good job for her because she got paid under the table, she could do all her family's laundry while she worked, and when she couldn't work because of practice or meets, Jeannine could fill in for her. She used her money for carfare and clothes and stuff we needed for swimming, like suits and goggles and fins. The team had dues but she didn't pay any because the parents had a scholarship fund and she got a scholarship. Pic had never set foot inside the pool, and I don't think she would have paid for anything even if she'd had the money.

Angel probably wasted some money on stuff she didn't need, like a fourteenth ear piercing or hair dye, since she changed her hair color a lot. But a lot of us wasted more money and it wasn't money we'd earned ourselves, either, so I felt she had the right. Anyway, she didn't usually have much money saved.

Her mother suggested that she go to her father. I'm sure her mother said it sarcastically, because Angel's father basically ignored her, but Angel didn't know what else to do.

"What about your aunt?" I asked, knowing that she frequently saw her mother's sister, Christine, who was her godmother. Among her many earrings, Angel wore a pair of tiny diamond studs that Christine had just sent for Angel's eighteenth birthday.

"Dude, Pic would kill me if I went to her," Angel said. "She hates Christine."

"What about your uncle, the older one? Isn't he some kind of general or something?"

"Yeah, right, a general. He's something big, I forget what, but he lives in Germany. I think I met him once when we lived with my grandmother. That's it."

Angel said that her father, Ray, must have read the article in the newspaper. Yes, he lived in Jersey, but she thought he must read the Philadelphia papers. If he didn't see the article, then she was sure one of his brothers would have told him, or maybe his mother, who couldn't read English but somehow knew all the news. They still lived in the old neighborhood in South Philly where Pic had grown up.

She figured Saturday morning would be a good time to

go to his house, because he worked nights in a casino in Atlantic City, or at least that's what he'd been doing the last time she'd seen him, a few months earlier, when one of her cousins got shot and they'd both gone to the funeral.

He lived with his wife and two kids in Jersey—not too far over the bridge, about half an hour from us. So the week before Orlando, we went over there after Saturday practice. It was a blazing hot day. The glass on the streets was shining in my eyes and the smell of tar was in the air. We rolled up the windows and turned on the air conditioner. The car reeked of chlorine from our wet hair and our swim bags full of wet gear, but it was better than hot tar air.

Just before the bridge to Jersey, there was a Dunkin' Donuts.

"*Stop!*" Angel commanded. "I'm starving."

"Four million fat grams a bite," I said. "No way."

Angel rolled her eyes. "*Stop.*"

I stopped. She ate constantly, all junk, and never gained an ounce. I, in contrast, was always trying to control my weight so CJ wouldn't tell me I was swimming slow because I had so much stuff to pull through the water. Angel dozed through CJ's lectures on nutrition.

"All right, then, pretzels," I said, pulling over to the curb where a guy was selling them.

"Okay," she said, sticking two dollars out the window.

"I heard these are fat-free."

"Yeah, right," Angel said, brushing the excess salt onto the floor of the car.

She had been holding a shoebox since we got in the car.

"What's in there?" I asked.

"A copy of the article," Angel said. "Maybe he didn't see it."

"Hmm. Why does it need to be in a box?"

"One of the medals is in there, too," Angel said. "I thought I'd give him one of the medals, you know, to hang up somewhere."

No, I didn't know. I couldn't understand why she would give him something she'd worked so hard for, when he didn't seem to care about her at all.

Angel was trying to read a map and tell me where to go. We got lost a few times and eventually ended up in a run-down development with curving streets, way more depressing than any neighborhood in the city. It was the kind of place that made me say, gratefully and passionately, "Thank you, God, that I am not growing up here."

"I wonder why they don't have sidewalks," Angel said, looking at the little single houses, cased in aluminum siding, on little lots that blended right into the street like waves flowing onto a beach.

"Maybe they don't need them," I said. "There's no traffic, so you can walk in the street, I guess."

We pulled up in a cul-de-sac of one-story homes. Angel looked back and forth between two of them, trying to decide which was her father's.

"They look different from the last time I was here. They must have painted them or something. Got new trees."

"You don't get new trees," I said. "It was winter when you were here before."

She thought she remembered the wrought-iron door painted white, but she hadn't been there for over a year.

"I'll wait here," I said, pulling over.

Angel nodded and picked up the shoebox.

A blast of hot air hit me when she opened the car door.

I rolled down the window. No one was outside. The only thing I could hear was some bees or locusts or some kind of bugs making noise. It was like hearing the heat sizzling.

Angel walked across the brown lawn, past a dented bike with training wheels, to the front door.

One really weird thing about Angel was that her mother had four daughters—Angel, Jeannine, Kathleen, and Joy—and her father had two children with this wife, and one of them was named Kathleen. So Angel had two sisters named Kathleen.

She told me about asking Pic how her father could do that, his Kathleen having been born second. Pic said, "Angel, he doesn't even know you have a sister named Kathleen. He doesn't care about anything, including you. Why don't you get it?"

Angel knocked on the door. In a minute, Bridget, her father's wife, answered. She tossed her head and talked to Angel through the screen door.

Angel's brother, Mikey was his name, came flying out the door and headed for the bike. He looked at Angel like he'd never seen her before.

Bridget disappeared for a minute; when she returned, she stepped outside onto the cement square in front of the door. She had on these high-heeled straw mules that made her taller than Angel, and Angel was about five-foot-nine. She handed Angel a pad and Angel propped it up against the door and scribbled fast.

"He's not here," she said when she got in the car. "Bridget's going to give him the stuff. He'll probably call me later."

I nodded and started the car and turned on the radio and the air conditioning full blast.

Halfway back to town, I yelled to Angel, "You know, the parents are having a car wash to help pay for the trip. My mother told me. I mean, I think *we* have to wash the cars, but they're setting it up. They're having a parent meeting on Tuesday."

Angel wondered out loud how many cars she'd have to wash to make $200 plus food money.

FOR one day I thought I might get to swim the relay in Orlando, because for one day I thought Angel might not come with us.

The day before we were leaving, we went to practice and the pool was down. For some reason the pump had shut off during the night and there was no chlorine in the water. At our pool, stuff like that happened a lot. Mr. Ramirez, the dumb fat maintenance man, was lumbering around, mumbling at everybody, dropping his tools. Valentine Russo, the smart creepy maintenance man, didn't seem to be around. Mr. Ramirez had dumped some powder chlorine into the water, and he kept telling CJ the pool was okay.

"You want their hair to fall out?" CJ yelled at him. "Don't you know how long it takes for the powder to mix?"

I was pissed because I always felt like I needed more work, but most people were happy.

"Fucking great," Angel said. "I need the rest."

Anyway, since we couldn't swim, a bunch of us decided to go to the IHOP for breakfast. Afterwards, I dropped Angel off at her house. She wanted to show me the second letter she'd gotten from the mystery admirer, so I went in with her.

It was still early, probably no later than eight. Their

front door opened directly into the living room, no vestibule or hallway or anything. When we walked in, not being especially quiet, Frank was asleep right there on the couch, with the TV on. Angel's eyes got wide, and she put her index finger up to her mouth with a signal to be quiet.

We tiptoed up the army green rug that covered their stairs and halls. "He wasn't home when I left," she whispered. "Asshole. He was out all night."

Her mother was at work.

Out all night? Then he just came home like nothing had happened? I couldn't figure that one out. "Out where?" I asked.

Angel shrugged. "Probably at the casino." She turned on the stair and grinned. "Maybe he was shooting craps with my dad."

She stopped at the top of the steps and listened. "They must still be asleep," she said. She wanted her little sisters to stay asleep, because if they woke up she'd have to take care of them.

Their house was pretty small. On the second floor there were three bedrooms and one small bathroom at the far end of the hall. Angel's littlest sisters shared one room and Angel and Jeannine shared another. Both rooms had bunk beds. The hallway was painted white but the walls were scuffed up and it was always dark. I think it was that dirty green rug that made it seem so small and close.

The little girls' bedroom was the middle room along the hallway. The door was open a little, but no light was on.

Angel motioned for me to follow her into the first room, the bedroom she shared with Jeannine. Just as she was opening her door, we heard a giggle from down the hall, from her mother's bedroom.

"Shit," she said with a sigh, and we went down the hall to look.

The bedroom was dim, and so messy that it was hard at first to see much. Clothes were piled on the dresser and the bed, and high on a straight-backed chair that was standing in the middle of the room. Stacks of bills and mail and empty food cartons and beer bottles were all over the place. But there were Kathleen and Joy, sitting on the floor in a pile of men's undershirts and underwear. They were both wearing big T-shirts, Angel's old swimming T-shirts, so they kind of blended into the stuff on the floor. They were sitting cross-legged, close together, sharing a look at one of Frank's *Hustler* magazines.

Beside Kathleen, half covered by a pair of jockey shorts, was Frank's gun.

Kathleen looked up at us, blank, like she didn't realize that she'd just been caught doing something wrong. Maybe she was relieved we weren't Frank. Then she saw the look on Angel's face and started to blubber.

"Shut up!" Angel growled. She yanked Kathleen to her feet and the magazine fell to the floor. "If your dad hears us, we're dead meat, so shut up."

She held Kathleen by the shoulders while she turned around to look at Joy, who was still sitting on the floor. With her long, messy hair, oversize shirt, and big, solemn eyes, she looked like a little street waif, something out of one of those Dickens novels my mom was always assigning.

"Joy, get up and go to my room," Angel said. "Right now, and don't make any noise. No noise at all."

Joy darted out of the room.

There was a cheap, banged-up dresser pushed against the wall a few feet away. Its bottom drawer was open. Ev-

idently the two girls had known there was something forbidden in there to look for, and had pulled stuff out of the
drawer until they found the magazines. There were a few
more scattered around with the clothes.

"Take her down the hall while I clean this up," Angel
said, pushing Kathleen at me.

Kathleen was only too happy to get away from Angel.

Joy was already curled up in bed with Jeannine. She
had two fingers in her mouth, and with her other hand, she
was twirling her hair around one finger. Kathleen climbed in
there too, and I stood around looking at all the stuff on their
dresser while Jeannine peppered me with questions.

"Where's Angel?"

"She's cleaning up a mess in your mother's room," I said.

"Is she mad?"

"She's really mad," Kathleen interrupted. "Like how Pic
gets mad."

"Oh, jeez." Jeannine sighed. "What were you guys doing?" she asked Kathleen.

"They were looking at porno magazines in there," I said.

"Oh my God." Jeannine groaned and slid further down
in the bed.

I didn't know what to say. I'd never even seen a porno
magazine myself, except the ones sitting on a newsstand.
Actually, I'd never seen a real gun, either.

I puttered around their room, fingering things on the
dresser. They only had one dresser between them. The
rest of their clothes and other stuff they kept in shoeboxes
and crates piled up in the corner. Jeannine had this thing
for keeping scrapbooks and writing in journals, and those
were stacked in a giant pile that was almost as tall as me.
They had a closet, but it was very shallow, and with the

clothing of two girls crammed in there its door wouldn't close. There were shoes and sneakers oozing out like lava. Angel had a thing for shoes.

I was always blown away when I went to Angel's house, because away from it, especially at the pool, we seemed a lot the same, just girls trying to swim fast and thinking about boys and clothes and other stuff. But when I visited her house, I couldn't help but see that our lives were really different. Like my bedroom, wow was it different from hers. For one thing, my house was always clean; my mother cleaned all the time. I had matching furniture in my room and my curtains matched my bedspread and I had a big closet. I had a phone and a TV in my room. Not that we were rich on my mother's salary, but she also had a word processing business at home. And my father paid child support every two weeks now, since he was working and they took it right out of his check. We definitely had enough to get by and then some. Pic worked as an aide in a nursing home, and Frank didn't work, although Angel said he made money "on the side." I didn't know what that meant and I wasn't sure I wanted to know.

The biggest difference, though, was that it was easy to be home at my house. My mother nagged and got into everybody's business a little too much, but basically she was really nice. To me, to my sister, and to our friends. Before going into Angel's house, you had to take a deep breath and hope it was a good day. Angel said that sometimes Pic and Frank locked themselves in their room and smoked pot and had sex in the middle of the day. At my house, we never even closed our bedroom doors unless we were playing loud music. My mother had boyfriends but they didn't sleep at our house.

But, actually, the top of Angel and Jeannine's dresser looked kind of like mine. There were tubes of hair gel and fruit-smelling lotions and little dishes with earrings and earring backs and a chain or two swirled together. There was a picture of their grandmother, who had died a few years earlier of cancer. Angel had strung a piece of yarn across the top of the mirror and hung some of her ribbons and medals from it. Taped to the mirror was the second letter she'd been telling me about.

There was also a small bookcase in the corner of the room. Jeannine read a lot. Angel told me she went to the library all the time, and she stole books from stores too. On top of the bookcase were all of Angel's trophies, sitting on one of our old gold and purple team towels.

It still wasn't nine o'clock, but it was hot. I turned on the window fan.

Angel blew into the room, steaming.

"What's the matter with you?" she hissed at Jeannine, yanking her head up off the pillow by her hair.

"I didn't know they were awake," Jeannine protested.

"Well, you have to know," Angel stammered, so angry she could barely speak. "Jeannine, they had Frank's gun on the floor beside them. A gun, do you hear me?"

"We didn't shoot the gun," Joy said, pulling her fingers out of her mouth with a smacking noise.

"God help us," Angel said, sitting down on the bed and taking Joy's chin in her hand, making Joy look at her. "Joy, you can't ever touch a gun, much less shoot the gun. Never, ever. Do you understand?"

Joy nodded soberly.

Angel turned to Kathleen. "She's four, but you're seven. You should know better," Angel snapped. "How could you look at those pictures? You know they're bad! And then to show them to her? What's wrong with you?"

To my surprise, Kathleen pursed her little lips and gave Angel a pouty, defiant look. Actually, it was an Angel-type look, a challenging look like I'd seen Angel give to teachers and to CJ a thousand times. Even though Kathleen was fairer than Angel, she looked like her, especially around the mouth with her full, wide lips.

"I'll smack you into next week, you little brat," Angel hissed.

I could hardly keep from laughing, hearing her use one of CJ's threats.

"You listen to me," she said to Kathleen. "Do you want me to tell Pic that you were looking at those magazines? And you were showing them to Joy?"

Apparently this was a scary threat, because Kathleen's expression changed real quick to one of genuine fear.

"No, no, don't tell her, Angel," she whined.

Angel held her by the shoulders again. "I'm going away for a week. You better be good as gold while I'm gone, because if you're not, I will tell Pic. When you get up in the morning you get Joy and you come in here and wake up Jeannine before you do anything. You got that? I'm going to call Jeannine every day and find out." She looked at Jeannine. "And you better get the fuck up."

"I don't think I can leave Jeannine," Angel kept saying to me the rest of that day. "She's not up to it."

But she was ready the next day when we picked her up to go to the airport.

chapter three

___

JEANNINE

When occasionally my mother noticed me, she yelled at me for startling her. "You're like a ghost, Jeannine," she'd say irritably.

She was absolutely right. I was trying hard to be a ghost, to slip through our house and through my life unnoticed.

And if I was a ghost, my bedroom was my sanctuary. When I was home, I spent as much time there as possible. I shared my room with Angel, the one person I didn't care to hide from.

Sometimes I spied on my family through the air duct on my bedroom floor. It was for the heating system, but we used kerosene or electric heaters, so it didn't matter that I had mangled the inside of the floor when I first pulled out the metal grid and dug around inside so I had a peephole to the room below.

Months before that, I'd realized that I could hear what was going on downstairs by putting my ear against the metal. My mother and Frank had gone out—together for once—to a wedding of someone in Frank's family. Angel had ordered our little sisters into Frank and my mother's bedroom, put on a video for them, and locked them in. Her boyfriend of the month was coming over, some guy from school named Chris. For a while she had a string of boyfriends all named Chris.

Angel knew that I would never come downstairs while he was there. I was reading, and after a while I heard a lulling sound, like a loud purr. It almost sounded like the watery rhythm of the machines at the laundromat, but we didn't have a washer. I was going to crack the bedroom door to figure out what it was when I passed the duct and realized the sound was floating up through the floor. I lay on the cool wood and put my ear to the metal, and heard Angel moaning.

I wanted to be sure to see next time, so one day, when only Frank was home, sleeping in bed, I pulled out the metal grate and dug around until I had a peephole that gave me a view of part of the sofa and a corner of the living room.

WHEN Angel came in from the three-day meet in Lancaster where the girls broke the record, Frank was snoring in the reclining chair beside the sofa, having drunk too much as usual. He started drinking beer right after his morning coffee. He had taken his hair out of the ponytail he usually wore, and it was bunched up around his neck. The bald spot on his crown gleamed like a beacon up to my peephole. He was surrounded by several baskets of unfolded laundry that I'd brought back from the laundromat. He stayed out late a lot, and I was waiting for him to leave or go to bed so I could fold them.

I did my best to avoid being anywhere near Frank. He usually looked straight through me like I was a pane of glass, but he was so unpredictable I didn't want to take any chances. It didn't take much for him to blow up at my mother or Angel, and when he did, he terrified me.

But Frank had his good side. When he didn't ignore them, he was pretty nice to his own kids, and sometimes he gave Pic enough money to buy me clothes and other stuff, as well as them. But nothing for Angel. They were always at war.

Pic was down the hall in their bedroom, watching TV and nursing her wounds with a little vodka and orange soda. They had been arguing all weekend about the same things they always argued about: He stayed out late, sometimes all night. She thought he was with women. He claimed to be with his buddies, or "on business." She didn't believe him. He didn't give her enough money. She spent too much money. He didn't help her with anything. She was a slob and didn't keep the house. And on and on. That day, waking him up after he'd only been home and in bed a few hours, it had been, why don't you take us somewhere? Where? The zoo. This is the zoo. Fuck you, Frank. Finally, he'd whacked her, having had enough screaming. She did have a screeching voice that got more and more annoying the longer she went on, fingernails on a blackboard that wouldn't stop.

My bedroom faced the street. I heard Alex's car door slam and Angel saying good-bye. When the front door opened, I pulled up the metal grid and spied.

Pic heard the door and went downstairs. From my viewing angle, I saw Frank open his eyes a slit and close them again. I could just see the top of Pic's orange-blond head as she sat on the bottom step and Angel's Nike sneakers and her gleaming ankle bracelet standing nearby, and I could also see her hand, nails painted black, holding her big meet bag.

Pic said, "You're finally home."

"The meet ended at nine. We were like, swimming in the dark. It was in Lancaster, Pic."

"I work the morning shift tomorrow. All week, in fact."

Angel let her swim bag, wet towels protruding, slip from her hand. "I have practice at five thirty. Alex is picking me up. I'll be back by nine thirty."

"I have to leave at six fifteen," Pic said. "I have to take the El. No one picks me up." She sprang up like a spooked cat.

Angel was immune to Pic's sarcasm. "He'll be here," she said, waving at Frank.

Pic fussed on the coffee table for her lighter. It was true, Frank would be there. He rarely got out of bed before mid-morning. For a while he had worked in some kind of warehouse, but then he hurt his back. That had happened two years before, but he never seemed very injured to me. When he wanted to move, he did. But he had a lawsuit and he was waiting for his settlement, so he had to act like he was hurt.

Angel knew he wouldn't get up with the little girls, even though he would be home. She made a stab at being reasonable.

"Jeannine'll be here, Pic. She can be in charge for an hour or two, if Frank won't get up."

"You won't do anything to help me, will you? Jeannine is twelve, Angel," Pic said, charging into the kitchen at the back of the house.

My mother had forgotten. I was thirteen, about to be fourteen.

"Yeah, well, when I was twelve I took care of her. And actually, Jeannine will be fourteen in October. And no, it's not true that I won't do anything to help you." Angel's voice was rising. "I'll come home right after practice. I'll take the kids to the playground before I have to go to work. I'll finish doing the laundry when I go to work." She kicked an overflowing basket. "But I won't miss practice because *he* won't get out of bed."

"Shut up, Angel," Frank groaned from his chair.

She moved toward where Pic had gone, to the kitchen, and I could no longer see them. I slipped from my bedroom and crept down four stairs to where I had a view of the kitchen archway. Frank had his back to me, but I huddled tight against the wall of the stairs, ready to dash up if he turned in his chair.

"Jeannine is too weak in the brain to babysit, Angel," Pic said, tapping her temple for emphasis about my brain weakness.

I winced, even though I was used to what my mother thought about me, or didn't know about me.

"Anyway, I thought this swim meet was the end," she whined, swaying back and forth on the balls of her feet. "You said it was." She poured orange soda into a glass, her cigarette bobbing between her lips.

"Jeannine is the smartest person around here by about a thousand IQ points," Angel said. "She can babysit just fine. And it's not the end because we qualified for Junior Nationals. Our freestyle relay broke the Middle Atlantic record today." Her voice was calm now, patient. "I made two cuts for Juniors—in my fly, and in the 100 free. I led off the relay and I made the cut and the relay made the cut too." Angel spoke faster, her excitement growing. "We're going to Orlando to swim at Junior Nationals!"

Pic stood barefoot on the cracked linoleum floor, quiet for a change, trying to comprehend. She stared at Angel, and put out her cigarette in the drip of water from the faucet.

"You're going to Disney World? You think you're going to fucking Disney World?" Pic snorted and thumped her glass on our speckled Formica counter.

"Not Disney World. I'm going to Orlando to swim." Angel sighed.

"You're not going to Orlando! I don't have no goddamn money for that," Pic said, preempting Angel's request, if she had any intention of making one, which I doubted.

"The team buys our plane tickets and pays our meet entries and they get paid back some of the money if we swim fast. I only need enough for my share of the hotel and food."

"Why don't you ask your father, who never gives me a fucking cent? I couldn't even afford to put these kids in camp this summer. You think I'm going to let you go to Disney World, you're out of your mind." Pic sounded desperate, like she was going to start crying.

"I'm definitely going. You could have put the kids in swim and golf camp at SportsStars for almost nothing. Don't throw that up at me, especially while he lies on his ass all day. The kids going to camp is not my responsibility," Angel hissed. "And actually, it's not *my* father's, either!"

"I wouldn't send my kids into that shithole. Just because—"

"Shut up, Rita. Since when do shitholes bother you?"

Frank broke in, sitting up and glaring at both of them. "Angel, you better shut up before I shut you up."

I raced silently up the stairs.

For once, Angel held her tongue. I pressed my face to the floor, looking and listening. I couldn't see anything. When I heard the refrigerator door bang, I put the grate back in place.

A few minutes later, Angel came into the bedroom with a pot filled with Frosted Flakes and milk. The bowls were too small for her. I was under the sheet on the bottom bunk, my bed, reading.

"Hey," she greeted me, sitting on my feet and slurping down her cereal.

"You won," I said.

"No. I didn't win. The relay won. You weren't listening carefully. What's this?" she said, pushing my book so she could read the title. "What kind of book is this, *Lonely Hearts of the Cosmos*—like, a love story?"

"It's about cosmologists."

She gave me the "I'm stupid, remember?" look.

"Astronomers."

She got up and lowered our window halfway. The night was loud with summer sounds, kids still out playing, the bass boom of car stereos, sirens.

"Guys looking through telescopes at the moon and stuff," she said.

"Right. Are you going to Orlando?"

"Yep. I don't give a shit what she says."

"Can I come?"

"Don't be ridiculous. How can you come? I don't even know how I'm gonna get there."

"Are you going to leave me here in the morning?"

Angel sighed as she zipped open her swim bag. She hung her wet suits on the doorknob. "Kathleen and Joy probably won't even be awake before I get back. Just give them some cereal and turn on the TV if they wake up."

"What if Frank wakes up?"

"What if he does? What's the difference?"

"I don't like being around him."

Angel sat down on the bed again. "No one likes being around him, the fat fuck. Don't pay any attention to him." She slipped out of her clothes and into a T-shirt. She set the alarm and climbed the ladder to the top bunk. "I have to go to sleep, Jeannine. Turn out the light."

I turned off the light and switched on my reading flashlight. I could hear Angel turning to the wall. I think she was asleep before I even turned a page.

I almost never slept at night. Instead I sometimes slept during the day when I should have gone to school, or, if I had to go to school, I often slept there. I read all night in my bed and ate candy. I loved gummy bears and orange slices and the spicy red fish. I think the only reason I still had teeth was because we had fluoride in the water in Philadelphia. I had only been to the dentist once, with my grandmother.

I can't pinpoint when I learned to read. In my memory it seems like I always knew how. Until I was in sixth grade, I read whatever came my way, usually books given or lent to me by friendly teachers and librarians—so usually children's books. I must have read every Hardy Boys and Nancy Drew mystery by the time I was eight, and then I moved on to the Little House on the Prairie series, then all the

Shoes books (*Ballet Shoes, Theatre Shoes, Dancing Shoes*), and then the Judy Blumes.

But that changed when Angel was in ninth grade and her English teacher assigned *Romeo and Juliet*. None of Angel's friends read the play, except maybe Melanie. Melanie's family had a VCR, so Angel and Mel and their friends rented the movie and watched it. They all agreed it was pretty cool—a story about gang fights, sex, and love you would die for. I didn't get to go to Melanie's, but I read the water-damaged paperback Angel had thrown into her swim bag and then dumped on our bedroom floor, and I loved it. I read it several times and then resolved to read every Shakespeare play, and that's when I began keeping a spiral notebook with lists of books I needed to read and checklists of those I'd already read, along with my own comments and reviews.

I remember when my grandmother, Nannie Lou, first realized that I could read.

Angel and I started living with her when I was six, when the court took us away from Pic. I loved her house the minute I got there. It was big and full of furniture and smelled like tomato gravy all the time.

The basement was sort of Nannie Lou's special place. There was an old sofa down there and an old television, and she would sit down there during the day and iron and mend and watch her stories.

On the days I was sick or pretended to be sick and didn't go to school, I stayed down in the basement with her. It was down there in the basement that I first started reading the paper. My grandfather—well, my step-grandfather— Pop, read the paper every morning while he was eating breakfast. That was also when he and Nannie Lou marked coupons to cut out and added items to the grocery list. After he left for work, Nannie Lou brought the paper downstairs. She cut out the coupons while she was watching the stories, and she read the comics. I would curl up on the sofa while she was sewing and read other sections of the paper with the drone of the television as background noise.

At first I just read the sports pages, because I heard Albert—my uncle, who, since he was the same age as Angel, seemed like my cousin—and Pop and Uncle Jimmy talking about sports all the time, and I had no idea what they were talking about. The special words they used when they were talking about football and basketball and hockey were words I'd never heard before, like "offsides" and "dunk." I could figure out how to read almost every word, though. There were a lot of words I didn't understand, but I loved looking up words in the dictionary. In fact, sometimes I just read the dictionary. So when I read the paper I always read the sports page and learned about how Randall Cunningham was replacing Ron Jaworski, how the Flyers kept losing to the Rangers, and how bad Temple's football team was doing. But eventually I started reading other sections too.

One day after school, Angel came downstairs to watch the stories, too. She was asking a million questions to get caught up on what was happening with the characters. As usual, I curled up with my newspaper.

"Why do you stare at that newspaper all the time, Jeannine?" Nannie Lou asked.

"I like to read it," I said.

"Well, it might be fun pretending to read, but day after day?"

"She's not pretending," Angel said.

"Of course she's pretending. No child of seven can read the newspaper."

"She can read the newspaper."

"We'll see, then. Jeannine, what are you reading about in there?"

"Drugs."

"Drugs? What do you mean, drugs?"

"Drugs—cocaine, like Pic takes."

"You call your mother 'Mommy,' and don't talk like that about her," she admonished me. "Here, read what the paper says."

I read, "'Two Philadelphia highway patrolmen made their third major cocaine arrest in North Philadelphia in five days yesterday when they stopped a car for reckless driving and seized a . . .' I don't know this word—k-i-l-o —'of cut cocaine with an estimated street value of $100,000.' What does kilo mean?"

"'Kilo' is like a pound in other countries," Angel said. "Does it say where in North Philly, Jeannine? We used to live in North Philly."

"It says 25th and Berks Street," I read.

"That's not near where we lived, is it, Nannie Lou?" Angel asked.

Nannie Lou was flustered by my reading and by the topic. "No, of course not. That's a terrible neighborhood. I can't believe you can read that, Jeannine. Here, let me see that paper." She turned down the volume on the television and settled in again beside me. She looked through the paper and chose something else, pointing it out to me. "Here, then, read this."

"'Although many colleges and universities have begun to downplay the importance of SAT scores for admission, most educators, students, and parents still see the tests as a ticket to a good college or a fat scholarship.'"

"What's a SAT score?" Angel asked.

"What's a fat scholarship?" I asked.

Nannie Lou stared at me, her eyebrows drawn together in a frown. "You're a little genius, then, aren't you?"

I didn't know what to say to that, so I said nothing.

We established a routine after that, where after school Angel would iron, Nannie Lou would mend, and I would read aloud to them. To me, everything was interesting, and I would just as soon read the obituaries as the news, but there were certain things my grandmother felt were inappropriate for me to read, and when I would start with something like, "'Two Philadelphia police officers discovered the nude body of a young woman . . .'" she'd speak up.

"Enough of that, then, Jeannine, go on to the horoscopes."

This newly discovered talent of mine gained me points in the eyes of my grandfather and my uncles. Pop called me "Sprite" because of the way I would just appear out of nowhere. "So, Sprite, what have you been reading in the paper?" he would say to me. I knew he wanted to hear something about sports, so I'd say something like, "Dwight Gooden says he's never taken any drugs and he doesn't drink either," and Pop and Uncle Jimmy would burst into gales of laughter. I had barely been able to speak in front of them before, but knowing I could please them made me bold.

Near Thanksgiving, Pop got a notice that he had to start working overtime at the post office, and instead of working from seven to three he went in at five. He and Nannie Lou were happy because he would get paid so much more before Christmas. He told me at dinner,

"Sprite, you can help your grandmother pick out the coupons and make the grocery list." I just nodded.

The next morning, while Nannie Lou was packing the lunches, I sat at the breakfast table with a pen and read the coupons out loud to her. Each time she said, "Mark that one," I drew an X in the corner. Once in a while I would start spelling out a word to her and she'd say, "Never mind. Go to the next one." Then, while she was drinking her coffee, she'd tell me things to write on the list. A few times I would say, "How do you spell that?" and she'd say, "Never mind, Pop will understand it."

All of a sudden, after a few mornings, I realized that Nannie Lou couldn't really spell or read.

IT wasn't too long after I'd dug the hole in the floor that I got to see what I wanted, plus something I didn't. It was a school day, probably in late May. Pic was at work, Joy at Head Start, Kathleen at school. Angel had gone to morning practice, and she must have known that Frank had some appointment so he could keep collecting his disability money, because instead of going to school from practice, she came home.

I was supposed to be at school, of course, but I didn't go that day. I was tired.

The front door banged. *Shit*, I thought. *Frank.* But then I heard MTV and I knew it was not Frank. I put my ear to the floor and heard a deep, low voice—a man, but not Frank. Quietly, I inched the grate out and peered through the hole. It was Jamal, Angel's new boyfriend, sitting on the couch, playing with the remote. Angel was in the kitchen, and he was calling to her.

"No, baby, just bring me some juice."

I knew there was no juice, we never had juice. Soda, milk, or beer, that was all.

Angel brought him a Coke, and he seemed satisfied, even though it wasn't much past nine. They must have dawdled around somewhere after morning practice and come to the house when they thought everyone would be gone. Angel was wearing a pair of shorts and a team T-shirt; Jamal had on his warm-ups. Evidently, they'd had no intention of going to school.

Angel put the chain on the door and wrapped herself around Jamal, so close she was like a second skin, making herself fit in all his nooks and crannies. He kissed her and bit at her lips and her neck, and then pulled her onto his lap, facing him. Angel pushed him away, and while he sat facing her, she looked him full in the face, lifted her T-shirt over her head, and undid her bra.

I had been watching my sister and her boyfriends for a long time, starting with our uncle Jimmy.

Jimmy was Pic's brother. He was seventeen, a senior in high school, when we moved in with Nannie Lou. He was so unlike Pic in every way I thought one of them had to be adopted, or maybe Pop had been his stepfather for so long that he'd rubbed off on Jimmy. He looked nothing like Pic; she had inherited the deep brown eyes and dark Piccola skin, while he was fair and had green eyes. He was consistently cheerful, helpful, and hardworking. He worked at a supermarket and went to Catholic school, where he played football well, swam not as well, and scraped by academically. His plan was to follow his older brother, my uncle Paul, into the army.

Even though we barely knew him, from the day we

moved in, Jimmy acted like we had been there all along.
By the time we got there I was barely speaking at all, except to Angel, but he sweetly persisted with me until he
broke through. He and Angel bonded instantly, partly because our other uncle in the house, Albert, who was Pop's
real son and just a few months older than Angel, did not
like us being there and did what he could to make us mis-
erable, especially Angel. He kept taunting us by saying
that our mother was an "alky" or a "tramp." He seemed to
forget that Pic was his sister—well, his half-sister.

During the summer, Jimmy worked at the supermarket
at night and on the weekends so during the day he could
be a lifeguard at the recreation center down the street
from the house. The rec center had a camp that Nannie
Lou made us go to, something Angel and I resisted fiercely
at first but which turned out to be the way Angel started
swimming. Jimmy taught her, coached her, and introduced
her to CJ. They practiced every day after camp, before the
public swimming time began. Sometimes he would stand in
the shallow water and shout directions at her, and sometimes he would wrap himself around her and move her
arms the way she was supposed to do the stroke. Sometimes he would get out on the deck and show her how to
move her legs or arms the right way.

I would sit on a bench by the pool or go to my favorite
tree and read. I could walk home with Albert, but most of
the time I didn't want to because he was so mean. I preferred to wait for Angel.

One late afternoon, I lay spread out under my tree
with my head on my backpack while they practiced. Even
then I could become totally absorbed in reading, and that's
what I did that day. Suddenly, a loud yell from the pool

distracted me and I realized that the public swim had begun. I got up and went looking for Angel.

I looked in the girls' locker room. There were a lot of girls from the neighborhood getting changed, but I didn't see Angel. I knew she wouldn't leave me to walk home alone, so I went across the blacktop to the main building. There wasn't anybody in the multi-purpose room. I could hear a basketball thudding and guys yelling in the gym so I poked my head in there, but I didn't see her.

Sometimes she took food from the kitchen before we walked home. The double doors to the kitchen were closed. I went over and pushed one open a crack.

Angel was sitting up on the kitchen counter in her bathing suit with her legs wrapped around Uncle Jimmy's hips. He was standing up with his back to the door, kissing Angel's neck and pulling the strap of her bathing suit off her shoulder. She was facing me, and in a moment she saw me. She didn't look startled or panicked. She just tilted her head ever so slightly, telling me I should scram.

I did, immediately. I went back under the tree and read my book. And after a while she came out and got me, her shorts pulled on over her bathing suit. She ate an apple as we walked home.

We never talked about what I'd seen, but we didn't have to. I accepted whatever Angel did, because she was the only person in the world I felt I could trust, and I couldn't let anything alter that. Besides, in the end, she always put me first, before anyone else, even the boyfriends she was sometimes so eager to please.

ANGEL and Jamal were lying quietly on the couch when the front door opened, caught by the chain. Frank's voice boomed through: "Open the goddamn door! Who's in there; is that you, Jeannine?"

Angel and Jamal leaped up and she followed him into the kitchen, pushing his sneakers and clothes at him as he headed for the back door. By this time, Frank was banging on the door in fury. Angel flew back in the room, pulled her towel from her swim bag, wrapped it around herself, and opened the door.

"I was in the shower," she said to Frank as he pushed by her into the living room.

He stopped. One of the things you counted on with Frank was that he was too lazy and self-absorbed to care much about what anyone else did. But today, he stopped. He looked at Angel in the towel, and then he looked at her clothes in a puddle on the floor. Lying next to them was Jamal's warm-up jacket, with his name embroidered on it, that he'd left behind.

"Yeah, right, you little liar. Who's here with you?"

He started looking around, even though you could see straight through the first floor to the back door, and there was nowhere to hide. Jamal was long gone.

Angel started gathering up her clothes, ignoring him. He grabbed her by the arm. He was a big man, and even though Angel was strong, she was no match for him. She said nothing, which infuriated him, and he yanked her arm tighter.

"Don't bullshit me, Angel. This is my house. I get to decide what goes on in here. So who the fuck was here with you?"

Then Angel made a very characteristic mistake. Instead

of a few more denials and a quick retreat upstairs, she had to let him get to her. She leaned back and gave him a wide, wry look.

"My boyfriend. Jamal. He fucked me right here on the couch. What's the matter, Frank?" She stared right in his eyes. "Not getting any?"

For a split second I saw her smile and I saw his eyes widen in disbelief. Then he let go with the back of his hand across her face, knocking her down.

"You little whore!"

She tried to gather the towel around herself and dodged him, shuffling toward the kitchen. She tripped on the loose floorboard under which he kept the pills and guns and cases of illegal cigarettes he sold in the neighborhood. He kicked at her and she leapt up, running for the kitchen.

He followed her, hollering, "You want to know about getting some, you stuck-up bitch?"

"Get the fuck away from me," she yelled, and I could hear stuff crashing around, but I could no longer see them.

They tumbled back into the living room, Angel kicking at him, Frank tearing at her towel, trying to hold on to her arm. I stopped looking. I put my face down on the bed, but I could still hear them.

Angel was shrieking, screaming at the top of her lungs, "Get the fuck off me, I'll kill you, motherfucker, I'll stab you in the middle of the night."

I put on Angel's earphones and turned Janet Jackson up loud.

It seemed like it went on forever, but really it was a short time. In a few minutes she flung open our door. She balked when she saw me. She was sweating and panting, holding her towel around her breasts. She put her fingers to her lips.

The scarred side of her face was already purple and swelling. Angel had a scar on her left cheek shaped like a starburst. It happened when she was little, maybe six or seven. In a fit of rage, Pic threw a glass vase and it hit a table where Angel was sitting and the glass flew into her face. She didn't mind the scar. I never heard her fussing over it, wishing it weren't there. She just said she was lucky the glass didn't put out her eye.

Angel closed our door and jammed our little chair under the knob. Then she came over to me and put her mouth to my ear.

"Don't let him know you're here," she whispered.

I nodded and slid far under my covers. I was crying. She sat on my bed, clutching the blanket, controlling herself, determined not to cry.

AFTER Angel's team won the relay and set a new record, she started getting these strange anonymous letters. The second letter came three days before the team left for Junior Nationals.

It was Saturday and she was packing. I was sitting on the floor in the corner, sketching, because she was using my bed to spread out her clothes on. I was drawing a pile of stuff I had heaped in the corner, including a couple of Angel's trophies, which stuck out of the pile like skyscrapers.

It had been hot and dry for a week—odd summer weather for Philadelphia—so dry that the ground had turned dusty and little grainy particles kept blowing in through our window, making the room dirty. Our screen was ripped, and when we'd tried to fix it with duct tape we just made it worse.

Angel was trying to pack everything into two large athletic bags. One was a new, roomy deck bag CJ had given to everyone making the trip. It was purple and gold, the team colors, and it had SportsStars embroidered on it. Angel said embroidering the whole name would have cost too much.

Angel had been handed the bag. She didn't know whether the other kids had to pay for theirs, or whether they were free for everyone. A week earlier she'd told CJ that she didn't have all the money for the trip—that she could get some, but she needed to borrow some. He'd told her not to worry.

"I just hope he went to Claire," Angel told me. Claire was Alex's mother, and she was always nice to us. "I don't want all those other mothers talking about me."

She muttered to herself as she studied the swim equipment scattered on the floor. CJ had told them to bring everything—all their equipment, their pull buoys, their fins and paddles, their kickboards.

She had the portable phone in our room.

"Dude, is he out of his fucking mind?" Angel said to Jamal or Alex or whoever was on the line. "Are we going down there to work out? I don't think so. We're going down there to race. Why do we need all this fucking equipment?"

She was trying to figure out how all the equipment, three or four suits, three or four towels, her warm-up, and her shoes were going to fit in the bag. She couldn't fit her shoes in her regular travel bag.

"Maybe I don't need all these shoes," she said, scrutinizing the pile.

I looked up. She had two pairs of platform sandals, two pairs of sneakers, one pair of ankle boots, and her deck shoes. She had a thing for shoes. Frank called her Imelda all the time. I had to tell her why.

"We might go to a club or something," she explained, holding up the ankle boots.

She dumped her travel bag all over the floor, intending to start over.

We heard movement in the hall. Frank passed by on his way to the bathroom, gave us a disinterested glance.

"Big moose," Angel said under her breath and pushed the door closed.

But for a big man he was incredibly light on his feet when he wanted to be. I wasn't the only one who snuck around. Our bathroom door had an old leaded glass window in it and more than once I'd spied him watching Angel through there. I told her, and after that she put a towel up when she took a shower.

I put down my sketchbook and picked up a book I had just started. It was a fat paperback.

Angel looked at it. *The Great Santini*, she said. "Where'd you get that?"

"At the supermarket."

"When were you at the supermarket?"

"One day on the way home from school."

"One day instead of being at school, you mean," she said. She knew I cut school a lot, but then so did she. "How did you pay for it?"

I didn't say anything.

"You better stop stealing stuff, Jeannine," she said.

"One day you'll get caught and they'll call Pic and she'll beat the shit out of you."

Angel didn't steal, even when she wanted things and didn't have the money. She would have gotten caught anyway; she was so noticeable, with her height, her colored, gelled-up hair, and her scar.

I was invisible. No one noticed me.

We heard the mail slot slam in the front door. Angel went down and returned with another letter.

It was typed like the first one. It read:

Good Luck in Orlando. You could make Senior Nationals, if you keep your mind on your swimming and out of the gutter.

"What the hell is this?" she said, flinging the letter to me and checking out the envelope.

The postmark was from the main Philadelphia post office, and there was no return address. Her name and address had been typed on the envelope.

She wondered out loud if one of the stupid boys on the team was sending her this stuff, letting the other guys in on it, waiting for her to mention it or even brag about it so he could build it up, the letters would keep coming, and in the end she'd be teased to death.

"Those fucking assholes," she said. "They're so immature."

And she tossed the letter in our trashcan.

After her bags were packed, I fished it out again and put it on our dresser.

That night, I noticed it was taped up beside the first one.

I hated it when Angel went away to swim meets. She was my connection to—and my shield from—the world outside my room.

In the past she had gone to meets for weekends, maybe for three days. Orlando was for a whole week. I was worried and frightened about her going.

I wasn't the only one who was unhappy. Pic was in a rage. After she first told Pic about the trip, Angel hadn't said a word. She figured that Pic wasn't going to give her any money, and might try to keep her from going, so she just went about her business making plans and packing bags. Angel could be aloof and provocative simultaneously. Pic watched her in a silent fury.

I'm not sure whether Pic and Angel had any other discussion about Angel's trip, but it's hard for me to imagine that Pic didn't talk to Angel at all about how the little girls were going to get taken care of while Angel was away. Maybe deep down, Pic knew that Angel wouldn't just desert us, or maybe she had a plan of her own and was waiting for Angel to be irresponsible.

On the morning of their flight, Alex's mother was picking Angel up to go to the airport. Angel's bags were sitting by the front door when Pic left for work.

"Why didn't you tell me you were leaving today?" she called to Angel, who was in the kitchen.

"What do you care?" Angel answered, not moving from the kitchen.

Pic walked back toward her. "Where'd you get the money?"

"Not from you."

"You taking a plane?"

"Yep."

Pic turned and left the house, slamming the door hard behind her. She'd never been on a plane.

The summers were hard on us because Head Start and school were closed and we had to worry about Kathleen and Joy. All summer Angel and I had been juggling, trying to make sure one of us was there with them. Sometimes I dragged them to the laundromat when Angel was at practice and I had to work for her. Angel was right, Pic could have and should have put them in the camp at Sports-Stars—Kathleen, at least. Joy, just two weeks away from turning five, was probably too young for camp. She was still wetting the bed, which caused a big problem while Angel was away.

ON the second morning after Angel left, Joy woke up when Pic was getting ready for work because her bed was soaked. It was only about five thirty. I was half awake in my bedroom and heard Joy pattering down the hall, crying and whining. Frank started yelling from the bedroom for quiet and Pic started yelling at Joy for wetting the bed, which made Joy cry more, which made Frank yell more, which made Pic grab Joy by the arm, rip her wet clothes off, and spank her before finally thrusting her into my room.

"Shut up," Pic was shrieking. "You're old enough not to pee the bed."

Joy was close to hysterical. I pulled her into my bed, naked and stinking of urine, and after a while she cried herself back to sleep. Later that day, we took her sheets and my sheets to the laundromat. But after that she was afraid to fall asleep, especially in her own bed. I would find her asleep on her floor, sucking her two fingers like she always did.

The week before she left, Angel had gone to a Baptist church a few blocks away and signed Kathleen up for vacation Bible school. They had it every day from nine to twelve, and she thought it would be better than me having both kids all morning. I thought it was a horrible idea, both for me and Kathleen, but Angel was right—it turned out to be a good thing. I took Kathleen there every day and went with Joy to a playground in the next block. She played and I sketched or read. There were always some other kids there, and Joy was happy. They had these big cement barrels, turned on their sides and painted bright colors, that were meant for the kids to crawl through. I sat inside one of them, curled against the cool cement, and read. I brought candy with me, and when Joy got bored she'd come inside the barrel and eat some candy and then go out and play again.

In the afternoon, we came home and watched TV or worked on my scrapbook project.

I kept everything, down to bus transfers and hall passes, and taped them into scrapbooks. I collected everything I could of Angel's, too, like programs from her meets, and put them in "Angel" scrapbooks. I didn't always have real scrapbooks, so I used spiral-bound tablets that were easy to steal. I gave one each to Joy and Kathleen, and got them to tape their stuff inside, like the pictures Kathleen was drawing in Bible school.

No one seemed to know that Kathleen was going to Bible school until one evening she started singing "Onward

Christian Soldiers" and eventually Pic came up to my room to ask me what was happening.

"Jeannine, we're Catholic," she said.

"I don't think they mind," I said.

A few days after Angel left, Pic's friend Linda and her three kids showed up at our house. They lived in the projects about four blocks from us, but their apartment was infested with fleas because Linda kept a lot of cats that she let out all the time and they came back with fleas. Linda and her kids took over Kathleen and Joy's bedroom, and the girls piled in with me.

"It's just for a few days," I heard Pic telling Frank. "Until they spray her place."

"She better not be bringing any fleas in here," Frank warned. "They could be in their clothes."

It wasn't ten minutes later that Pic showed up at my bedroom door, wanting to know if I was going to be working any shifts for Angel at the laundromat and would I take Linda's family's clothes and run them through with hot water and put them in the dryer on the hottest setting.

"I can't carry them all down there," I said. "There's too much of our stuff."

So Linda and Pic helped me carry all the clothes to the laundromat when I went to work Angel's evening shift, leaving Kathleen in charge of Joy and Linda's kids. Linda and Pic started sorting through the clothes, dumping them into washers.

"I can do this," I said, thinking about how Kathleen might decide to torment Linda's two- and three-year-olds.

"Maybe you could come back at ten and help me carry them home."

Most of the time, I enjoyed being at the laundromat. There was an easy chair in the little back office where I could sit and read, and all I had to do was fill the soap machines when they got low and occasionally do laundry for people who'd paid to have it done rather than do it themselves. I even liked folding laundry, the clothes warm and pliant. I stacked the folded clothes by elaborate color and shape schemes I devised.

It was living at my grandmother's that prepared Angel and me to work at the laundromat. Everyone at Nannie Lou's did chores, and ours was the laundry. The washing machine and the dryer were in the basement, as well as the ironing board and Nannie Lou's sewing machine. But unless it was bitter cold or pouring rain, Nannie Lou liked to have all the laundry hung outside. She was convinced that the fresh air was good for the clothes, "kept the fabric longer," and that the dryer "drove up the electric." Even sometimes in bad weather she had us string lines and hang the clothes inside. I didn't think the basement was a very good place to hang up laundry because there was certainly no fresh air—it was dank and musty and sometimes smelled of Nannie Lou's extinguished cigarettes. But when Angel and Nannie Lou were ironing there was a very good smell as the warm steam and the sweet fragrance of the spray starch mingled. Nannie Lou, who was shorter than Angel, would stand behind her and give commands—*never iron collars first, they'll get wrinkled again while you're ironing the rest; put the spray starch on the inside of the shirt because sometimes it flakes; always iron the upper part of the pants first and leave the crease for last; you must iron the crease on both sides or it will not stay*; and so on. No amount of persuasion by Angel could change her mind about these facts.

Filling the iron was also an exercise; it had to be filled with distilled water, because Nannie Lou was convinced that regular water rotted out the inside of the iron. She also felt that the iron had to be unplugged and cooled before water could be added or we would get electrocuted. When she told us that, it was the first I'd ever thought about that way of dying.

BY ten o'clock I had all our laundry and Linda's folded and packed into our baskets and pillowcases and was waiting for someone to show up and help me get it home. By ten thirty, no one had come, so I rearranged our stuff, putting mine and the girls' clothes in one big basket, and stored the rest in the office. I put the big basket on my hip and walked the two blocks home.

When I came in, all the kids except Kathleen were asleep in the living room, on the sofa or curled up on the floor. Kathleen was lying on the sofa, her legs over Joy, eating cereal from a box, watching some crime show on TV. She looked at me vacantly. She was sleepy.

"You should go to bed," I said. "Bible school tomorrow. Where's Pic?"

She shrugged.

I took the basket upstairs, dumped it in my room, and heard Pic and Linda laughing from Pic's bedroom, Linda's Spanish curses punctuating their conversation in English. I floated silently down the hallway and peeked in. They were draped on Pic's bed, smoking a joint, drinking beer, giggling wildly. I went on into the bathroom without them even noticing me.

ANGEL called me every morning to check on things. She had to call before they went to the pool for the morning warm-up, but it was late enough that Pic was gone. That next morning, though, Pic was late and she was still home when Angel called. We had a portable phone in the living room and I had been sneaking downstairs late at night and getting it so I'd have it in the morning. Pic heard it ring.

"Where's the phone?" she yelled up the stairs. "Frank?"

Frank was sound asleep, of course.

I had the phone and was whispering to Angel when Pic flung my door open.

"Who is it?"

"Angel."

She put out her hand and I turned over the phone.

"Hello?" she said, pacing around my room.

"Where are you, Angel?"

"I know you're in Florida, I mean, where are you calling from?"

"Is it nice?"

"Is it hot?"

"Why are you calling?"

"Jeannine is fine. Everything's fine. Why wouldn't it be?"

She hung up and Angel was lost to me until the next morning.

She handed the phone back to me, then took it away again, to take it back downstairs. "Why was she calling?" she asked.

"She's just checking on us," I said.

"What does she think, we can't get along without her?"

Exactly.

"I bet you'd like to be with her," she said, checking out her makeup in my mirror. "In a nice hotel."

She turned and looked at me, cuddled up under my sheet. "No, probably not," she corrected herself. "You're really weird, Jeannine." She noticed the laundry basket in the corner. "Where are my clothes?"

"At the laundromat, with Linda's. You were supposed to come and help me last night."

She looked puzzled for a moment. "Oh, yeah. Well, I have to go to work. Will you go back and get them?" She came over to the bed, bent over me, and pinched my chin lightly.

"After I take Kathleen."

"I'm late," she said, and left.

She was nicer to me when Angel wasn't around.

chapter four

———

ALEX

T his place is funky, funky," Angel crooned, doing a little "Walk Like An Egyptian" dance on the pool deck.
She sniffed and snorted and pretended she was
throwing up.

We were wandering around the old YMCA pool in Orlando, waiting for CJ to finish his business. The place was
sweltering, like chlorine soup.

"Pool's supposed to be fast," Jamal replied.

"I don't see how," Melanie said. She was inspecting the
old concrete deck and ancient gutter system. "God, it's hot
as hell in here."

We were checking into the meet, a long process where
all the swimmers had to sign various papers, including
permission for drug testing. That done, CJ had to provide
proofs of all the times he had entered.

"You know, what the fuck is the matter with US Swimming?" Angel complained. "They put the summer meet in
Florida and the winter meet in Buffalo."

"Angel, shut up," CJ warned, approaching just in time
to hear Angel·curse.

"Girl, you want to be in Buffalo?" asked Aisha.

"You're right, you're right. Let it be a hundred and twenty, I'm glad I'm here. When're we going to Disney World?"

"Right now you're going to the locker room," CJ said. "We're swimming."

CJ always made us get right in and swim as soon as we arrived anywhere. He believed that every pool has a particular character, a set of idiosyncrasies, and you have to get comfortable with a pool in order to swim well in it. In a way, he was right. Like, the backstroke flags are the same distance from the wall at every pool, but when you're swimming on your back looking up, you need to get familiar with everything else you see in order to respond to those backstroke flags just right. And every wall is different to turn against—one can be slippery tile, while another can be rough cement. You need to know what you're going to feel before you feel it in a race.

So we all got in and swam to get familiar, to get comfortable, while the natatorium filled up with other teams registering. Parents milled around everywhere. My mother sat up on the old wooden bleachers, chatting with Melanie's mom and Kim's dad, the other parent chaperones. I looked up from the pool at my mother, and saw her talking with Mr. Simmons. We were glad to have him traveling with us because Kim, our wonder-child Senior National breast-stroker, was only fourteen and sometimes a pain in the butt. In the pool she was ageless, but on the deck she acted fourteen a lot, and it got annoying. She had a hard time being modest, and she didn't understand how incredibly lucky and talented she was. Some of us had worked twice as hard for five times as long and still weren't there. Plus, she asked a lot of dumb questions.

When we got tired of her, we threatened her with going up to the bleachers to sit with her dad.

I watched my mother entertaining Mr. Simmons, making him laugh. The girls all speculated about him because he was single and good-looking. He reminded me of Dr. J, tall and lean, turning gray, sophisticated-looking without being handsome. I wondered what my mother thought when she looked at him. The last time she had a serious boyfriend she was sad for months after it ended.

Whatever she thought, I figured she could worry about him or any other guy after I left in a year for college. I liked our female household, where you could walk around in your underwear whenever you wanted and hang your hand washing everywhere. From what I could see from my friends and relatives, living with a man was more of a curse than a blessing. A man in the house meant having all life revolve around someone else, like the remote is always in someone else's hand.

My mother and Mrs. Johnson were rooming together. CJ always had the kids stay in rooms together, because he felt we needed each other to get psyched up to swim fast. He usually put four girls in a room, two to a double bed, but only two boys to a room, because he thought boys should not sleep together in the same bed. Angel always argued with him about unfair that was, how incredibly sexist that was, but of course he ignored her and did it anyway.

After our swim, we changed and headed for the hotel in the vans we had rented at the airport. Instead of getting us two rooms or squeezing all five of us into one room, CJ had gotten the girls a suite—I actually kissed him when I saw it.

Left alone, we managed to make a mess out of it before my mother and Mrs. Johnson popped in fifteen minutes later to check on us. Our swim bags and travel bags were dumped in the middle of the living room floor, Gatorade and water bottles were sweating rings onto the nightstands, our rubber deck shoes were kicked off all over the place. Aisha had already made the complementary microwave popcorn and we were eating it sprawled on the two queen beds, watching TV.

Except for Angel, who was out on our little terrace, hanging our wet suits and towels over the railing.

"Who's going to sleep out here on the pull-out sofa?" my mother called from the living room area.

"Me," Angel called in. "I'm the oldest. I get a bed to myself."

Yeah, right, I thought. The reason she was getting a bed to herself, out in the living room while the other four of us were in the bedroom, was so Jamal could sneak in at night.

"Girls," my mother said, "CJ wants to go out to dinner across the street at Friday's at five thirty. Don't be late."

"We won't be late," I said. "We have to get back here and shave."

Shaving. All season we let our hair grow, or some of us let some hair grow, in the belief that the hair created drag in the water, and that when you shaved it off before the big meet your new, smooth skin would make a tiny but critical difference in the resistance of the body in the water. Was it true?

Maybe for very hairy girls, and maybe for most boys. But no doubt it was a psychological boost. It did feel different to be hairless in the water, smooth and silky, like the water had suddenly become softer, more slippery. Besides, it was symbolic of being ready. Shave, taper, put on the paper. Work hard all season, then a few weeks before

the big meet, start to taper, to bring the yardage down, to
rest. Shave all the hair off your body. Put an expensive
swimsuit, so thin it seems made of paper, onto your hairless body. And swim like hell.

But being hairy all season was really disgusting, especially for the white girls. The black girls generally didn't
have as much hair, and they were more comfortable with
their legs being unshaven. Me being both, I didn't have as
much hair as the white girls but wasn't comfortable with it
like the black girls.

CJ and Andrew laughed at our embarrassment.

Most of us shaved our underarms. We couldn't go that
far. Angel shaved her legs, too. She thought the whole
thing was stupid, blowing CJ off whenever he told her she
was undermining her own success. Yeah right, she would
say. Gorillas really swim fast.

The white girls—well, besides Angel, there was only
one other white girl, Sharon, who wasn't fast, and Salsa,
who was very white for a Hispanic girl and also very hairy
—tried bleaching their dark leg hair and, when it got really
out of control, wore tights at practice. CJ liked that—it
created more drag.

That evening, after dinner, we put on our bathing
suits, got out the razors and the shaving cream, and went
to work. Thinking back on it, wearing our bathing suits
was crazy. We traveled together, we slept in the same beds
together, we shared the same bathroom, but we couldn't
be naked together. Even in the locker room we showered
with our bathing suits on. Once I asked Wrench if the
boys wore their suits in the shower and he told me I was
stupid. Of course not.

Melanie and Kim sat on the edge of the tub and started

on their legs while Aisha leaned against the sink and let me shave her back.

Angel, in shorts and a T-shirt, wearing her deck shoes, supervised.

"Oh my God, this is disgusting," Kim said, giggling, as clumps of hair clogged the razor. We had to rinse the razor heads after every stroke.

Aisha pulled down her bathing suit straps. She was short, thick, and muscular—built like me, really, but firmer. No loose skin anywhere. I sprayed the shaving cream onto her back and spread it around, feeling the hard muscles underneath.

"Ooh," she said, "almost as good as a massage."

"Dude, let's do a massage," said Angel.

"You know some of those big teams bring their own massage tables," said Melanie. "They have a trainer with them who gives massages."

"Maybe I'll just work myself in," Angel said, swishing her hips.

I started shaving Aisha's back in short, careful strokes; I definitely didn't want to cut her. There was hardly any hair at all on her back. We rotated, shaving legs, backs, arms. Angel finally let me shave her arms, where there was very little hair anyway.

When we were finished, hairless and smooth, Angel turned on the shower and swished a washcloth around the bottom of the tub, directing all the stray hairs down the drain. Then she pulled the shower curtain across.

"Dudettes, get in," she said, shooing us in. "Rinse off. You'll make the beds gross if you don't."

She waited until we were all in there before reaching in and quickly turning off the hot water.

"Bitch!" I howled.

"Aah!" screamed Kim, jumping out of the shower, shaving cream in hand. Dripping and shrieking, she chased Angel through the suite, spraying shaving cream everywhere except on her target. Angel, the only one dressed and dry, dashed out the door and into the hallway.

An hour later we sat on the sofa, Angel's bed, munching snacks and watching television in our pajamas. Angel had brought along a manicure kit and several bottles of purple and gold nail polish—for spirit, she said. We painted each other's nails while Angel sat on the carpet and, one by one, gave us pedicures.

SOMEHOW Orlando was everything we had hoped for and anticlimactic at the same time. There were thirteen of us, eight boys and five girls, and I was really just along for the ride, since I had no individual cuts and wasn't even on the relays. I could warm up every day, but I wouldn't compete unless for some reason one of the other girls couldn't swim in one of the relays—fat chance.

I guess we'd had such a great summer season at home that we went down there with inflated ideas about what we could do, and CJ hadn't brought us down to earth for fear of demoralizing us before we even got there. But after a day or two we realized we weren't even going to score in the top ten at the meet. There were at least five teams that had twenty-five swimmers, and one had over forty. Our girls' relays had made the cut, but barely, and they certainly wouldn't score.

But I was so glad I had gotten to go because for me especially, without the pressure of competing, it was like a weeklong pajama party with hundreds of kids. The hotel, a Residence Inn with a pool and game room and barbecue pits, was full of teams, and the less swimming you had to do, the more fun you could have. I spent a lot of time with kids from all over the country, working on my tan at the hotel pool, playing video games, and renting movies in other kids' hotel rooms—CJ always blocked the movies in our rooms because he thought we wouldn't get enough sleep. We went to Disney World, Universal Studios, and Wet and Wild (a lot of jokes got made about that place).

Unfortunately, the swimming wasn't going all that well. Jamal swam great in the sprints, winning the 50 free with a faster Senior cut than he had before and making a new one in the 100, and one or two of our other guys scored, but the competition was intense. We realized that this was a different level—like, hello, Toto, we're not in Philadelphia anymore. By the fourth day, Angel was sitting glumly on the edge of the warm-up pool, procrastinating about getting in to swim a few hundred yards before the 100 butterfly. So far, the week had not gone exactly as she had hoped. Her 100 free time was almost the same as her entry time—no real drop. Her swim in the freestyle relay had been flat, a disappointing swim. And Kim had made a Senior cut in the 200 breast, matching the one she already owned in the 100, which pissed Angel off immensely.

"It's because your training is for shit, Angel," CJ said to her after the 100 free, when she hurled her goggles into the wall.

She was stalking around the deck, cursing. An official came over and warned her to knock it off.

CJ came up in her face and stalked with her.

"Lancaster used you up. You're a one-meet girl, because you don't have anything behind you. You think you'll make Seniors the way you train? Everybody has a wall, Angel, and you might have already hit yours. You might never swim faster than this. You can't get over that wall unless you really work for it. Work, you hear me?"

Her eyes six inches from his, Angel stared her meanest stare.

"You think I'm going to shut up? You think you can bulldog me into shutting up? I don't think so. And don't even think about telling me to shut up, cause I'll smack you into next week."

She turned away but he pulled her back.

"And another thing. Staying up late with these boys ain't helping either."

Angel rolled her eyes but kept her mouth shut.

"Don't give me that. I know you been in that idiot's room at least once this week," he said, jerking his head toward Jamal. "His mind's not always where it should be either."

"Well, CJ, he won an event yesterday, remember?" Angel retorted. "I can't be distracting him that much,"

"Yeah, boy did swim. So you must be distracting yourself."

CJ knew what he was doing. He was making Angel determined to prove him wrong.

THE next day, when she stood behind the block, waiting for her heat in the 100 Fly, she looked calm and focused. She was seeded in the middle of the pack; about thirty girls had faster times, about thirty slower. In order to make a night swim she needed to be in the top twenty-four, but in order to be able to score at night, she needed to be in the top sixteen. The third heat was what they called a "bonus heat" and what we called "the boner heat." It was almost better not to have made a night swim at all.

"You get in there with the idea that you're going to win your heat," CJ had counseled a moment earlier as Angel left us to go to the blocks. "You win the heat, you might make it back tonight."

Behind the block, Angel stretched her head from side to side and rolled her shoulders. We were standing on the deck, getting ready to cheer for her.

The heat before hers touched and Angel's heat climbed onto the blocks. All along the row of swimmers, girls were shaking their arms, kicking their legs, cracking their necks. Angel stood perfectly still, staring down the 50-meter lane of bright blue water, the exact color of the small gem pierced into her nose. When the starter called "100-meter butterfly, take your mark," all eight girls bent at the waist and grabbed the end of their starting blocks. Angel's long legs tensed, and at the tone, she shot off the block—a strong dive.

"Yes," panted CJ, pounding the air. He was missing his golf club.

Angel popped out of her dive and breathed. CJ shook his head in disgust; he'd told us ten thousand times never to breathe out of the breakout. Then she kept her head down for half the pool. Next time she breathed, we all yelled in unison, making a hooting noise, deep and easy to hear. I looked at the clock when she turned. Another girl was ahead of her by a little, but the two of them had a good lead on the other swimmers. The time at the turn was fast, I thought, and since CJ wasn't cursing but instead was hooting too, I figured Angel was doing all right.

She stayed with the other girl all the way, riding her hip. Sometimes at the end of a butterfly race your stroke falls apart from fatigue, but Angel was rolling along like a snake slithering through tall, wet grass. I guess the other girl was just a bit stronger, because she touched just before Angel did. Angel was second, but with a fast time, more than a second faster than her entry time.

She leapt out of the pool and into CJ's arms, getting him totally wet.

"Angel, I'm sure you made it for tonight," he cried, hugging her.

He started to critique her swim, but we grabbed her and dragged her off toward the warm-down pool.

Ten paces away, Angel turned and yelled down the deck, "Yo, CJ. What's that you were saying about my wall?"

AISHA swam just as badly in her butterfly heat as Angel swam well in hers. In fact, Aisha had been having a terrible meet—not just a flat meet but a downright awful one. She was swimming slower than all her entry times. That's not supposed to happen, not when you've killed yourself working all season, you're healthy, and you've tapered, and yet it happens to everyone, and usually more than once. It's hard to know why. We would speculate that maybe "she missed her taper," meaning that the reduction of yardage started too far ahead or not far enough ahead of the big meet. Or people would say that it was a head problem, that the swimmer having a bad meet was in a bad frame of mind—over-confident, under-confident, caving from the pressure, something psychological. Rich teams had sports psychologists helping them with that stuff. We had CJ telling us to shut up and swim fast.

In any case, after her heat Aisha stumbled over to the warm-up pool, sat on the edge, and just cried.

I felt for her. I knew too well how hard it is to feel like you're doing your best and then come up short.

Angel slithered up and out of the water and pulled Aisha through the doors, away from the crowded deck. I followed. There was a little tanning area outside with some lounge chairs, used when the pool was set up for recreation. The sun was hot, but at least we weren't breathing chlorine. Angel sat beside Aisha on an extended chaise lounge and put an arm around her.

"Hey, don't worry about it," she said. "Everybody has a bad meet."

"I have a bad meet every meet. I can't even swim the time you just swam," I added, trying to make her feel better in comparison with me.

"Yeah, but I can swim faster than that. I already have." She sniffed.

"It's just a swim meet," Angel said.

"It's not just a swim meet," Aisha wailed. "It's my first Junior Nationals!"

"Yeah, so it probably won't be your last. We'll all probably get to go to Buffalo in the winter. Even Alex'll make it, right?" she said, grinning at me.

"CJ's so disappointed in me," Aisha said. "He's barely talking to me."

"Oh, screw him," Angel said irreverently. "He just feels bad because he probably got your taper wrong."

"You think that's what it is?"

"Who knows?" Angel said, rubbing Aisha's shoulders. "But if you keep on worrying about it, you won't swim good tomorrow either. You still have the two fly, girl. You need to forget what just happened. Tomorrow's another day."

Aisha nodded, trying to convince herself.

I knew what she was struggling with. Once you have a couple bad swims in a meet, it's very hard to turn it around.

"You know what?" Angel said. "Let's get out of here. We haven't had a chance to do anything fun since we've been here. Except for you." She scowled at me.

"And do what?" I asked.

"You think your mother would let you drive the car?" she asked.

"No," I said. "I think you have to be twenty-five to drive a rented car. We have to go sleep. Well, *you* have to go sleep."

The rule was very firm: if you made finals, you went back to the hotel and slept all afternoon so you'd be ready to swim that night.

Angel waved her hand; screw that.

"I think I know someone who can drive," she said.

And she did. On the deck she'd been talking to some guy named Adam from a team right around Orlando, and of course he was interested in her. So it didn't take much for her to convince him to take us to Daytona Beach, a mere hour away.

Melanie, goody-two-shoes, wouldn't go because she was afraid her mom would figure it out, but she wasn't going to tell anyone either. So we got the shuttle back to the hotel on the pretense of Angel needing to sleep, threw some stuff into a bag, and took off with Adam.

~~⌒~~

WE passed the famous racetrack as we approached the beach. Adam said it could seat half a million people. The beach itself was totally different than what we were used to in New Jersey. Adam could drive his car straight onto the sand, a hard, flat ribbon that extended for 100 yards before the water lapped up. Cars were parked in a line, and people rented beach chairs and umbrellas right there from a guy who sat under one himself.

It was paradise. The water was deep blue, the waves small, and it was clear enough that you could see your toes when the water was at your neck. We flopped onto our rented chairs, ate the pizza we'd picked up on the way, and soaked up the sun. Adam made passes at Angel, which she casually deflected, and we talked swimming. When we got hot we went dashing into the surf and played and splashed to exhaustion.

Angel slept all the way back in the car, and I worried about explaining my sunburn.

That night Angel made her Senior cut, and the next day Aisha swam a decent two hundred fly.

WHILE we were in Orlando, Angel called Jeannine every morning. She had to call very early, because we left for warm-ups very early. She said Jeannine snuck downstairs in the night and brought the portable phone up to her room.

The first two days, Angel went down to the lobby to make her phone call. She had brought a whole bag of quarters with her. She set her alarm for five forty-five, pulled on her warm-ups, grabbed some of the free coffee in the lobby, and got on the phone. After two days, I asked my mother if Angel could use our phone credit card. It seemed ridiculous for her to go to the lobby when there was a phone right beside her bed. Anyway, her alarm clock woke the rest of us up, and who needed to get up even fifteen minutes earlier than necessary!

She was keeping us awake at the other end, too, because Jamal snuck in every night. I was sharing a bed with Melanie, across from Kim and Aisha in the other one. I figured it was like being in a dorm, which I was looking forward to.

I had been sharing beds with Melanie all my life. We stayed over each other's houses a lot, and slept in the same bed then, and when the team traveled, she was usually my bedmate. She was a quiet sleeper. There was something very cozy about snuggling up under the comforter in the dark, icy, air-conditioned room with Melanie next to me and the other girls in their bed, across an alley of tangled clothes, teenage magazines, and food wrappers.

Angel made us go in our room and close our door early, because she liked to sleep. She was in bed and out like a light by ten. She had given Jamal her key, and at some point in the night he would slip in and wake her up. The first night we practically had to gag Kim to shut her up. She wanted to crack our door so we could listen to them. We made it clear that we weren't going to eavesdrop, nor were we going to say a word to anyone about Jamal being in the room.

But I sympathized with Kim. It's hard to be a teenage girl, lying in bed with your girlfriends, knowing that just through the wall another one of your friends is in bed with her boyfriend having sex. It's almost impossible to sleep knowing that.

The most I had ever done with a boy was kiss and a little more, hook-ups at parties. I'd never had a steady boyfriend, never been on a real date. Wrench and I went to the junior prom together—buddies—and I figured we'd probably go to the senior prom too. Sometimes it upset me, but not much. My sister Vanessa had her first real boyfriend her sophomore year of college, and it had turned out to be a nightmare.

Vanessa is lighter than me, and her hair is wavy. No kink at all. She can pass. I pity her for that. It means that with every person she meets, she has to decide whether and when to tell them that she's half black. With me, people can tell by looking that I'm not all white. She didn't tell this white boyfriend until they had been dating a few months and the holidays were approaching, and we were going to drive to Massachusetts to get her. She knew she had to say something, or tell him I was adopted.

She said something. He dumped her.

We listened to Angel and Jamal, we put pillows over our heads, and finally the delicious exhaustion of swimming would put us to sleep.

I met Angel at a recreation department swim meet the summer I was eleven. Every summer we went to this meet, but only our newest, mostly youngest, kids swam. Most of us were way too fast to compete fairly against kids who were just swimming at their rec centers for the summer. CJ took some of us older kids to support our youngest swimmers, who were competing for the first time. And CJ went to recruit. He was like a celebrity at those meets, two or three stopwatches hanging around his neck, coaches from other rec centers following him, trying to get him to look at their swimmers.

The summer we recruited Angel, she won every event in her age group, coached by her uncle, who worked at the rec center pool in her neighborhood. At the end of the meet, CJ grabbed Melanie, me, and a few other kids to meet Angel.

Angel's uncle, Jimmy, brought her over to us. I remember her that day. She was a year older than me but she looked five years older—tall, muscular, curvy, and confident.

"You had a very good day, young lady," CJ said in his deep, growly voice.

"Thanks." Angel smiled.

"You think you might want to try out for my swim team?"

"I have to try out?" Angel asked. "This wasn't good enough?"

CJ laughed. "This was a good start. A very good start. And I have no doubt that you can learn to swim fast—very, very fast. But it's hard work. Haaaarrrd work, you hear me, girl? It's not all about racing, now. It's about training."

"Yeah, I want to do it," Angel said, with no hesitation.

I felt like warning her that she didn't know what she was getting herself into, but CJ was right there.

"You better talk to my mother," Jimmy said, leading CJ over to where Angel's grandmother was sitting.

CJ took off his hat. Underneath he had short, thick hair that was getting gray.

"Mom, this is CJ Rhodes, coach at the Center for SportsStars. It's the best team in the city. CJ, this is my mother, Louise Litrenta. Mom, CJ wants Angel to swim for him."

CJ held out his hand. "Nice to meet you, Mrs. Litrenta. You have a fine athlete here."

Angel's grandmother flushed with pride. "Thank you."

"I'd like her to come for a few weeks and practice with us. Let's see after that if she wants to do the work."

"When do you practice?" Angel's grandmother asked.

"Every day." CJ grinned. "In the summer, twice a day. In the school year, every day after school, and Saturday mornings. Sundays, too, if I can get a lifeguard. And the older kids swim before school, too, at five, but she wouldn't do that for a while."

"Oh. I don't know. Angel's schoolwork's not too good . . ." her grandmother said.

CJ smiled, steady and calm. "Well," he said quietly. "I care about the schoolwork. My swimmers' grades usually improve. If she swims for me she'll be bringing me her report card and we'll be talking about it."

That left Angel and her grandmother speechless.

"Angel, this here is Alex," he said, pulling me closer. "She's been swimming with me since she was five. Meet your new best friend. She'll be your buddy, show you the ropes, help you out. Jim, you know where the pool is. Have her there on Monday. Six thirty. *Six thirty a.m.*," he added, with emphasis.

He smiled, nodded, and walked away, replacing his hat.

From that day on, Angel and I spent a lot of time together. She took CJ at his word, and relied on me for a lot. She started asking me questions as soon as CJ walked away, like "Six thirty in the morning?" and "What's the deal with the report cards?"

We got tight, but she never let the other girls, like Melanie, very far into her personal world. She was a good teammate to them, but not a close friend.

IN the darkness of our Florida room, we couldn't hear much through the wall—sometimes low talking, sometimes Angel's throaty laugh, one night an aching moan that could have come from either one of them. Mostly I just snuggled with my pillow and tried to imagine what it was like, and then tried to stop imagining.

In the morning, Jamal was gone and Angel was up, making her phone call and packing her swim bag like nothing had happened, nothing had occurred the night before that would impact the day that stretched ahead.

It was then that I made a connection between the way Angel swam and the way she did everything else. She lived in the moment in a way I could barely comprehend. When she stood on the block to race, the rest of the world, the rest of her life, melted away, and there was only her and the lane of water waiting for her. She put her whole self into that race. If she won, great; if not, oh well. And when she had sex, with Jamal or anyone else, there was only that moment, which at that moment meant everything, but later, oh well, it was over.

I drove myself nuts thinking about it, trying to figure it out. What makes people like that, able to be so absorbed in the present instant? Was it a sign of being very talented? No, that couldn't be, because geniuses, scientists, artists, had to stay focused on something for a long time to create or discover something. Was it a sign of being crazy? I didn't think so, because although Angel was different, she absolutely never seemed crazy, never depressed or anxious. Quite the opposite, in fact; most of the time she was up-beat and strangely practical.

Whatever it was, I wanted a little of it, that ability to surrender to the moment, body, heart, and soul.

THE day after the meet ended, we were finally going to Disney World. CJ was being nice to us, letting us stay in Florida an extra day. A lot of teams were doing it; there was a big social that night for all the swimmers.

The meet was over and we weren't leaving for Disney until noon, so we slept in. When I got up and came into the living room, it was about ten. Angel was sitting on the sofa bed, talking on the phone and looking grim. I stopped and gave her an inquiring look. She pointed to the coffee machine, and I obediently went over to make a pot. No one drank coffee but her.

I could hear only her end of the conversation.

"So where is he now?"

"I guess Pic's asleep, huh?"

"What about the girls?"

"I think I should talk to Aunt Christine."

"Well, let me give you this number. When she wakes up, tell her to call me back."

I poured her some coffee and mixed it with loads of cream and sugar, the way she liked it. We went out on the little balcony and sat down. Our room looked out over the pool, where hotel employees in tropical shirts were cleaning up from the night before. It was already blazing hot.

Angel was spilling over with the story. "Saturday night, Frank never came home, so Pic decided she was going out.

Jeannine said she was in a bad mood anyway because she had to work yesterday and it was Saturday—she should be happy, it's overtime. So when she came home from work, Frank wasn't there and by nine or whatever he still wasn't home so she was like, 'fuck this, why should I sit around waiting for him, I have a life too, I'm going out.' So she went out with that ho friend of hers, Linda, who, I find out, has been staying at our house with her kids."

She stopped and gulped some coffee. "How can you eat that shit for breakfast?" she asked me, making a grossed-out face at my Power Bar.

She was eating a package of Little Debbie's pastries. I knew there wasn't any point in arguing about which was really shit. "Was she going out to find Frank?"

Angel shrugged with disgust. "Who knows? Who would want to find that fat fuck anyway? So anyhow, at some point she and Linda go to some club and there's Frank with a girl."

"Oh my God," I said, trying to imagine this scene.

"So I guess they're all drunk and Pic goes ballistic and she goes at the girl. I don't know exactly what she did, but Jeannine said they had to take the girl to the hospital."

"Oh my God," I said again.

"She wasn't hurt that bad," Angel said, scooting her chair over and propping her long, tanned legs on the balcony railing. "They let her go. So meanwhile, the cops got called and Pic got arrested. They didn't charge her with anything that bad, not assault, but she was drunk, and finally someone called my aunt and she came and got her. Jeannine said they didn't get home until eight this morning. She said Christine called from the police station to talk to me, she didn't know Jeannine was there alone.

Anyway, Christine was really freaked out when she realized Jeannine was alone with Joy and Kathleen and Linda's kids too, so when she brought Pic home, she stayed. Jeannine tried to tell her it wasn't the first time she was alone with the kids but I guess Christine is worried about what might happen if Frank comes home or if Pic wakes up and isn't okay." She stopped abruptly and sighed. "Linda came and took her kids home."

I had no idea what to say. "It'll be okay. Your aunt will stay."

"Yeah. Don't say anything to anyone."

"I won't."

I was surprised that Angel could have a good time at Disney World, but she seemed to. She stuck close to Jamal and the two of them rode on Space Mountain over and over. She and I spent some time in a gift shop. She had a little money left, so she bought her little sisters black Mickey hats with big ears and their names embroidered on them—except for Jeannine, who she got a *Little Mermaid* beach towel.

She didn't talk again about what had happened.

TWENTY minutes before CJ wanted us to be in the lobby to check out, Angel was sitting on the bathroom floor with Kim, who was puking her guts out.

"You tell Tyree I'm gonna fucking kill him," Angel snarled at me.

The social the night before had wound down into lots of small parties in people's rooms, and Tyree, one of the guys on our team, had taken Kim with him to one. Then he had proceeded to let her drink beer after beer, and then disappear for a while with some guy from another team. It was an unwritten rule on our team that the older swimmers watched out for the younger swimmers, and the boys watched out for the girls.

"Should I get her father?" I asked.

"No, please," Kim choked through her vomit.

"I could get my mother," I said.

"No, don't get anybody," Angel said. "Don't put your mother in that position, where she'll feel like she has to tell Kim's dad. Just go pack her stuff. And go down the hall and get a Coke."

She grabbed Kim by the shoulders. "You have to get it together. We're not missing that plane."

She stood up, stripped, and dragged Kim into the shower with her.

Half an hour later, Kim and Angel emerged from the elevator. The rest of us were all huddled around the desk while CJ was paying the bill—in cash, as usual. We didn't have a team credit card. Angel parked Kim on a chair with all the carry-on luggage and came over.

CJ turned and looked at her. "Everything okay?"

Angel nodded. "Yeah."

He looked over at Kim.

"She's a little tired," Angel said. "We stayed up too late watching TV."

CJ gave her a long look and went back to counting the money.

Fortunately, our seats were split up all over the plane. Angel asked for seats in the same row with Kim and me. Again, CJ gave her the look, expecting her to sit with Jamal. He didn't know that Angel was furious with Jamal because at one of the parties the night before she'd found him alone in a room with some blond girl from some other team. I told her maybe he was just talking, and she shook her head at my stupidity.

"Please," she said. "The lights were off."

We put Kim in the window seat and made sure she had a few puke bags. My mother, Mrs. Johnson, and Kim's dad were way up at the front of the plane. Two people could get upgraded to First Class, so of course CJ and Andrew had gone up there.

After the plane was in the air and the seat belt sign went off, CJ came back and crouched in the aisle next to my seat. Angel was in the middle. I was sure he was going to grill us about what was going on with Kim.

Instead he said, "We have to leave for Seniors in five days. I already got reservations for everyone who already had cuts. Now I have to get a few more." He grinned.

Angel looked at him. "I can't go."

"What do you mean you can't go? Why?"

"I don't have any money."

"You don't need money. The team can pay."

"I can't go."

"Angel, we've worked for this for years. You're gonna be a senior. This is your time."

"I can't go. I can't leave my family right now."

"What's this about? Your mother? She won't let you go? I'll call her."

"Get up," she said to me.

She pushed past me and she and CJ walked up toward first class. In a minute, Andrew came by and motioned for me to move over next to Kim. I did because I didn't want him near her. She was dozing, but when the stewardess came by I asked her for a Coke anyway, just in case.

Andrew was CJ's protégé. He had been one of CJ's first swimmers, and certainly was his earliest success. Andrew went to Howard on a swimming scholarship and then came back home to work with CJ. He had a degree in business, but basically he just wanted to be around the pool.

"So, what's with her?" he said, indicating Kim.

"Nothing. Just tired," I said, pulling down the window shade to keep the sun off of her face.

"Sure." He laughed. "What's up with Angel?" he asked.

"She can't go to Seniors. CJ's upset."

"Oh man, she has to go to Seniors. That's ridiculous."

"Andrew, her family thing is really screwed up. She has a lot of responsibilities at home."

He took off his glasses and cleaned them with the end of his T-shirt. "She could be so good. She just doesn't do the work."

"You're not hearing me. There's a lot of other stuff going on in her life."

"Yeah. Like Jamal."

I sighed. He wasn't going to understand. His parents were together, they both had good jobs, they always did everything CJ wanted, they did everything they could for Andrew and his sister to do well in school and swimming. He just didn't get it.

I pulled the airline magazine out of the pocket and started reading. Andrew closed his eyes and dozed. When Angel came back, he got up without a word and went back to his seat.

"What's his problem?" she asked.

"You," I said.

"He'll get over it. CJ's cool, so Andrew will be too."

"CJ said it's okay?" I was stunned. I figured he would give Angel a really hard time.

"I just told him the whole story. Do you think anyone wants to go more than me? But I can't. I can't leave Jeannine again right now. I just can't. He understands."

I thought about that. Behind his pig-headed focus on us swimming well, CJ had a life that would make understanding Angel pretty easy. He grew up in the projects in West Philly with three sisters and no dad, because his father died when CJ was eight. His mother, who sometimes came to our swim meets, had been a custodian in our school district and was a serious, church-going lady. CJ talked about his mother all the time, especially when he was mad at us. "My mother could swim that set faster than you," he'd say if we disappointed him. He gave her all the credit for the way his life turned out.

CJ came up through the Y and the city's rec system, and played all the ball sports and even did some swimming at the Y. He was a good athlete and got a football scholarship to University of Delaware, which kept him from going to Vietnam. That changed his life, but not the way anyone expected. He got hurt in his freshman year, and started swimming to keep in shape while healing. He never went back to football. He married as soon as he graduated, had three kids, and raised them in the church, the pool, and school. One of his daughters, who was the same age as Andrew, got a swimming scholarship to college. Before their kids were grown, CJ and his wife started taking in foster kids. They always had a few children living with them—some of them swam with Andrew. Those kids had lives like Angel's, only worse.

"Listen, you know what else he said?" Angel went on.

"He said two of his college guards have to leave to go back to school, so while he's away, until Labor Day, actually, we can take their places, make almost ten bucks an hour."

I didn't say anything right away. I had been planning to go down the shore where my sister was working for the summer.

She looked at me. "It'll be like $300 a week."

"Okay."

My mother didn't want me to go and hang out with Vanessa's college friends anyway.

chapter five

———

JEANNINE

I liked to read about space. When I felt hopeless, which was occasional, the unexpected order of the universe encouraged me to believe in some sort of meaning greater than myself, and when I felt helpless, which was often, the vastness of the universe made my helplessness seem comical.

The Milky Way galaxy is what is known as a pinwheel galaxy. We are located on the inside of one of the graceful arms that flies out from the wheel. Our sun is 30,000 light years from the center of the galaxy. Light moves at 186,282 miles per second. There are 31,536,000 seconds in one year. So light travels 1,147,975,152,000 miles in one year. Times 30,000 to get to the center of the Milky Way. And there are at least 100 billion other galaxies in the universe, all of them much farther away than that.

When the events of my personal existence overwhelmed me, I could rely on the facts of our collective existence to put things in perspective. How much could sadness and fear in my little life matter?

One night while Angel was in Florida, Pic went out and didn't come home. She left with Linda to go to a club, and didn't come back that night or the next morning. Frank had gone out too, and he didn't come home either. They left me with Linda's kids and Kathleen and Joy. Thank God for television. We never went upstairs that night. I brought all the blankets and pillows downstairs and we made a snuggly nest on the floor. It was okay until the middle of the night, when they were all asleep and I was afraid to go to sleep. I watched movies all night. Some of the time I spent sitting on the back of the sofa, looking out the window at the street.

Once in a while you have an eerie out-of-time moment when you think you've been in this exact scene before. Déjà vu. I'd read about it, but that night I learned what it was firsthand. Curled up in front of the TV, I had the profound sense that I'd been there before. And in a way, I had—it amounted to how we ended up living with my grandmother.

The thing I remembered best about that night was how the dogs kept barking.

They were two mutts with a lot of pit bull in them, one a dark, creamy brown and the other a nutty beige. They had come to us with names from some rap song, but the names were meaningless to me, so I called them Chocolate and Butterscotch. They weren't huge dogs—in fact, they were mangy and skinny—but they seemed enormous to a tiny girl like me. I'd never had a pet, having a pet had never even occurred to me, and they hadn't been raised with us nor with any other children, so we ignored each other. They liked Angel, though, because she fed them.

We'd inherited the dogs when Pic's boyfriend went to jail. At first they were barking because they were hungry.

Angel had already fed them all the food she could find. Pic had been gone for a long time, had left late at night, and then another night had gone by.

We didn't know she was gone that first day until we got up in the morning. It was a school day, and even though Angel walked me to school every day, and I knew perfectly well how to get dressed, and we could always find something for breakfast, she decided we should stay home and wait for Pic. She let the dogs out back in the little fenced-in place where the trashcans were kept. The dogs knocked them over, making a noise like cymbals clashing, and a man raised up his window and started yelling. Somehow, Angel got them back inside.

We watched television off-and-on all day, and at every commercial Angel went to the window and looked around the shade to see if Pic was coming. I played with Angel's old Barbies and read my books over and over. "Do you like green eggs and ham? Yes I like them, Sam-I-Am." Angel painted her nails with Pic's polish, and then she painted mine. She put makeup on me, sparkling blue eye shadow up to my eyebrows. I kept skidding into the bathroom and climbing up on the sink to look in the mirror. Once I didn't stop in time and smashed into the edge of the sink. My tooth punctured my lip and it started bleeding, dripping bright red polka dots onto the white ceramic floor. We didn't have any ice, but Angel got a washcloth and ran it under cold water and I held it on my lip for a while. The bleeding stopped but my mouth was all swollen.

We had an apartment then, down a long hallway. We had lived in so many places I have trouble remembering each one, but I remember that our bedroom was in the back, because that's where we went when the dogs really went crazy. The bedroom was small, with a single mattress that Angel and I shared. There was a window that faced the window of another building, and Angel had covered it with a pink sheet.

When it got dark the second night and Pic still hadn't come home, Angel called our grandmother, Nannie Lou. There was no answer, even though Angel tried and tried. She also tried to call her father, but his phone was disconnected. We didn't know that he had moved. We ate Pop Tarts and cereal, a perfect dinner as far as I was concerned.

We cuddled up on the sofa in the living room where Pic slept, with the television going. I was freezing, so Angel wrapped me in the blanket from our bed and put me under Pic's blanket. Angel herself was never cold—or hot, for that matter. While Angel slept, I lay on the couch studying the headlights from passing cars that skimmed the ceiling, made a right angle at one corner, and disappeared.

Chocolate and Butterscotch paced around in the night, pushing against us with their cold noses. Their claws clattering on the bare floors sounded like Pic's fake nails drumming on the kitchen table while she talked on the phone. The dogs were in my dreams or I was partly awake all night, I'm not sure. They woke us up early in the morning with their whining and barking. We ate dry cereal and gave them milk when we couldn't find more dog food. We were afraid to let them out again, and they carried on yelping and thumping their tails on the floor like cavemen banging clubs. Butterscotch finally shit in the kitchen and Angel tried to clean it up.

Sometime that morning Angel got Nannie Lou on the phone. Poor Angel. I couldn't hear Nannie Lou but Angel got very confused and then frustrated trying to answer her questions, and had to keep repeating things, all the while with the dogs barking and whimpering. When she got off the phone Angel wasn't clear on what Nannie Lou had said she was going to do.

Sometime later there was banging on the door to our apartment and the dogs went crazy, barking and growling and jumping up against the door, their claws raking the wood. Angel went up to open the door and Chocolate turned on her, baring his teeth and dripping saliva from his mouth. She yelled and kicked at him and we ran into our bedroom and closed the door.

For a long while we could hear the alternating sounds of knocking and barking, continuous but uneven, like a thunderstorm.

Eventually the knocking stopped.

"Shit." Angel sighed, disgusted, and peeked through our keyhole to see if it was safe for us to go out to the rest of the apartment. She decided no, the dogs were pacing around the door in a circle, so we curled up on the bed and she braided my hair and then she fell asleep. I sang songs I knew from school, including the Bingo dog song, which I sang loud by the door, thinking the dogs might like it and would calm down.

Then there were crashing noises, and barking and growling, and then explosions like cars make on the street. Then quiet.

"What the fuck?" Angel said.

She peeked through the keyhole, and opened our door a sliver.

"We're in here," she called.

A deep voice was just on the other side of the door, telling us to wait a minute. We heard voices whispering.

Finally, Miss Evelyn, our social worker, came in our room.

"What did you do to our dogs?" Angel asked.

"The police are taking them," Miss Evelyn said. Then she looked at me. "Don't come out. Wait here."

She came back in with a wet towel and washed the makeup off my face, clucking about my fat lip, and helped Angel put some clothes in a grocery bag. I got my books.

"Where are our dogs?" Angel asked again when they let us out of our room.

When we were at Miss Evelyn's office, Angel whispered to me that the dogs were dead.

THE night they left me alone, Pic and Linda went to a bar and discovered Frank in there with a woman. Pic went crazy and started a fight, and she got arrested. My aunt Christine went and got her out and brought her home, just after I finally went to sleep. Christine stayed at the house with us until Angel came home from Florida. Angel had asked her to over the phone. It was only one extra day.

When Pic finally woke up, she was inconsolable. She cried, she wailed. She sobbed so hard she was choking. All she talked about was that moment of walking into the bar and seeing Frank sitting at the bar with his arm draped around the bare shoulder of some woman. How could he do it to her? What was wrong with her, why didn't he love her? What did that other girl have that she didn't have?

And then she was angry, shrieking from behind the closed door of her bedroom. But it was that other girl she was enraged with, not Frank.

I couldn't understand it; how could anybody mourn Frank?

Later, Angel explained to me that Pic wasn't mourning just Frank. She was mourning every man she'd ever had, every man who ever cheated on her: my father, whoever and wherever he was, and Angel's father, with his missing child support, and all the rest. She was howling with frustration. Frank was just one more thing.

And anyway, I asked Angel, was it possible that Pic didn't know anything about Frank's secrets—his porno magazines, his girlfriends—when we knew?

People know what they want to know, Angel said.

Pic stayed in her room. For the most part, Christine stayed in there with her. She tried to get Pic to eat, to drink tea.

Christine put all the beer from the refrigerator outside in the trash, and poured bottles of vodka and whiskey down the drain. She was worried that Pic would start drinking because she was so upset. She thought Pic was straight and sober. Pic didn't usually drink beer, mostly she drank orange soda morning, noon, and night, but it was often mixed with vodka.

"You need to throw away the pot," I said to her.

She looked at me in surprise. "Is it Frank's? Do you know where it's at?"

"In the bedroom somewhere. There's usually bottles of liquor in there, too."

"Well I'm not sure I can get to that," she said.

I had never spent two straight days with my aunt. In fact, I hadn't even seen her since my grandmother's funeral. She was Angel's godmother but Pic didn't like her and kept her away. Sometimes she came to Angel's meets or visited her at the pool. She was quiet, but very deliberate. She took charge. She told me exactly what to do: give the girls breakfast, brush Joy's hair and put it in a ponytail, pile all the dirty laundry into these baskets, take the girls outside. I did exactly what she told me. I didn't want her to leave.

Christine made us chicken and rice for dinner. Pic wouldn't come downstairs, so it was just the girls and Christine and me, sitting at the kitchen table. There were only four chairs anyway. Christine tried to keep it light, talking to Joy about starting kindergarten, asking what the girls' favorite TV shows were, what they liked to eat. When Joy and Kathleen said spaghetti, Christine said she was sorry that Kathleen and Joy never got to meet her mother, our grandmother, Nannie Lou, who made great spaghetti—and ravioli, and lasagna.

I nodded and rocked in my chair. Nannie Lou had always made me plain "macaronis" as she called them—just butter and salt.

"And you never got to meet my father," Christine said to me.

I shook my head. Nannie Lou's first husband, Paul, had died before I was born. "But I met Pop. I really liked Pop."

Christine smiled. "Isn't he wonderful? We visit him all the time."

I was stunned. I didn't understand. After Nannie Lou died, Pic never talked about Pop, Nannie Lou's second husband and the only grandfather I ever knew. Pic told Angel that he'd moved away. "You do? Can I visit him?"

"That's up to your mom," said Christine, tight-lipped. "She never got along with Pop. She never got over our father dying."

"What did he die of?" I asked.

"He had a heart attack. It was very sudden. Really quick. He was talking to one of the neighbors outside, came in and turned on the TV to watch the football game, and just keeled over and died. I was fifteen, your mother was thirteen. She took it very hard. She was his favorite. Always. She was a really good softball player and he practiced all the time with her and went to all her games." She got up and put some foil over the leftovers, and carried the dishes to the sink.

"She kind of went crazy, started acting really bad. She was so angry when my mother married Pop. But she never understood. Jimmy was three when our father died. My mother had no way to support us. She was lucky Pop came along. He was good to us, real good. Your mother got pregnant with Angel pretty soon after Nannie Lou got pregnant with Albert. She was so upset that Mom got pregnant, like she couldn't stand the idea that Mom would have a baby with someone besides our father. When she got pregnant herself, it was like she was throwing it up in Mom and Pop's face."

"Where did Nannie Lou meet Pop?"

"At church. His sister was involved with activities in church with my mother. He was single, never married before he married Mom."

She sighed and put the leftovers into the refrigerator. I wondered how many more secrets there were to know about my family. There was the big one that I wanted to ask about. When Kathleen and Joy skipped away from the table, happy at being fed so well, I did.

"Did you know my father?" I asked to her back as she stood at the sink washing dishes.

She stood still a minute and then turned around. "No, I didn't." When I didn't answer, she said, "I'm sorry."

"Do you know who he was?" I asked.

She came close to me and put her hand on my arm. I didn't shake it off even though I usually didn't like people touching me, except my sisters.

"Your mother was going through a bad time. I don't think she was ever sure who he was."

"How can that be?" I asked. "She must have known who she had sex with."

"Jeannine, she was drinking a lot then, doing some drugs. I think there's a lot of things she doesn't remember from back then. But what you need to know is that when she realized she was pregnant, she went into rehab. She cared enough about you to get sober."

"Yeah, for a while," I said.

ALEX and Claire dropped Angel off the next afternoon. Kathleen and Joy and I were watching TV when she came in. She was tan. She dove into the sofa on top of us and wound my hair around her hand. She kissed my forehead and gave us all presents. The house was different with her there—it was like she brought the Florida sun home with her.

That evening, Christine ordered pizza for us. While Kathleen and Joy and I ate in front of the TV, Angel and Christine huddled in the kitchen talking. I sat on the floor of the living room, keeping my eye on the girls and listening to them. Pic still hadn't come out of her room. Frank hadn't come home and we didn't know where he was. Christine was afraid of what he would do if he came home.

"He won't do anything," Angel said, dismissing him with a wave of her hand. "He's a pussy."

"Angel!" Christine said, acting shocked.

"It's true!" Angel replied. "He'll get tired of being out there and come home. He doesn't have anywhere to go. You should be more afraid of what Pic will do."

"Your mother needs to go to work," Christine said. "I called them yesterday and told them she was really sick, but she's got to go back tomorrow or the next day."

Angel nodded and sighed. "Frank better come home. We can't pay the rent without him."

"Look, Angel, we're going down the shore for two weeks. I'd take Kathleen and Joy with me, but your mother would flip out, I think," Christine said.

"That would really help. I have the chance to make some money lifeguarding, but I can't do it if I have to leave Jeannine here all day to take care of them."

"I'll take her too, if you want," Christine offered.

Angel looked in at me. "Bring me some pizza, Jeannine," she said. "The one with sausage."

She and Christine were sitting at the kitchen table. I brought them the pizza box. I liked my aunt, but the last thing I wanted was to go to a strange house at the shore with my uncle, who I could barely remember, and my two cousins, and Kathleen and Joy. I gave Angel the "don't make me do this" look.

"If Aunt Christine takes Kathleen and Joy down the shore, will you go to the pool with me while I work? You can help me, or read, or something. Maybe you can do some shifts at the laundry."

I nodded and slipped into a chair. They kept talking like I wasn't even there.

"I think it'll be fine with Pic if you take the girls. It's just for two weeks," Angel said, ripping a big chunk of pizza off with her teeth.

Christine lowered her voice. "She gets paranoid. She always thinks I'm trying to show her up. She'll think it's a criticism, like I'm saying she can't take care of her kids."

"Well, actually she can't, but whatever. If I tell her that I can't babysit because I have to work at the pool, she'll get mad and say she has to go back to work. Then you can offer to take the kids, and I'll tell her I'll give her half the money I earn for the rent. Then she'll go back to work."

Christine laughed, but she looked sad. "You've had to grow up too fast, Angel."

"Hey, I'm eighteen."

A little later I helped Angel carry her bags upstairs. She swiftly sorted everything into piles: wet towels, T-shirts, shorts, and warm-ups went into one basket, dry dirty clothes into another; dry clean clothes on my bed; shoes in the corner by our closet; wet bathing suits over the doorknob, as always.

"I have a shift at the laundromat tomorrow," she said. "It's a good thing, too. Go get the girls' basket and put it down by the front door. I'm going to try to talk to Pic."

We went into the hall together. I ducked into the girls' room and pulled their laundry basket into the hallway. Angel was standing outside Pic's closed door. She knocked.

"Pic. It's me, Angel. Can I come in?"

Silence.

Angel looked down the hall at me and shrugged, then knocked again, this time a bit louder. "Pic, come on, answer me."

"Go away, Angel," Pic said quietly. She sounded so weary.

"No. I can't. I have to talk to you." Angel turned the doorknob.

"Angel, please," Pic whimpered.

But she didn't say any more, and Angel walked right in. I edged down the hallway until I was just outside the door. I sank onto the floor and peered into the bedroom.

"You look like hell," Angel said, chuckling a little.

"Oh thanks a lot," Pic said, but her voice seemed a little lighter.

She did look bad. Her hair, fried from bad dye jobs, hadn't been washed or combed, and it stuck out from her head the way lightning looks in a cartoon.

"What are you doing out there, Jeannine," she said to me, with that strange brusque tone she used so often, the one that kept you guessing about whether she was mad, or just Pic. I was accustomed to not answering her, and she was accustomed to not having me answer.

"Come in here," she commanded, and I obeyed, edging to the bed and sitting on the corner, out of her reach.

She turned her attention back to Angel. "I guess Christine told you what that bastard did to me," she said, her voice turning bitter.

"He didn't do it to you," Angel said. "He just did it."

"Yeah, how do you know so fucking much?"

"I know. I have a father, a stepfather, an uncle"—she emphasized that last one—"and a cheating boyfriend. And other boyfriends before. Men cheat, they'll fuck anything that moves."

Pic shook a mangled pack of Winstons and one popped out. Her hand shaking, she lit a match, and the room filled

with the smell of sulphur, a smell that always for some reason reminded me of winter. Meanwhile, it was August in
Philadelphia, humid and dirty, and the only air conditioning we had was in this room, and it wasn't on.

"I feel like shit. I feel like a piece of shit," Pic said, a
sob rising.

"He's not worth it. Fuck him. Worry about yourself."

"You always hated him, always!" Pic accused Angel.

Angel sighed. I sympathized. Talking to Pic was like
walking in a field of landmines. One false move and she'd
blow up on you.

"It doesn't matter how I feel about him," Angel said.
"In less than a year, I'll be gone."

There was silence. Pic's face drained of anger for a
moment, and I could see her confusion, just like my own,
the bewilderment and fear that took my breath away whenever the subject of Angel going to college came up.

"You're not going to college, Angel," she scoffed. She
took a long drag on her cigarette and blew the smoke in
Angel's direction.

"Oh yes, I'm definitely going to college," Angel replied,
waving away the smoke with her hand. "I swam really well
in Orlando. Really well. A couple different college coaches
talked to CJ about me." She walked over to the air conditioner and flipped it on. "Jesus, Pic, it's disgusting in here."

Pic tossed her head. "I'm taking a shower," she said,
dismissing us.

"Wait a minute, Pic. I need to talk to you about something. CJ asked me to lifeguard at the pool for the next
three weeks. Starting in two days. I can make some money."

"What about the laundromat?" Pic asked. "What about
our laundry? There's tons of it."

"Yeah, I know. I can do that, too. I have to work there tomorrow. I can ask for an evening shift for the next few weeks. If it's a problem, Jeannine can do a couple shifts for me."

"Well, I need one of you to take care of the kids. I have to go back to work."

"Oh," Angel replied, as if we didn't all know Pic would go back to work right away. None of us were worried about that. "Are you going back tomorrow?"

"Yes, I am," Pic said, the defensiveness evident in her voice.

"Well, you know what Christine just told me? She said she would take the girls down the shore with her kids for two weeks. Isn't that a break? This way we can all work. They're going to pay me nine dollars an hour to guard."

"Nine dollars an hour? That is SO fucking unfair. That's more than I make!"

"I'll give you half of what I make for the rent," Angel said.

"Damn straight you will," Pic sputtered.

"Are you hungry, Pic?" Angel asked. "There's some pizza downstairs. Why don't you come down and have some? You're looking very skinny."

"What's that supposed to mean?" she asked, suspicious.

Angel was already heading for the door and beckoning for me to follow. "It's not supposed to mean anything, except that you should eat."

IT all happened just about as Angel said it would. The next day, Pic went back to work, and while she was there, Angel went to the laundromat, did all our wash, and then came home and packed for Joy and Kathleen to go away with our aunt. They left the following morning.

That night, while Angel and I were getting ready for bed, I heard the front door.

It was Frank. We could hear his voice, calling Pic.

Angel froze halfway up the ladder to her bunk. "Fuck," she hissed. "He's back."

Pic went running down the stairs in her nightgown and then stopped midway, like she'd just remembered she was supposed to be mad. I found myself feeling relieved that she had cleaned up the bedroom, and cleaned herself up. I didn't want Frank to see that he had devastated her.

I flattened myself to the floor and peered through the grate at him.

"What're you doing here?" Pic asked, sounding both angry and desperate.

"Baby, I missed you," Frank said, moving toward the steps.

"Yeah, fuck you, you missed me," Pic shrieked, stopping Frank in his tracks. "You didn't look like you missed me so much when you had your arm around that slut."

"Rita, you overreacted to that, babe. That girl wasn't nothing to me." Frank kept his voice smooth and low.

"Oh my God," Angel whispered, creeping closer to me on the floor. "If she believes that, she's even more stupid than I think she is."

"She didn't look like nothing to you. Even though she was ugly as shit." Pic spat out her words, but there was a hopeful lilt to her voice.

"You didn't give me time to explain, baby. You just went crazy. She was just a girl my brother Howie used to go with. We were just talking, drinking, you know, having a couple laughs."

"I never heard Howie talk about any girl named Lisa."

Pic had come down the stairs and was standing in her bare feet near the front door, her hand on the door knob, like she might fling open the door and order him out at any moment. "Where've you been for the past week?"

"Staying at my cousin Steve's."

"I could call him, you know. Ask him."

"Go ahead."

"Right, what's Steve gonna say?" Angel whispered. "Oh no, Rita, Frank's been fucking that girl Lisa every night."

"Baby, come here," Frank said, moving toward her. His big arms, once muscular but now fat, reached out for her. "I brought you something. A little make-up present."

He pulled a small cellophane bag out of his pocket, dangled it in front of her face, and smiled.

I don't know who looked more shocked, Pic or Angel.

Frank tossed the bag on the table and came thumping up the steps. Down he went again, and put Pic's makeup mirror on the table. He went into the kitchen and got a paring knife. He lit a joint, took a deep drag, and passed it to Pic. He dumped some of the white powder on the mirror and began chopping it with the knife and arranging it in thin lines.

"Where'd you get this?" Pic asked. But she was sitting down beside him, right by his elbow.

"Hey babe," Frank said, turning to her. "I know some people. Just a few hits, and we'll work at making up." He grinned, clutched her to him, and kissed her hard on the mouth. She relaxed and kissed him back.

He reached into his pocket, pulled out a bill, rolled it

tight, and, holding one end to his nose, bent his head toward the mirror. He inhaled deeply through his nose, and one of the lines disappeared. Then he handed the bill to Pic. She hesitated a second, then down her head went and she snorted in a line.

"Jesus Christ," Angel said. She climbed up the ladder and lay on her bed, staring up at the ceiling. "What an asshole. He didn't even ask about the kids. He doesn't even know they're not here."

Pretty soon Frank went into the kitchen, looking for beer. "Shit, don't tell me we're out."

Pic hadn't replaced it since Christine tossed it. "Get some soda, Frank. Get me some too. Come on over and do another line," she coaxed, lighting a cigarette.

After he did, she stuck her finger into the powder and rubbed it along her gums. "Mmm," she said, reaching between Frank's legs and cupping him in her hand.

Angel leaned over the bunk and looked down at me. "What's going on?" she said.

"They're making out."

"Get in bed, Jeannine," she said.

When I had, she put her head over the side again and said, "That's cocaine."

"I know."

"Why would he do that?"

"I guess he wanted to come home," I said.

"Selfish prick," she said.

IT was August in Philadelphia, hot, wet, and tempestuous, and like the weather, Angel stormed through summer's waning weeks bent on causing discomfort and despair.

She had come back from Florida furious with Jamal and open to opportunities for revenge. Our neighbor Ramon was the perfect, if unwitting, accomplice.

Ramon lived with his sister and her boyfriend and their kids across the street and one house down. Everybody said he sold drugs, and since he clearly wasn't running off every day to a job, maybe he did. But he never seemed preoccupied, or clandestine, or wary, like the other dealers in the neighborhood. Angel said that people just said he dealt drugs because he was Puerto Rican.

He and his friends spent a lot of time on the stoop and on the corner. I saw them all the time but they never saw me.

But Ramon saw Angel.

Sometimes he cried things out to her, like, "Hey, my Angel, fly to me." Sometimes he followed her down the block. Sometimes Angel thought he was funny and strung together meaningless sounds in a Spanish accent, and then he laughed at her while she was laughing at him. Sometimes she dismissed him with a toss of her head.

But the day after she got back from Florida, on the way to her shift at the laundromat, she stopped at his little porch when he called out to her. He was sitting alone, drinking a beer. She leaned against his railing, long, tan legs extending from her jean shorts, green toenail polish gleaming in the bright sun. She only stayed a minute, chatting and laughing, but it was long enough for him to get that dazed look I'd seen on Jamal.

The next night, after we were in bed, she climbed down the ladder and opened our door a crack. Pic and Frank, up late and noisy the night before, were asleep. Angel came over to me and whispered, "I'm going over to Ramon's. I'll be back."

"When?"

"In a while. Don't worry. Read your book."

She was so quiet that I didn't hear her shut the front door, but when I got up and peered out our window, I saw her crossing the street and climbing the steps to Ramon's porch. Then suddenly he stepped out of nowhere and grasped her, planting his hand on her butt and pulling her against him. They slipped into the shadows of the porch and I couldn't see them anymore.

I did read. I was reading *Coming of Age in the Milky Way*, which I had actually checked out of the library. It made me want a telescope very badly, and I spent a lot of time pondering how I could get one and whether it would be possible to steal one.

Angel came home two hours later, climbed up the ladder, and fell asleep instantly.

THE next day, one day before the boys and Kim left for Seniors, Angel and I arrived at SportsStars to begin Angel's lifeguarding duties. It was such a relief to get up and leave with Angel and not to have to worry about Joy and Kathleen, or be in the house alone with creepy Frank. We took the subway and then walked as far as possible underground to avoid the heat, although it was still early morning. The tunnel smelled of piss and damp concrete but it was better than frying in the street.

CJ was sitting at a desk in the pool office, filling out timesheets for the coming weeks.

"Angel!" he said, rising from his chair and hooking his

arm around her neck, happy to see her. "And who's this?" He squinted at me, eyes the same dark brown as his skin. "You're Jeannine, right?"

I nodded.

"Well, you're grown," he said, smiling widely.

"Grown?" Angel scowled. "She's not even fourteen yet." He hadn't seen me for a while. I must have looked bigger.

"You gonna help Angel?" he asked.

I looked quickly at Angel, but she had walked over to one of the bulletin boards and was reviewing the results from the younger kids' championships. So I nodded at CJ.

"Good," he said. "Angel tells me that you're real smart. Well, I need someone to remember to fax these timesheets over to Ms. Debbie every Thursday. Maybe you could do that, what do you think?"

"Okay," I said.

Angel turned. "Whose timesheets?" she asked.

"Well, mine and Andrew's," CJ said. "And Ramirez, and Valentine's. And yours and Alex's."

"How will we know how much everyone has worked?" Angel asked.

"I'm filling them out ahead of time. You just have to remember to send them in."

"Oh, I see," Angel said grumpily. "So when Ramirez doesn't show up for two days, we still send in the forty-hour time sheet, right?"

"Who's talking to you?" CJ said. "I'm talking to your sister."

The front door opened and Jamal and a few of the other guys came in, laughing and joking and eating food from McDonald's. "Yo, CJ," one of them called, tossing him a bag.

CJ grinned and pulled out a breakfast sandwich.

Angel swept past Jamal like he had a disease and went out on the deck.

"Whoa," CJ said, sucking deeply on a bottle of water and pretending to shiver. "Just got cold in here!"

I followed Angel, not knowing if he was talking to me, or to Jamal, or just to the room in general.

The pool was surrounded by a narrow concrete deck and lined with old metal benches on three sides and old wooden bleachers on the fourth. There was one lifeguard chair, positioned along the side near the deep end.

Down at the shallow end of the pool, Andrew had a group of little kids in swim lessons. He was in the water and Alex was down there, standing on the deck, watching. I hadn't seen her since Angel had convinced her to lighten her hair. Swept up in a clip, it gleamed in the pool lights.

In a few minutes, CJ and the Seniors team came onto the deck, the four guys and Kim. They congregated on the bleachers and listened as CJ gave them a pep talk about flying out the next day, getting focused, being prepared. They were just getting in to "swim around" as CJ put it. Nothing too strenuous. Just getting in to keep their feel for the water, to stretch.

They stripped to their suits, dumping sweats and jeans and T-shirts onto the bleachers, then pulled their equipment bags to the starting blocks at the deep end and sat on the side, waiting for CJ to pick up his club, walk down, and call out the workout.

Angel was standing by the lifeguard chair, on the side of the pool by the deep end. She pulled off her sweat pants, revealing the bottom of a Speedo two-piece workout suit. The girls never wore them to practice because CJ wouldn't let them. The bottom was like a tiny pair of low-slung shorts, cut low enough to reveal Angel's new belly button ring with its jade stone. Then she yanked the sweat top over her head.

Even though these guys saw her every day, day in, day out, in a bathing suit, somehow seeing her in this black-and-white two-piece suit—even though it was a Speedo, and even though it was sold right out of the equipment closet right there at the pool, despite all that—the guys couldn't take their eyes off of her. There was her six-pack rising above the shiny silver ring, and there was the hint of cleavage, and there were her nipples, hard and shaped like stars, visible through the fabric. And right on her chest, right near where the swell of her left breast emerged from the suit, was a very large, very purple hickey. A remnant of her night visit to Ramon.

Jamal looked quickly away, enraged and humiliated. Exactly as Angel had planned.

RAMON was also part of Angel's plan to torment Frank. But first she confronted him about Pic. Things between him and Pic seemed mended, at least for the moment, but Pic had a haunted look that scared me and infuriated Angel.

"I'm really worried about her," Angel told me. "Weed is one thing, but the coke." She shook her head. "I don't get her thing with men."

That seemed a little ironic to me right then, but I let it go.

But Pic was back at work, leaving most days on time for the early shift, as usual. Angel and I were up early too, going to the pool. One morning at about eight we went downstairs to eat. I was sitting at the kitchen table, reading and nibbling on a butterscotch Tastycake, and Angel was standing at the counter making coffee. In walked Frank, dressed and ready to go out.

"You're up early," Angel said, hostility vibrating under the control in her voice.

"You making coffee?"

"Yeah. You going out to buy some hits for Pic? The dealers are probably still asleep."

"Shut up, Angel," he said. "Goddamn it, why can't you ever just keep your mouth shut?"

"No Frank, I can't shut up," she said, whirling around from the counter. "What are you doing? First you're cheating on her, and then to keep her from being too upset, you're getting her high?"

"Mind your own fucking business, Angel."

"This is my business. She's my mother."

"Listen to you. All of a sudden, 'she's my mother,'" he mimicked.

"She's only fifteen years older than me, Frank. The mother-daughter thing has always been a little torqued."

"Yeah, well, she can decide things for herself. She's a grown-up."

"She's always had a bit of trouble making good decisions for herself, have you noticed?" She made a disgusted noise and started pulling things out of the cabinet, looking for cereal.

"Stay out of it, Angel. I mean it," he said, menacing and close to her back as she bent over.

No response. Frank realized I was there, glared at me, and then stomped through the living room and left the house.

"Torqued?" I asked.

Angel grinned, energized by her confrontation. "I made it up. I think. Is it a word?"

BEING at the pool every day with Angel and Alex was a dream come true. It had interesting moments, and was totally undemanding—for me, anyway. I could just watch, and if there was nothing to watch, I could read. I could have done it for years.

Things were very quiet in the morning. Angel or Alex checked the chemical levels in the pool every day, because they didn't trust the maintenance men. They taught me to do it, too, measuring out the liquid in the little tubes and checking the color against a color card. Sometimes Mr. Ramirez was cleaning the bathrooms or putting out the trash, and Mr. Valentine Russo, the intellectual mechanic, was either in the pump room tinkering around or outside smoking and reading about World War II, his obsession.

It was fairly cool early in the day, before the heat outside and the heat of all the bodies inside had time to raise the temperature. The only windows in the building were hard to open and located high up along the ceiling, to keep people from throwing stuff through them and sending glass flying around. My school was built the same way.

At about ten o'clock, moms starting filtering in with their kids for the swim lessons that started at ten thirty and went on until noon. Alex was teaching and Angel was guarding because Angel had just gotten a tattoo of a dolphin on her shoulder and she wasn't supposed to go in the water for a little while. Sometimes I would get in the water then, when it was calm and quiet, and float around or dive to the bottom with the goggles and pick up junk that had fallen out of people's pockets during the free swim time the day before. Usually I found change, but also occasionally a key, and once a switchblade.

Free swim time began at one and lasted all afternoon. Most of the kids didn't know how to swim. They were totally wild in the pool, splashing and shrieking, and because the ceiling was low, it was really loud in there. I often went in the air-conditioned office then and read. Mr. Ramirez was usually asleep on the couch and Valentine was sitting at his desk, doing paperwork or reading. Sometimes he talked to me about Hitler, sometimes about Angel.

"You're not much like your sister," he said to me one day.

I had been sitting at CJ's desk, reading, and I could feel that Valentine was studying me.

I kept reading.

"She should stay away from that hot-head Jamal," he said.

I looked up.

"She can do better than that."

Why, I thought, *because he's black?*

He was weird and I didn't like him. He thought he was really smart, which maybe he was, but he liked to make other people feel stupid. One day he was going on to no one in particular about the wimpy French and how complacent they were, how they idiotically believed that the Maginot Line was an impenetrable barrier. I was listening.

"The Maginot Line isn't a steamship company, by the way," he said to me, seeing that I had stopped reading and was looking up at him.

"Right," I said. "Even if they had extended it into the

mountains, I don't think it could have kept the Germans out."

His jaw dropped. Actually, I knew a lot about World War II. In fact, I learned about Hitler and Frank on the same day, during a snowstorm.

ANGEL and I lived with Nannie Lou and Pop for a little more than a year while Pic was in rehab. After being in a residential unit for a while, she moved into a transitional house with a few other women. They were all trying to get their kids back. For the first time, Angel and I were able to visit her overnight. Our first visit was right around Valentine's Day. I remember taking the bus with Pic from Miss Evelyn's office to the house. It was very cold, and Angel was in a bad mood.

"It's freezing," said Angel. "Put up your hood, Jeannine."

I was wearing my new very puffy, very warm coat that Nannie Lou had bought me. It was bright yellow and had a big hood. Angel called me Tweetie all the time, but I was warm. Angel wouldn't agree to wear a coat like that, so she got what she called a "pea coat," which was short and navy and had buttons with anchors on them. She also refused to wear gloves.

Angel wandered away from us and looked into the window of a luggage store while we waited for the bus.

Pic looked at me hard. "I wonder if you can get on for five."

"I'm seven."

"I know how old you are. But five and under don't have to pay. You look very small, Jeannine. Just get on and walk right past the driver to an empty seat."

There were no empty seats and we had to stand up. Then we had to transfer to a second bus, and by that time Angel was very grumpy. She wasn't too happy about giving up every Saturday to visit Pic in the first place. She had made some new friends at school and she wanted to hang out with them. Nannie Lou said that was normal for someone who was twelve, but she had to visit her mother anyway.

The house was a deep twin in a neighborhood that I later realized was near to where Alex lived. Pic led us upstairs, past the bedrooms of the other residents.

"What about Ruth, your old roommate from the rehab?" Angel asked. "Is she here?"

"No. She went AWOL from the program," Pic said. "You know, she left. Back on the street."

Pic's room had a single bed, a nightstand, a dresser, and a laundry basket. We sat down on the bed. On the dresser was a big Valentine's heart full of candy. Pic bounced up. "Want some candy?" She opened it up. It was still almost full. "You can have all the ones with nuts, Jeannine. They're the ones that look bumpy. You know I don't like those."

Angel took a big milk chocolate and bit in. There was caramel inside and she pulled the piece still in her hand away from her teeth and made a long string out of the caramel. "Where'd you get these?"

"From a guy named Frank," Pic said, like she was telling a secret.

"Is he your boyfriend?" Angel asked.

"Maybe," she said. "We're not supposed to have boyfriends while we're still in treatment. His sister's in the program. I met him when he came to visit her. Then he started visiting me."

"Hmm," said Angel. Pic's string of sleazy, stupid, loser boyfriends had ceased to interest her. "Your room's nice. Where'd you get the furniture?"

"It belongs to the house."

"Where's our furniture from our apartment?" asked Angel.

Pic shrugged. "It was all junk. We'll get nicer stuff."

"So someone else lived here with this furniture before you?" I asked.

"Yeah."

"Where is she?"

"She got her own place. You don't stay in the program forever. I'll be out of here pretty soon. I'll get my own place and you can move back with me."

A clap of thunder sounded in my head. Somehow it had never occurred to me that things would change again. I had never thought about Pic being out of the program, of us moving out of Nannie Lou's and back with her. I looked at Angel—did she know about this?

She gave me the "don't worry about it" look.

There were some large workbooks on Pic's nightstand. I picked one up and leafed through it. They were for her GED, they all said "GED Preparation Series." The one I was looking at was about sentence parts. It showed you what was the noun, the verb, the adjective, etc. You had to mark the parts and the answers were in the back. I put that book down and picked up the next one. It was about history. It was divided into sections. I snuggled into Pic's pillow and started reading about World War II and ate all the candy with nuts.

After a lunch of jelly sandwiches and chips, perfect for me, Angel and I curled up inside our sleeping bags on

Pic's sofa and I read about World War II all afternoon while Angel slept in front of the TV. Pic stayed upstairs and talked on the phone and painted her toenails. Once she came down to have a cigarette and see what we were doing.

"Are you still reading that book, Jeannine? Maybe you can take the test for me!" She laughed at her joke, said, "I'm taking a bath," and went back upstairs.

It had started to snow. I dragged my sleeping bag over to the window and watched. First the trees and the grass were covered, then the cars, and finally the street. It started to get dark and the streetlight came on. I looked up into the light and all I could see was snow, thick flakes whirling down. It made me think about a quote from the book, about the ashes whirling around the camps all day while they burned the bodies of the Jews.

The phone rang and then Pic came downstairs and said Pop was coming to get us.

"It's supposed to be a blizzard," she said. "If he waited till tomorrow, he might not be able to get you."

I was glad to see Pop. The ride home took a long time because the streets were already clogged with snow. That was okay. I pulled the sleeping bag around me and pretended I was in a sleigh.

I whispered to Angel, "Did you know that Hitler killed six million Jewish people?"

Angel was still waking up from her long afternoon nap. "What are you talking about?"

"World War II," I said.

"Jeannine, I do bad in school," she said. "I don't know anything about World War II."

From up front, Pop said, "What's that, Sprite?"

"She's asking about World War II," Angel said. "She says . . . what did you say?"

I leaned toward the front so he could hear me. "I read that Hitler killed six million Jewish people. It said he put them on trains and took them to camps and put them in ovens."

"Yep, that's right," Pop said, blowing out smoke from his cigarette.

When we got back to Nannie Lou's she made us some hot chocolate and Angel started nagging Jimmy about taking her sledding in the dark and finally they went out bundled up, dragging Jimmy's toboggan. All night long I watched the snow get higher and higher and thought about the Jews in the ovens.

ANGEL was slipping out to see Ramon almost every night after lifeguarding. Sometimes when we got home from the pool and didn't have to go to the laundromat, and he was sitting on the stoop, she'd go hang out over there.

One evening, just past dusk, Angel was over there when Frank pulled up outside. You could hear him coming up the block because his car made so much noise.

I was reading in our bedroom with my chair pulled up to the window, both to get some air and to watch the street. Pic was asleep in her bedroom, tired out by working and drinking and waiting for Frank.

It was a typical August night in Philly, air dense and moist, almost no breeze, no sunset, no sign of moon or stars. A thunderstorm had rumbled through earlier and another one was brewing. Music from cars came and went, I could hear mingled snatches of Spanish and English wafting from the street, and across the way I could see a cigarette glowing from Ramon's porch in the near-dark. He was sitting on the narrow concrete steps, one leg dangling off the side, Angel beside him.

Angel jumped to the sidewalk and worked herself into the V between his legs. She flattened herself against him, pulled his face to her, and kissed him. And kept kissing him. She was wearing her cut-off jean shorts, so short that if she flicked her hips the curve of her butt flashed. She had on a tiny white sleeveless T-shirt that exposed a band of skin along her waist.

Frank didn't get out of the car. I couldn't see him, only the top of the car, but I knew he could see them, was sitting in the car watching.

ANGEL had been home from Florida about two weeks when another letter came. Like the others, the envelope was typed. The contents had no words. It was just the drawing of a naked girl from the back, with a dolphin on her shoulder.

"See?" Angel said, waving it at me. "I knew it was from the pool. No one else knows I have the tattoo."

"Well, they might," I said. "You can see it when you wear a tank top."

And it was so hot she was wearing tank tops all the time. So anybody at the laundromat or on the subway or on the block could see it. She frowned at me and shoved the picture in our underwear drawer.

THE paychecks came to the pool every Friday. On our way home the first time she got paid, we stopped at the check-cashing place around the corner from the house. It was a combination check-cashing, bill-paying, lottery-selling pawnshop. We sometimes went in there to get our subway tokens. The guy who was usually behind the counter had a front tooth that was rimmed in gold.

Angel cashed her check and then we went next door to the Chinese take-out place. She got sweet-and-sour something, and spare ribs, and shrimp fried rice, and she got me white rice and fortune cookies. Then we went home to eat.

It was still light, and Pic was home alone. She was very agitated, up and down off the sofa, opening the front door, looking down the street, smoking, switching channels on the remote, going back to the door. Frank wasn't home and she was upset. Whenever he was late now, she got upset— which was a bad thing, because he was never on time.

"Want some Chinese?" Angel asked.

Pic shook her head. She was drinking a spiked orange soda and smoking a cigarette.

"Did you get paid?" she asked Angel.

"Yep." Angel pulled a wad of money from the pocket of her backpack and counted out $150 for Pic.

"You'll spend this on the rent, right?" she asked.

Pic looked stunned, then furious. "What are you talking about?"

"You know exactly what I'm talking about. We're short for the rent and you might spend it on something else."

"I don't know what you're talking about."

"Shit you don't."

"You know what, Angel? You're too fucking busy. Mind your own business."

"You know what, Pic? I think I should call Miss Evelyn and talk with her."

Pic started at the mention of our old caseworker. She breathed out heavily and clenched her teeth. "Don't you dare threaten me."

"I do dare. I am threatening you. Because this sucks for us and it sucks for you," Angel said, not yelling but still loud and firm. "Frank is not important. Vodka and weed and whatever else are not important. The kids and your job are important. If you can't put them first, Joy and Kathleen shouldn't even come back here."

"Frank wouldn't let that happen. Don't mess with us this way, Angel, by threatening to take away his kids."

"Us? Have you lost your damn mind?" Angel said, exasperated. "He doesn't give a shit about those kids. I don't even think he realizes that they're not here!"

Pic jumped up and came at Angel. "Who do you think you are, you little slut? Frank told me about that scene across the street."

"I'm sure he did, because he couldn't get out of his fucking car. He couldn't stop looking," Angel retorted, taking a step back. "Have you noticed that, Pic? That he can't ever stop looking at any girl older than thirteen?"

Pic swung out and slapped Angel hard across the face.

Angel held her ground, and it struck me that Pic was actually the same height as Angel. It never seemed that way because Pic usually stood with rounded shoulders.

Angel put her hand to her face and rocked slightly forward, toward Pic.

"Don't you do anything you'll regret, Angel."

"I never regret anything I do. Never."

IN September I started high school. Like so many other kids, I had missed a lot of school. In eighth grade I was absent over seventy days, almost half the year. It really wasn't such a big deal; in my school, a third of the kids were out every day.

Virtually all my absences were unexcused, except for times when I had to stay home because Joy or Kathleen was sick; Pic didn't know when I went to school and when I didn't, and I never asked her to write a note. I didn't have to. When you were absent, the school made this automated phone call to your home phone after advisory, and our advisory was after second period, past ten o'clock, because if they had it first thing in the morning, so many kids were late that they would have to mark half the school absent every day. So the automated call came in the early afternoon, when no one was at my house to answer the phone, and we didn't have voice mail. So, no problem.

Unlike most of the truant kids, I was scoring in the ninety-ninth percentile on the stupid standardized tests, and in classes where the teachers gave make-up exams, my grades were As. Still, in some other classes I had Cs because I missed tests and didn't turn in homework, which most of time was so deadly boring I couldn't make myself do it. That, combined with the absences, kept me from getting into Kennedy, despite Claire's best efforts. Along with 2,700 other kids, I was assigned to my neighborhood high school.

The ninth graders started a day before the other students, for orientation. Because of the drop-out rate and the failure rate, the freshman class was four times the size of the senior class. Half of us were first-time ninth graders, and half of us were repeaters. Some of those kids looked old enough to be my father.

Angel and Kathleen didn't have school until the following day, so Angel stayed home from practice to take care of the little girls and make sure I went to school. Joy was starting kindergarten but for some incomprehensible reason they didn't begin until two weeks after everyone else, so one of us was going to have to stay home each day until then to take care of her because Pic had to go to work and Joy couldn't go to Head Start anymore. Angel said we'd take turns but I was thinking I would gladly watch her for two weeks instead of starting school.

Angel and the girls walked me. It had rained the night before, a thunderstorm, and it felt like a summer morning, not a school day. We threaded around the soggy sidewalk trash, sidestepping along with the sleepy hookers who were on their way home.

When we got near my school, the kids were lined up halfway down the block because it took a long time to get everyone through the metal detectors. Angel said that once everyone got used to it the line went much quicker; you knew to take off your jewelry and stuff before you got to the door.

She stopped at the corner. "Do you want us to come all the way with you?" she asked. "They're gonna think I'm your mother, and then someone will make fun of you."

I looked up at the building, four or five stories of gray stone, a square block around, bars on the bottom set of windows. A gothic prison.

Angel read my mind. "You can do this," she said.

I looked down the block, and now it seemed very long,

the end of the line of kids very far away. The sun was working its way over the building, and it was already getting hot. I felt dizzy.

I shook my head. *No.*

"Okay." Angel shrugged. "You'll try again tomorrow."

She had no particular reason to make me go, having no conviction herself about the value of school. So we went home, made pancakes, and watched TV.

Later that day, Angel dug through her swim bag and pulled out a book. She tossed it to me.

"Did you ever read this?" she asked.

I nodded. "Why?"

"We were supposed to read it this summer and write an essay. I forgot all about it until Claire reminded me. She was typing Alex's essay. Isn't it weird? The whole senior class has to read the same book."

"It's a really famous book," I said. "Also lucky for you, pretty short and easy to read. Didn't you ever hear of it?"

"No. What's it about?"

"It's about this guy who's born into some white trash family but he's really determined to be wealthy and powerful and it's all tied up with this woman who he loves, but he doesn't really love her, she just represents the money and the upper-class society he wants to belong to. He makes a lot of money by being a gangster."

"And?"

"He gets killed."

"Oh. Well, the essay is . . . wait a second, I wrote it down." Angel dug a crumpled piece of paper out of her swim bag. "Explain the American Dream as a theme in *The Great Gatsby* and explain the relevance of the American Dream to contemporary American society."

"Well, that's easy," I said. "You can write that without even reading the book."

"I don't think so."

"Definitely," I said. "What's the American dream? What does everyone in America want?"

Angel thought it over. "To be rich and famous."

"Right. But, are rich and famous people usually happy? Are they satisfied? Are they good? No."

"So that's what I say? That doesn't seem like I could write a whole essay just with that."

"You have to give examples. Drug dealers are a good example. You could even use sports. Basketball and football, especially, you know, how they all want to get out of the neighborhood and they make all this money and then they act like they never left the neighborhood, getting shot up in bars or arrested for beating up their girlfriends. You know, they haven't really gotten anything except the money."

She nodded and paused. "Could you write it for me? Come on, Jeannine, it'll take me ten times as long as you. Claire said she'd type it for me if I wrote it."

"Sure," I said. It wasn't the first time I'd written papers for her. "How long does it have to be?"

OF course, eventually I did start going to school. I was in a Spanish I class with all these Puerto Rican kids who didn't know the first thing about grammar and cursed in dialect at the gay Cuban guy who taught the class. I had algebra but we didn't have a teacher, so some days there were subs but a lot of days there weren't and we got sent to sit in the lunchroom with an aide. Because there wasn't a teacher, they didn't give us books, which was great because it meant we couldn't do any work, so I just wrote in my journal and sketched the kids.

My English teacher was a geeky young white guy who was afraid of us. We had this anthology and he assigned the black writers in it because he thought the kids would read the stuff that way, but they didn't read it anyway and he didn't know what to do. I don't know why he thought they would want to read "Sonny's Blues." He should have started with rap lyrics, but there weren't any in the anthology and he probably didn't know any himself.

They put me in a science class called Earth Science that every freshman had to take. It was like a combination of geology and oceanography and zoology, but basically they made it up to replace physics because they knew most of the kids in the school could never make it through physics. This way the kids who made it through eleventh grade could still get credit for three years of science: earth science, biology, and chemistry. Lucky for me my science teacher was bored too, so he had started an astronomy club. His name was Mr. Washington, and one day in early October he asked me to stay after class.

"You've barely been here all month," he said.

I nodded.

"How did you get such a good grade on this test?" he asked, waving the first chapter test at me.

I shrugged.

"Jeannine, did you read the chapter?"

I shook my head. *I never got a textbook, you idiot.*

"So?"

"I already knew the answers," I said.

"How?"

"From reading other books."

He considered. "Why are you out of school so much?"

I shrugged.

"That's not good enough, Jeannine. Is something wrong at home?"

I shook my head.

"Then why?" he persisted.

"School's boring," I said.

"I see. Do you also read books about astronomy?"

I nodded.

"Then why don't you join my astronomy club? We have a monthly sky watch, and we meet every week in school. Every Thursday afternoon. I give the students articles to read, and we discuss them. And we map the sky, we go to the astronomy meetings at the planetarium. It's fun. And in your case, it might help you with your attendance problem."

I don't have an attendance problem. You have a problem with my attendance. "Okay."

THE first sky watch was near the end of October, a night when there was no moon. Angel didn't get it.

"Your teacher's going to drive you? That's weird, Jeannine. They don't drive you places. Maybe he's some kind of a pervert."

She walked me to school. Mr. Washington was there, along with another teacher I didn't know and about six kids.

"You're Jeannine's mother?" Mr. Washington asked when Angel approached him. He looked appalled.

"I'm her sister," Angel said, checking out the scene and Mr. Washington's mini-van. "What time are you coming back?"

"Around eleven. We can't really see anything until it's very dark, and it takes a while to set up and break down the equipment," he explained. "Can you pick her up?"

"I can meet her back here," Angel said.

"You're welcome to come with us," he offered.

"I don't think so," she said.

"Are you still in school?" he asked.

"Yeah." She nodded. "I'm a senior at Kennedy."

"Oh," he replied, impressed. "Jeannine should be at Kennedy."

"Yeah," Angel agreed. "She belongs there a lot more than me. It just didn't work out."

We drove a long way, out of the neighborhood, the houses gradually getting bigger and farther apart. It looked like the suburbs, but Mr. Washington said we were still in the city. We turned onto a windy, uphill road that led into an arboretum. There was an old house there with a few lights, but once we passed by, it was completely dark. No lights.

Other people were already there, setting up telescopes. Every month people from different astronomy clubs came together in some dark place and looked at whatever the sky was offering that month. I found the constellations and their movement only mildly interesting, and the moon less so. But I was fascinated with the ideas that looking through the telescope suggested—like, if there was a Big Bang, what was there before it? And if the universe had been expanding ever since that explosion, would it go on forever? And if not, what would stop it?

I was also obsessed with the notion that when a telescope captures an image of deep space, it records an image of the past. It's called lookback time. The farther out you go, the farther back you go. I kept revisiting this idea, that light I was seeing might be coming from a star that was long dead, from a quasar that I could never really see from any telescope. What I was seeing were fossils—light that was emitted near the beginning of creation and had taken this long to reach us.

By finding the boundaries of the universe, the scientists were attempting to map the beginning of time.

I think Mr. Washington thought that all of this stuff would excite me and make me want to come to school. Actually, exactly the opposite happened. School seemed more irrelevant than ever. Who could care about solving a problem about where John and Harry would meet if they began 100 miles apart and one traveled at 35 miles an hour and the other at 40 when the earth was hurtling through the sky like a runaway train?

chapter six

———

ALEX

When Angel joined the team and CJ told me it was my job to be her buddy, he meant that I was supposed to get her used to the routines of the team and help her understand competitive swimming (rules about practice, how to interpret time standards and meet entries), and help her deal with our special environment— water that was usually about ten degrees below normal because the pool was ancient (coat yourself with Vaseline and put on tights and a leotard under your suit), roaches in the locker room (hang your swim bag on a hook and don't ever put food down, just eat it!) and racial issues (swim teams at suburban meets will treat you like you're black only worse, since you're white but with a black team and you have a black coach).

It turned into so much more than that.

Angel started swimming for us at a good time, near the end of the summer, when the younger kids were already finished with competing and we were just swimming to stay in shape. The workouts were pretty easy. In the afternoons while he worked with the older kids, CJ made Andrew take us places on the subway. He didn't want us to go home to empty houses and he thought there were important things for us to see. Usually those important places were outside because inside places like museums cost money. That's how we found ourselves one day standing in a long line with a whole lot of tourists to see the Liberty Bell. It was blazing hot and we were not happy. Even though she was new, Angel was not quiet.

"This better be worth it," she complained, frowning at Andrew. "They rang this bell for the American Revolution?"

"Yeah," he said.

"No," said a tourist in front of us. "It was the bell for the State House."

"What State House?" asked Andrew.

"Independence Hall used to be the Pennsylvania State House," the tourist said, gesturing across the street to the old brick building.

"So if it wasn't for the Revolution, why are we seeing it?" another swimmer asked.

"Because CJ said to see it," Andrew said, his tone suggesting we should shut up.

Finally, it was our turn to get near the bell. The park ranger stationed there asked us to gather close and he began his well-rehearsed explanation of the history of the bell. When he concluded, with us understanding very little of what he had said about this symbol of freedom, he asked if we had any questions.

"It looks broken," Angel observed.

"Well, it's cracked," said the ranger.

"Does it ring?" Angel asked.

"No," said the ranger. "It hasn't been rung for almost 150 years."

Angel turned to me and the other swimmers and said,

"So CJ sent us all the way down here to get hot standing in line to see a broken bell?"

The snickers were loud and Andrew quickly led us to a nearby stand and bought us popsicles. From that day, every time we found something disappointing, highly overrated, or not operating as it should, we called it a broken bell.

SOON we were at the beginning of the school year and that meant the start of a training cycle. The yardage and pace we were swimming would build slowly through the fall. Even so, Angel, like everybody else who was new, found those first practices almost impossible. Kids were crying all over the deck or throwing up in the pool gutters from the exertion. We began every season with a bunch of new swimmers, but most left within a month. They just couldn't take the work. Angel was stubborn, though. She took the whole thing like it was personal challenge from CJ to her, and she wasn't going to let him win.

Most of the time, Angel had no way of getting around except on public transportation. Sometimes her grandfather would come and get her, and once in a while her Uncle Jimmy would drop her off or pick her up, but he was in school and working too, so most of the time she was on her own. My mother often gave her a ride home, especially when daylight savings ended and it was dark when we left practice. Angel started staying at our house a lot on Friday nights, and going to Saturday morning practice with me. Then sometimes I'd go home with her after practice and hang out with her.

She and her sister lived with her grandmother and

step-grandfather because their mother was in rehab. I knew a lot of people in school and on the team whose fathers or brothers were on crack or alcoholics or in jail or even dead, but I didn't know anyone else with a mother in rehab. It was all hard to imagine, because Angel's grandmother was so normal, with a clean house and a full refrigerator and decorations for Christmas going up the day after Thanksgiving.

Slowly, Angel talked to me about her mother.

"She's so annoying," she said to me one day after she missed Saturday practice because she had to visit her mother in the social worker's office. "She told me I looked like I was growing. I said, hell yeah, I'm eating like a cow because Nannie Lou makes us great food all the time. She got, like, pissed off. Like she's jealous that I want to eat Nannie Lou's food."

Still, once CJ started entering her in meets and she was winning ribbons and medals, she would put them aside to take to show her mother.

Angel and I became friends quickly. She was only a year older than me, but in some ways she seemed like an adult—I was fascinated by her familiarity with and confidence about getting around the city on her own, the way she took responsibility for her sister, how much she knew about sex, drugs, and stuff like food stamps. But about other things she was clueless—like, she'd never been out of Philadelphia except a couple times to New Jersey, she barely knew what college was, and she couldn't ever remember having been to the doctor, so when Nannie Lou made appointments for her, Jeannine, Albert, and Jimmy, she was scared to death.

I remember one time when Angel first joined the team

and we went to a meet in Delaware. It was a two-day meet and we were staying overnight. We were young then and were staying in a hotel room with my mother. When we first got there, Angel raced in first and then came running back out into the hallway, panting in amazement. "Hey, we have our own bathroom in there!" she said.

And I realized that I was a novelty to Angel. She hadn't made any new friends since going to live at her grandmother's, and she didn't have any from before because she had moved so many times and been in so many schools.

CJ insisted on parent participation with the swim team. He had a parent meeting once a month and expected every swimmer's family to be there. "I can't do the whole damn thing myself," he'd say, urging parents to volunteer to work at meets and raise money to buy us equipment and pay for meet entries.

So one day, after Angel had been swimming with us for six weeks or so, my mother stopped in to talk with Angel's grandmother. Angel and I hung around the kitchen and ate eggs and Scrapple while they talked.

Nannie Lou was a sweet lady who seemed to be mildly confused most of the time. She listened to my mother, nodding and smiling.

"And when are these meetings?" she asked. "I don't drive, you know."

"The first Wednesday of every month at six thirty," my mother said.

"Down there at the pool?" She looked helplessly at Angel, as if the pool was in a different universe instead of a few miles away. "Well, maybe Pop will drive me." She stopped to consider. "What if my son came?"

She meant Jimmy, Angel's uncle, who was only a senior in high school.

My mother looked at me. "Well, I'm not sure. I can ask the coach."

So once in a while Angel's grandparents came to the meetings together, shy and completely baffled by the swimming talk but proud of Angel nevertheless, especially when they looked at the bulletin boards and saw her name highlighted so often in the meet results.

The real problems began when Angel went back to living with her mother.

Eventually, Pic got discharged from her treatment program and the courts let her have Angel and Jeannine back. She had gotten married shortly before that, and by the time Angel and Jeannine returned to her, she was very pregnant with their sister Kathleen.

Pic had no interest in swimming, couldn't see any point in Angel doing it, and thought Angel needed to be home helping her take care of Jeannine and the new baby. She had a job that she couldn't lose because of the case worker who was still checking up on them, so when she went back to work the baby had to go to a neighbor's and Angel had to take the baby there every day and then walk Jeannine to school. All this happened just at the time when CJ wanted us to start coming to morning practice a few times a week. He didn't believe that Angel's mother wouldn't want to see her be successful, wouldn't understand that she was very talented and that swimming would open a lot of doors for her. He finally got tired of hearing what he thought were Angel's excuses and one evening he showed up at the house to talk to her mother.

When Pic answered the door, she was already in a

mood because she had worked all day and the baby was fussy.

She was astonished to see a big black man, hat in hand, standing on her doorstep.

CJ held out his hand, introduced himself, and asked if he could come in. It was chilly outside.

Pic handed Kathleen to Angel, who was also astonished to see CJ, and then stepped outside instead of inviting him in. "What can I do for you?" she asked.

CJ proceeded to explain how talented Angel was, how much promise she had, how she could be a ranked swimmer, how she could get a college scholarship but needed to be able to come to every practice to make that happen. And he needed Pic to come to parent meetings and get involved in the team.

Angel heard Pic say, "Angel's not smart enough to go to college. I think I know my daughter. I don't need you to tell me about her. And I sure as shit don't need you to tell me what I should do."

And with that she went back inside.

FOR students at Kennedy, senior year was about getting into college. So while the prom and graduation loomed out there in the far-off spring, the fall was a very tense time. For some kids, like Melanie, there wasn't too much pressure to have the best trimester of your life—her AP courses and grades from junior year would hold up. For others, like Angel, all Bs would be a really big help. For everyone, the last shot at the SATs was fearsome. I felt really sorry for the kids who didn't have athletics to help them get in somewhere. I had a B average and a lousy 1120, but I knew that was enough for some coach somewhere to be glad to have me at his school and help pay for it too.

The previous spring, CJ had us all make a list of ten schools we were interested in. Mine included a lot of the schools where I probably had little chance of getting any money because I wasn't fast enough—Penn State, Syracuse, Villanova. Angel's included schools where she'd be able to swim and get some money but where she'd never make it academically—UVA, North Carolina, Michigan.

"Williams, back to the drawing board," CJ said to me, looking at my list. "Don't you want to be able to score? At these schools you might not even make the traveling team."

"Alex," my mother said, "think. You can probably get into a school that you wouldn't be able to otherwise. You can get a better education and a degree from a more prestigious school than you would be able to with just your academics. Choose a great school with a mid-level team."

I thought about Penn, but everyone knows the Ivies don't give athletic scholarships.

"That's a lot of bullshit," CJ said. "If they want you, they'll figure out a way to get you some money, whatever they call it. But look at some Division I schools that are a level below Big East and Big Ten schools. How about American?"

In the end, American was on my list. So was U Mass, and Fordham, and William and Mary.

"Girl, we have to get you out of high school first," CJ said to Angel.

CJ was getting calls about all of us and the coaches were calling us at home while they still could; once we started competing for the winter season, they'd have to leave us alone until spring. Some of the guys, like Jamal, signed early. He had just about the same grades and scores as me, but two Senior cuts. That made all the difference. By October, he knew that he was into school and that it would all be paid for.

By NCAA rules, we were allowed four official, paid recruiting trips. Some of the schools had these big recruiting weekends where twenty kids came at the same time. A number of us got invited to visit Rutgers, and with CJ's blessing, Melanie, Angel, and I decided to go. It was a Big East team, but it was near the bottom of that conference.

"Kind of boring, isn't it? I mean, it's an hour away, *in New Jersey*," my mother said. "If they're paying for these trips, why not go somewhere you haven't been, somewhere far—Arizona, California? At least look."

I didn't want to say it to her but I didn't want to go too far away to school. I wanted to be able to get home whenever I wanted to, and without taking a plane. I knew I wouldn't have money for planes.

She had a point about Rutgers, though, because we'd all been there plenty of times. Rutgers had one of the newest and best facilities in the Northeast, and a lot of club meets were held there. In fact, we usually swam there twice a year, once in the winter and once in the late spring.

But CJ thought we should go for the visit. Swimming there in a meet with your club wasn't the same as spending a weekend with the college team and meeting the coach, he reasoned. "Decent team, coming up, and all y'all," he said, waving his hand at the three of us, "could find the right academics there. They have programs for everyone, even you," he added, winking at Angel.

Before we left, he took us aside to give us a little lecture. "Remember that you're representing all of us back here. No drinking. Those college kids do a lot of drinking, but you don't need to. And no wild shit." He frowned at Angel.

Angel wasn't thinking about any wild shit. She had a lot of other things on her mind. Besides troubles at home, she hadn't been feeling well for weeks.

"Maybe you have mono," I said to her one day at practice when she dragged herself out of the pool, unable to finish the workout.

"Why would I have mono?"

"Why wouldn't you?" CJ chimed in. "We all know you been kissin' too many people."

She scowled at him, swept her equipment bag up, and stomped into the locker room.

I think all three of us were a bit nervous about our visit to Rutgers. I drove, Melanie sat in the front, and Angel stretched out in the backseat and complained about the music. I wanted to listen to Aerosmith and Melanie was into Janet Jackson.

"That's all right," I said to Melanie. "You can put that on."

"Come on, dude," Angel groaned.

She put on her headphones for a while, and when she pulled them off I could hear Coolio booming from her Walkman. She leaned up to us and said, "Why do we have to stay in different rooms? I don't want to stay with someone I don't know."

"They want us to get to know the other kids," Melanie said. "We already know each other."

"Well, I hope they don't put me with some geek."

"Well, at least they'll put you with someone like you—
a white girl."

"Yeah, well, they'll probably put you with a white girl,
too, Mel, 'cause I don't think they got any black girl
swimmers up here," Angel said, and we all giggled.

"That's what I mean!" Mel said. "I'm probably the only
black person in the whole place."

"Hey, what about me?" I said.

"Do you count?" Mel nudged me. "Just kidding. I mean
people who are already there."

"All kinds of people from New York go there. There's
probably plenty of black kids," I said.

"Yeah, what do you got against white people, anyway?"
Angel joked.

It turned out we were all right. There were no black
swimmers on the team, which was no surprise, because
there were very few blacks swimming in all of Division I.
But there were a lot of black students on campus, and
there were a lot of black athletes, just not swimmers. And
Angel did get stuck with a very geeky girl as her buddy for
the weekend.

We got there on Friday evening and had dinner in the
dining hall with the whole swim team, the head coach, one
assistant, and about fifteen recruits. It was like eating at
TGI Friday's except it was mostly buffet.

"Oh my God, I love this place," said Angel, filling up
her plate for the third time.

After dinner we were invited to go to a party at "the
boys' house." There was a lot of drinking, just as CJ had
warned. They had a keg. Athletes from some of the other
teams were there. The girl I was staying with, Tara, told
me there were parties every weekend.

"How do you get up for practice?" I asked, knowing that they had Saturday morning practice early, just like we did.

She shrugged. "You get used to it."

"Not me," Angel said. "I need my beauty sleep."

The girl that Angel was staying with was clearly out of place at this party. Her name was Sheila. She swam the same events as Angel—100 free, 100 fly—only slower, and had been recruited from Ohio. There wasn't one girl on the team who had a Senior cut, which made Angel a choice pick. The coach had spent a lot of time talking to her at dinner.

Sheila told us she didn't dance or drink ("I think she's from some religious cult," Angel told us later) and told Angel at ten thirty that she was leaving and Angel could go back to the dorms with someone else if she wanted to stay. Angel wasn't drinking either, not that she did much anyway. She always said that wine and other liquor tasted like cough medicine and too many beers made her have the runs. That night she was sipping on a Coke and said her stomach was upset.

"Maybe it has something to do with eating enough dinner for five people," I said.

"Come back with me," she said.

"No. Stay here and come back with me."

"Please," she whined. "I don't want to go back with her."

"So, stay with me. We'll go back by twelve, I promise."

In the end she stayed and had fun flirting with some basketball player from Newark. When we left at midnight to go back, the party was in full swing and Melanie was still there, drinking beer and dancing her little heart out. She was going to have fun in college, I could tell.

When we got back to the dorms, Angel decided to stay

in the room with Tara and me rather than go down the hall to Sheila's room. Tara's roommate was there too, so Tara climbed in her bed and Angel and I shared a bed. We fell asleep head to toe, watching TV.

The next day we were to shadow the swimmers as they went through their workout. It was against NCAA rules for recruits to practice with the swimmers, but we could get into the second pool and do a workout sent by our coach. The reason for that was supposedly that you were in training and you shouldn't miss a day of training, but really it was to make sure the coaches got to see you work out.

Angel put on a show, had the best workout of her life. After practice the team went to the weight room, where they had the same trainers as the football team.

"Jesus Christ!" Angel said, looking at the stack of weights the girls were using on the incline presses. "This shit's hard. Does everyone have to do this?"

"The sprinters do more," Tara said.

Angel groaned.

"But they do less yardage," Tara said.

We toured the campus, which was so big and spread out that we had to take a bus. We saw the classrooms, labs, the library, all the athletic facilities, the stadium, the gyms, and the sports medicine and trainers' offices.

In the afternoon, Tara took us for a walk through town. She showed us the bookstore—it seemed awfully far away from the dorms and the classrooms, I thought, imagining lugging all those books back once they were bought—and the best ice cream place. There were kids everywhere; it almost seemed like a little city inhabited totally by people between eighteen and twenty-five.

We drifted in and out of stores and boutiques and

found ourselves in the Gap, my kind of store. We weren't in there ten minutes before Melanie had a pile of stuff draped over her arm.

"She shops," I said to Tara. "Seriously."

Angel and Tara and I leafed through clothes on the rack and tried on some hats. Tara took a few pairs of jeans into the dressing room while Angel and I looked at the summer sale rack, the super markdowns. If Angel had a style of dressing, it was some weird combination of punk and slutty—but athletic punk and slutty. She might dress like Madonna, but she moved like Jackie Joyner-Kersey.

Melanie came out of the dressing room, dumped her take on the counter, and whipped out her credit card. Her parents gave her and her sister pretty free rein with money, especially for clothes. My mother made me ask for shopping money in advance—no credit cards, no impulse shopping. Angel bought all her own clothes, of course. That day she bought a five-dollar camisole-type top with a sequined star on the front from the sale rack, probably the only such thing the Gap ever carried.

THAT night, lying in bed, Angel whispered to me, "Let's go here."

"How do you know we're going to the same place?" I said. "You're way faster than me. They might want you but not me."

She dismissed that with a hiss. "Don't be ridiculous. Of course they'll want you. I'll tell them I'm not coming unless they take you."

A few minutes later, just as I was drifting off, she shook my shoulder lightly.

"Alex. Hey."

"What?" I asked sleepily.

"I was thinking I might be pregnant," she whispered.

ANGEL, my mother, and I sat in our kitchen drinking tea while my mother grilled Angel. Our table was by the window, looking out on our little backyard. My mother had a bird feeder hanging near the window, filled with seed. It was a beautiful October afternoon, late, red and yellow leaves all over the grass.

On our way home from Rutgers we stopped at a CVS, me telling Melanie that I needed tampons. I bought one of those instant pregnancy tests; you pee on the stick and you know within a minute. Angel used it as soon as we got home, and the telltale pink line appeared, bold and bright, before the minute was out.

"When was the last time you had your period?" my mother asked.

Angel sighed. "I don't know. Before Juniors."

"Before Juniors!? That's three months ago!" I said.

"Two," Angel retorted. "August to September, September to October."

"Yeah, but Alex is right in a way," my mother said. "You could be ten weeks pregnant. That doesn't leave much time. Haven't you noticed any symptoms? Are your boobs sore?"

"Mom!"

"Really, Alex. If we're going to talk about this, let's talk."

Angel nodded. "Yeah, maybe. I guess I just wasn't thinking about it. I have been feeling a little sick. To my stomach."

"Angel, didn't you use anything?"

Angel looked embarrassed. "Well, sometimes."

"Well, sometimes doesn't keep you from getting pregnant."

"I know," she said, shaking her head at her own stupidity. "Sometimes I had rubbers with me, sometimes I didn't. Sometimes it wasn't . . . I don't know. Convenient."

I stood up and got a box of ginger snaps. I couldn't believe we were having this conversation. I kept wondering how this same conversation would be going if it were me who was pregnant.

"You could get AIDS," I said.

"I don't have AIDS," Angel said, dismissing me with a wave.

"Well, you could get AIDS. You should use a condom just for that reason," my mother said. "You're sure you want to have an abortion?"

"Oh God, yeah. I can't have a baby. I'm going to college." Angel slipped a couple cookies out of the pack. "I'm not going to do what my mother did. Do you have any soda?"

My mother went to the fridge. "What about insurance? Whose name is the insurance under?"

Angel shrugged. "I don't know. I don't even know if we have insurance."

"Well, what happens when you go to the doctor? Do you have cards that you give them?"

Angel frowned, thinking. "I don't know. I haven't been to the doctor for years. I might not have been to the doctor since I lived with my grandmother, I can't even remember."

"Can't she just pay for the abortion?" I asked.

"Yeah, how much do you think it is?" Angel asked.

"I don't know. I'm sure it's a lot. We need to find out about the insurance. Angel, are you sure you don't want to tell your mother?"

Angel shook her head violently. "There's no way I'm telling her. No way."

"What about Jamal?" my mother asked. "If you have to pay for it, he should pay some too."

"No," Angel said. "We can't tell him."

"But, Angel," my mother protested, all caught up in the fairness of things.

"Claire," Angel said, staring her straight in the eye. "I'm not sure it's Jamal's baby."

That stopped my mother dead in her tracks. "Oh!" was all she could say.

"I'm sorry." Angel sighed. "You must think I'm really awful."

My mother took a deep breath. "No. No I don't." She put her hand on Angel's arm. "We all do things we regret later."

Really, I thought.

"So," my mother continued. "You've never been to a gynecologist."

Angel shook her head.

"Well." She rooted in her purse for her phone book. "You'll have to go to mine."

FIVE days later, Angel went to my mother's gynecologist for an abortion. The procedure was performed right in the office, which was in a hospital. The doctor had agreed to do it for cost, and my mother paid for it, with the agreement that Angel would pay her back, sometime, when she could.

The worst part of the whole business happened afterwards, at the pool. On the first day that Angel didn't show up for practice, CJ fumed. On the second day, he yelled at me. "Where the hell is she, Alex? I know you know."

I knew this was an argument I couldn't win, so I said nothing.

"You tell her I want her here tomorrow for morning practice. I'm holding you responsible. *You.* Do you hear me?"

I went home and told my mother. Angel had stayed with us the night of the abortion, at the insistence of my mother. The next day she had gone home, but not to school or the pool.

"What am I supposed to tell him?" I asked.

My mother thought it over. "I'll come with you in the morning. I'll talk to him."

So the next morning, my mother got up at three thirty and showered and put on her work clothes and came to the pool with me and Melanie for morning practice.

CJ glowered at us when we came in without Angel, but he knew my mother was there to calm him down and protect me from having to explain, so he said nothing until we were stretching on the side of the pool.

Then, to my mother, he said, "I'm gonna call her house."

My mother shook her head. "Don't, CJ. There are enough problems."

"What problems? Her mother? I'll get with her mother."

"I don't think that will help right now," my mother said. "You have to trust me that she's not here for a good reason. She has to take a little time off."

CJ, still looking skeptical, motioned us into the water

and called out the warm-up. Then he handed the workout book to Andrew.

I lingered on the side, pretending to adjust my goggles.

CJ and my mother stepped back a little bit.

CJ caught my mother's eye. "She's pregnant."

My mother flinched visibly. "Was pregnant. How did you know?"

"Do you think I've been working with kids all these years for nothing?"

"No, of course not. I just didn't know . . ."

"No, they don't tell me stuff like that because they know I won't approve. And I don't approve. That girl needs to clean it up."

"CJ, she doesn't drink, she doesn't do drugs, and she's trying to do what she's supposed to do—for you, at school, for her sisters. Angel has a crater inside of her the size of the Grand Canyon. For Christ's sake, how's she going to fill it? Why do you think she has all these boyfriends, anyway?"

"Well, that's the wrong way to make up for what she doesn't have," CJ retorted. "She could pray. And work harder," he growled. And then, "Is she all right?"

My mother smiled grimly. "She will be. She'll be back in a few days."

If that had been the end of it, all might have been well, but of course, it wasn't. Andrew had overheard and, as usual, couldn't keep himself from repeating what he'd heard, thereby proving himself to be better than Angel and Jamal because he had never let anything like that happen to him. So it wasn't long before Jamal knew why Angel hadn't been at the pool.

She came back to practice a week after the abortion.

They had told her to stay out a month, but she knew that was impossible. A month out and her whole winter season might be sacrificed. Besides, we were always having the experience of doctors and the school nurse telling us crazy stuff about staying out of the water, like take off a week when you have an ear infection or don't swim when you have a cold. She knew she would just have to use double tampons and suck it up.

When she came back and strolled into the locker room, all the girls just acted normal. The older ones all knew where she'd been and no one was about to bring it up, and the younger girls were so cowed by Angel that they'd never ask. She didn't look any different in her suit than she usually did.

When we walked out on the deck, though, Jamal got up from the bleachers where the guys were waiting for CJ and walked right up to Angel and took her by the arm. She looked at me, letting me know it was okay to walk away, and she let Jamal lead her down beyond the diving well. They stood there talking for a few minutes, and then their voices started rising and Angel yelled, "Fuck you, Jamal," and turned to walk away. He tried to turn her back around, and she tried to pull away from him, so he yanked her, and she resisted, cursing, and then he yanked her harder, so hard that he pulled her arm out of the socket.

She howled in pain and sank to the deck. By this time half of us were down there, and the guys were pulling Jamal away, and just then CJ came out on the deck. He came running and bent over Angel.

"Call 911," he said to no one in particular.

"No!" Angel groaned.

"Angel, this has to get fixed by a doctor."

"You drive me then," she begged.

"Okay. Okay. Williams, you come with us." He turned to Jamal and pointed at him. "You go home and wait for me to call you," he said quietly, his low even voice scarier than if he'd been hollering.

At the hospital, Angel told them that we'd been horsing around on the deck. When they started asking questions about supervision, she spoke up and said that CJ had been there, had told us to stop, and we hadn't, and it just happened in an instant. No one's fault.

And she actually felt that way.

"Jamal has a reason to be mad," she said later, her arm in a sling.

chapter seven

———

JEANNINE

Kathleen was old enough to walk to school by herself, but we didn't trust her to watch Joy, so on days when Angel had morning practice, I walked them. When Angel took them, she got them there at seven thirty. Then they had to wait outside in the yard with a swelling group of kids until the building opened at eight for breakfast. Kathleen kept a double Dutch rope in her book bag and pulled it out before even hitting the yard. She and her girlfriends jumped until breakfast while Joy sat on the sidelines, sucking her fingers and staring happily at the activity all around her.

But when I took them, they often just made it in time to grab some breakfast, which made Kathleen furious. She loved her pack of friends and her double Dutch and wanted to get there as early as possible. Their school was six blocks from our house, but at Joy's pace it sometimes took a half hour to get there. She was a dreamy kid who could get lost staring at a pile of junk on the sidewalk. Meanwhile, Kathleen would keep walking ahead, and then I'd have to herd them back together before we crossed the one busy street just before getting to their school.

One October morning started out no different than any other day. Angel woke me up as she was leaving for morning practice, but since I had just gone to sleep an hour or so earlier, I immediately conked out again. She put the phone next to my ear before leaving, as always, and called me again from the pool, about five minutes before the alarm clock she set went off at top volume.

Joy had been sleeping up above me in Angel's bed, so with all the noise, she was already awake. I went in and got Kathleen up, and we got dressed. We looked alike, because the three of us had new jackets—all the same, all red, paid for by Frank. They were windbreakers Pic had gotten at Kmart on sale, which had left her money to buy some stuff for herself. My real size was only one larger than Kathleen, but Pic had gotten mine three sizes larger so it could be handed down to Kathleen when hers was handed down to Joy.

Our route to school was a little nicer now that the weather had gotten cooler. People weren't hanging out so much late into the night, leaving their bottles and baggies and used condoms scattered all over the place, and the drier weather meant that most of the homeless people were sleeping in the park, not on the street, so we didn't have to step over bodies bundled in dirty blankets when we walked by the steps to the El. Plus, on some streets there were trees and the leaves were turning and they were beautiful.

The girls' school looked a lot like mine, just not quite as big; including the schoolyard and the teachers' parking lot, it took up a full square block. The building was made of grey stone and was several stories high, with bars across all the windows to keep flying objects thrown from the street from breaking the glass. The schoolyard was an asphalt rectangle with grass poking up in lines where there were cracks and two netless basketball hoops at each end.

I knew it was just before eight, because the yard was full of kids playing and fighting—no breakfast yet.

There were two entrances to the yard: one on the street where we walked, and the main one on the perpendicular street. Kids were still arriving through both, some in the tow of an adult or older sibling. On the corner, a crossing guard wearing a bright orange vest was stopping traffic so kids could cross.

The crossing guard was an older Hispanic lady who everybody called Titi. She was known for giving out peppermint Life Savers. If you were unruly waiting to cross the street, she scolded you, but if you shaped up, she gave you a Life Saver.

Some things seem to happen in a rapid blur and in slow motion at the same time. We were almost at the entrance to the yard when Titi, at her post in the middle of the street, fell. I didn't hear the shots until after I saw her hit the street. A young guy with a do-rag who was crossing with a little girl flew onto the sidewalk and buried her with his body. I turned to the right and saw the kids in the yard racing toward the school door, shepherded by adults. A car was slowly cruising down the street perpendicular to us, guns blazing at some guys on foot who were running right past the main entrance to the yard. They were shooting back at the car.

The principal appeared at the door, and then suddenly I tuned into all the noise, him yelling for the kids to hurry, run inside, kids screaming, adults hollering, shots cracking. We were still right outside the schoolyard, too far to get to the door. We would have had to run all the way across the yard. I had two choices: run the other way, or try to hide.

Right near us there were three wire trashcans, filled to overflowing, attached by chains to the schoolyard entrance gate. I shoved and yanked Kathleen and Joy behind them and crouched down with them. Kathleen stepped right into a big pile of dog shit and started shrieking, but I held her hand tight and made her stay down.

Peeking over the top of the trashcan toward the yard, I saw the principal, a big black man, running across the yard toward the shooting. I wanted to jump up, yell to him, *Stop, what are you doing?* Then I saw why. Lying on his back near the main entrance to the yard was a boy, still, his face streaming blood. The principal bent down beside him.

By now I could hear the sirens. The gunfire had stopped, and Kathleen was vomiting.

The police came and they made us go inside. They made everyone go inside. Teachers and police were everywhere, trying to get control of the kids and answer questions from adults. They wanted the kids to go to their classrooms so they could count everyone, but neither of my sisters would let me go, so we all went to Kathleen's classroom. She was sobbing, covered with dog shit and vomit. Joy looked vacant and bewildered, sucking her fingers, her other hand grabbing tightly to my jeans.

All the kids were clustered at the windows, looking out at the yard. The school was ringed with cops, fire engines, ambulances, and TV vans. Titi and the boy were no longer there.

The teacher had a clipboard and was trying to figure out who was there and who was not. I explained to him that I had Joy, so he went to the classroom phone and called someone to report that a kindergartener was safe in his room. Families were being called to pick up their kids, but some people, having heard about it on the radio or following the commotion in the neighborhood, were already at the school. I explained to the teacher that I could take the girls home, but there was no way he was going to let me go.

"You can call my sister," I said. "She goes to Kennedy."

The teacher shook his head. "What about your parents?"

"My mother's at work. She won't be able to leave."

He looked at me, puzzled.

"They don't pay her if she leaves. You can try our house. Maybe my stepfather's home."

Another man came in the classroom, took the teacher aside, and told him something that made him gasp and hold his head in his hands. The kids quieted right away. The rumor they had been repeating was true: the boy shot in the face was named Zahir, and he sat in the second row, third seat, of that very classroom.

After a while, Frank showed up at the classroom door. He came to us, but when he saw and smelled Kathleen, he backed up a little.

"Why didn't you clean her up?" he complained to me. Then he turned to the teacher. "This is a goddamn disgrace. I'm taking my kids out of this school."

He picked up Joy and nodded to me to follow with Kathleen.

That night on the news, we found out that Zahir had surgery and would be all right, but Titi was dead.

Kathleen was very upset about Titi. "Is she in heaven?" she asked us.

"Yeah," Angel said. "She was good. She's in heaven."

"Do you believe in heaven?" I asked Angel later.

"I don't know," Angel said. "I don't ever think about it. But what am I going to tell her?"

"You don't think about it?" I asked. "I think about it all the time."

"You think too much, Jeannine."

Frank never did take the girls out of that school, but we all got to stay home for the rest of the week.

ONE evening in early November, I was home alone with Joy and Kathleen when suddenly all the lights went out. We were watching television, cuddled up under my comforter, and snap, it was dark. The lights and the television and the electric heater all stopped. Joy dug her little fingers into my arm when I tried to get up from the sofa.

"Let me go," I said. "I'm going to turn on the stove."

I didn't know what else to do. We had a gas stove, so the burners provided a little light and a little warmth. The oven was scary to light, though. You had to do it with a match and sometimes it made a loud pop.

After lighting the stove, I went to the front window and looked out. The streetlights were on, and there were lights in other people's windows, so I knew it was just our house.

I called the pool and asked the maintenance man who answered to get Angel.

"The coach don't let them get phone calls," he said.

"It's an emergency," I pleaded. "Please tell CJ it's Angel's sister. It's an emergency."

A few minutes later, Angel picked up the phone and I told her what was happening.

"Where's Pic?" she asked.

"She didn't come home yet," I said.

"The phone works, the stove works. Probably they just turned off the electric," Angel said. "There's nothing you can do. I'll be home in about an hour."

I opened all the curtains so light from outside would come in. The living room was dim and murky, like the morning just before dawn, but we could see. I grabbed a big bag of chips and we snuggled on the sofa for a while, munching. I was so tired. I tried to get the girls to be quiet and calm, hoping maybe they would just fall asleep there with me until someone came home.

But Kathleen was whining. She was bored. She was cold. We put on our coats and took the comforter and sat on the front steps. Everything outside was normal, which was reassuring. Cars went up and down the block, some pausing for a minute or two by the dealers on the corner and then whizzing away. The bus went by, stopping to let people off who were coming home from work. Our neighbors came and went from their houses. Earlier, Kathleen had shown me two books from the school library—they were supposed to take two books home each week and read. One of them was *Charlotte's Web*, and Kathleen started reading it to us now by the light from the streetlamp. She was really a bad reader, though, and I couldn't tolerate listening to her stumble over every other word, so I took the book from her and started reading it to them.

We were on Chapter Four when Alex dropped Angel off in front of the house. *Salutations!*

"Come back inside," she said. "It's cold out here."

"It's cold in there!" Kathleen complained.

Angel went inside and rummaged through the kitchen

cabinets, cursing. "Goddamn it! Don't we have a freakin' candle around here?"

We couldn't find one so we had to make do with the stove. We made peanut butter sandwiches, and Angel opened a few cans of chicken noodle soup. We stood around the stove drinking it from cups, warming our hands.

"Okay," she said when we'd finished eating. "We might as well go to bed. Can't do anything else."

She turned the stove off and guided us up the stairs and we all went into our bedroom. I got out my reading flashlight and we piled into bed with our coats on, Kathleen on the bottom with me and Joy up top with Angel. Ever since the shooting, Kathleen slept with us most of the time.

"We could have used that earlier, dude," Angel said, motioning at my flashlight.

"I didn't think of it," I said.

I whispered more of *Charlotte's Web* to Kathleen until her eyes closed, and then kept reading it to myself. I always liked Templeton, the outcast packrat who's a good guy in the end.

Half an hour later, they were all sleeping, I was still reading, and Frank came home. It only took him a moment to realize something was wrong.

"What the fuck is going on?" he hollered. "Rita!"

Angel stirred above me. "Oh God, shut the fuck up," she moaned.

No chance. He came stomping up the steps and pushed our door open. "What's going on here?"

"We're sleeping, obviously," Angel replied in her "level but deadly" voice.

"You know what I mean, wiseass," Frank shot back. "What's with the lights?"

"They're off, obviously."

"Where's your mother?"

"Haven't seen her," Angel said.

"I'm gonna fuck her up. I gave her plenty of money to pay the bill." He moved closer. "Give me that flashlight," he said, and grabbed it from me.

"Didn't Pic pay the electric bill?" I whispered to Angel when he'd left.

"Probably not," Angel said and yawned. "Go back to sleep."

Kathleen was already nodding off again. I didn't know what time it was, but I estimated that it might be about ten.

When I heard Frank in the living room I crept out of bed and pressed my eye to my peephole. He had propped the flashlight on pillows from the sofa so that it was lighting up his hiding place. He lifted the floorboard and began rummaging around. He pulled out a few plastic bags and sorted through the stuff inside, removing large pill jars, opening some, and counting out pills into smaller bottles. Then he knocked into the flashlight and it fell and rolled, causing him to drop some things. Cursing, he set up the light again and continued.

I got cold so I got back into bed. Pretty soon I heard Frank's car roar and rumble away. I wanted to sleep, but I was afraid I wouldn't be able to, so I slipped out of bed and felt my way down the stairs, looking for my flashlight so I could read.

It was dumped with the pillows on the sofa. I turned it on and went into the kitchen and got a glass of water to take back upstairs. As I was following the narrow beam of light across the living room to the steps, I tripped over something. I shone my light on it and saw that it was a small bottle of pills. I picked them up and took them upstairs and hid them in one of Angel's summer shoeboxes.

Back in bed, I picked up *Charlotte's Web*. A while later I heard the door, and then there was some bumping around and cursing, and then quiet. Pic was home.

I got near to the end of the book and stopped reading. I hated the way it ended. I didn't see why Charlotte had to die after saving Wilbur and creating her babies; it seemed so unfair. I dropped the book over the side of the bed, buried myself deep under the covers, spooned up against Kathleen, and drifted to sleep.

WHEN it was still dark, the phone rang. Angel had it in the upper bunk with her. It was Alex, giving Angel the morning warning—I'm leaving now to pick you up for practice, be ready. Angel stumbled down from the bunk, cursing at the cold, threw stuff into her swim bag, and went downstairs, where she would doze on the couch until Alex was outside beeping. She had slept in her sweats and her coat, so she didn't have much to do to get ready.

I peeked at the window and saw the deep gray sky of early morning. No electricity, no alarm clocks. It was a school day, a work day for Pic, but I wasn't going to be the one to jump up and get everybody going. I could stay in my bed all day, no problem.

The next time I woke up, the sun was shining and Frank was hollering down the hall. At some point Joy had climbed down from Angel's bed and snuggled in with Kathleen and me. She popped her head up when Frank started yelling. I put my finger to my lips, climbed out of bed, and quietly slipped the chair under our doorknob. I knew that if Frank wanted to push our door in he could, but Angel always put the chair there and it made me feel safer. The house was freezing; I scurried back under the covers.

I couldn't make out everything Frank was saying, but he was yelling at Pic about the electricity. Then she was shrieking back at him, her high-pitched wails more and more hysterical. Then suddenly she stopped, and we heard Frank go down the steps and out the door.

Angel called from school at lunchtime. "I knew you wouldn't go to school," she said. "Is the electricity back on?"

"No. It's cold in here."

"Why don't you take the girls to the library?" she suggested. "But wait until around two thirty so they don't get suspicious and think you're truant or something."

It was a good idea. We got dressed and went into the kitchen. We ate some cereal and I put some candy in my pockets for later and on the way to the library we stopped at the corner store and got some chips and Pepsi. I didn't steal from that store because the owner, some old Korean guy who told us to call him Poppy, was always really nice to me. I didn't need to steal from him. Like Templeton, I had some things squirreled away for emergencies, like batteries, change, and candy.

Joy and Kathleen liked the library. I had taken them there many times. I always brought spare notebooks and markers so they could draw, and there was a big children's area where you could sit on the floor against pillows and look at as many books as you wanted. I read to them for hours. Then I left them alone for a little while so I could look something up.

Lorazepam. Lorazepam is used to relieve anxiety, nervousness, and tension associated with anxiety disorders. It is also used to treat certain types of seizure disorders and to relieve insomnia.

Yes! I was looking forward to relieving my insomnia.

Anxiety disorders. Generalized anxiety disorder (GAD) is much more than the normal anxiety people experience day to day. It's chronic and fills one's day with exaggerated worry and tension. Individuals with GAD are unable to relax, and they may startle more easily than other people. Often, they have trouble falling or staying asleep.

Wow. Me explained in a few lines.

When the library closed at eight, we went home. The lights were back on and Angel was in the kitchen, cooking eggs.

"Want some?" she asked the girls, and proceeded to use the whole dozen.

I made cinnamon toast.

While we were eating, Pic came downstairs, dragging her blanket, and threw herself on the couch. She turned on the television and didn't say a word to us. One side of her face was bruised and her eye was swollen shut. Angel went over to the couch but Pic turned her face away into the pillows.

"Hey, no problem," Angel said mildly. "There's a cold pack in the freezer left over from when I hurt my shoulder, if you want it."

PIC made a big deal about how she was going to cook a turkey for Thanksgiving. The year before she had worked on Thanksgiving and we'd just had leftovers from the nursing home. This year, though, she'd won a big turkey at a raffle at the nursing home.

On Tuesday, she got a ride home from work and brought it with her and put it in the refrigerator. She said it would be thawed in time to cook it on Thursday. When Angel went shopping, Pic told her to buy some cans of cranberry and yams and bags of stuffing. She said she was going to get a pumpkin pie, too.

Joy and Kathleen were really excited about Thanksgiving. At school, Joy had been making different kinds of turkeys—one a tracing of her hand with multicolored feathers glued on to it, one an apple with multicolored toothpicks stuck in for feathers, and one made from multicolored Play-Doh.

The problem was that on Wednesday night, Pic didn't come home after work.

"Alex says the night before Thanksgiving is a big party night," Angel said as we were lying in our beds. "She said her sister comes home from college and stays out all night at the clubs."

"So is that where Pic is?"

"Maybe she's thinking about going to college," Angel said, chuckling.

EARLY the next morning, I was dozing and heard Pic being very sick down the hall. I could hear her groaning and vomiting. I woke Angel up. She slid down from her bunk and stomped to the bathroom. I trailed behind. Pic was curled on the bathroom floor near the toilet. She was trembling and looked blue. Her nightgown was stained with diarrhea and there was vomit everywhere.

"Oh, Jesus." Angel sighed. "Go downstairs and get the bucket and some cleaning stuff," she said to me.

Joy was standing in the doorway to the bathroom.

"Get her out of here," Angel said. "Take her downstairs and put on the TV."

"I have to pee," Joy squealed.

"Pee in a pot," Angel growled.

I took Joy downstairs. On the way I peeked in at Kathleen, who was still sleeping, thankfully, since lately she'd been waking up almost every night, wandering around the house, and bothering me when I was trying to read.

I got the bucket out from under the sink. First I let Joy sit on it to pee, which she thought was really funny. Then I tucked her into the sofa, gave her a bag of cheese curls, and turned on the TV. By the time I got back upstairs with the bucket, a rag, and some Lysol, Angel had put Pic in my bed.

"Sorry," she said to me. "Frank's in their room."

She had taken off Pic's soiled nightgown and was wiping her face with a washcloth.

"Could you go downstairs and get the spaghetti pot? I'm afraid she'll puke again."

I dumped the trash from our plastic trashcan on the floor. "Just use this."

"Good thinking, dude."

I went into the bathroom and cleaned everything up. I preferred doing that to trying to take care of Pic; Angel was better at that.

"Go get the phone," she whispered to me when I came back into our room. "And can you put some water in the kettle? I think we should make her some tea."

Pic threw up a few more times into the trashcan, dozing in between. Angel had gotten her into a clean night-gown and was sitting on the bed beside her. I brought her the phone.

"I'm calling Christine," she whispered, and went into the hall. I sat on the floor and looked at my mother—curled in a fetal position, eyes sunk into her cheeks, mouth open, breath raspy.

I could hear Angel asking Christine questions. How do you know when someone has overdosed? Do they vomit and have diarrhea? Coherent, Christine asked? Yeah, sort of, Angel said. Should we call 911? Should we give her any medicine? Should we wake her up and make her drink something? Water? Tea? Soda?

By ten, Pic was sleeping soundly. Angel had consulted a few more times with Christine, and they had concluded that she was in no danger, just sick and hung over from some combination of drugs and liquor, and mostly needing to sleep. Christine wanted us to come there for dinner, but Angel wouldn't even consider it because our uncle Jimmy and his new wife were going there, and she was permanently angry with Jimmy.

No problem, Angel told Christine. We're fine.

Kathleen was up, watching TV with Joy. The pre-show for the Thanksgiving parade was on and the girls were chattering about turkeys.

"A turkey's just a big chicken," I said. "It's no big deal."

Kathleen scowled at me. "Shut up, Jeannine."

Angel pulled the turkey out of the refrigerator. "This thing's still frozen." She frowned, poking it.

She picked up the phone and talked for a minute with Alex. "I think this whole Thanksgiving dinner thing is a broken bell," she said.

Alex's mother Claire got on the phone. It's pretty frozen, Angel said. How many pounds? Let me look. Twenty-two. She's sick, so I was thinking I would cook it. How hard could it be? Hey, that would be really great. Are you sure it's okay?

Angel shoved the turkey back into the fridge and sat down on the floor near the sofa to talk to us. "Guess what, dudettes?" she said, shaking Kathleen's arm to get her attention. "See the parade?" she said, pointing at the TV. "I'm going to take you there."

Joy and Kathleen bounced with excitement.

"Go get their clothes," she said to me. "Really warm clothes. It'll be cold standing outside."

"What are we doing?" I asked. The last thing I wanted to do was go stand in the cold and watch some parade.

"Alex is coming to get us and we're going to the parade. Then we're going to Alex's for dinner. You *will* have a really good time and you *will* eat something normal there." She turned to the girls. "Pic is too sick to make Thanksgiving dinner, so we're going to Alex's. Her mom's going to make us dinner."

I almost froze to death at the parade. The weatherman had been saying that this was one of the coldest Thanksgiving days on record; in fact, the whole month of November had been unusually cold. Luckily for me the swim team had gotten new swim parkas that fall so I'd gotten Angel's old one. It was lined with fleece and it had a hood and it was too big so it went almost to my ankles. But I was still cold. Angel and Alex bought us hot chocolate twice, so that helped.

On the way back to her house, Angel sat in the front with Alex and I sat in the back with Kathleen and Joy. Alex told us who was going to be there for Thanksgiving.

"My great-grandfather's there. And my uncle, you know, the gay one. My great-grandfather doesn't know it, so he keeps talking about fixing my uncle up with all these women."

Kathleen pressed up against the front seat. "I know what gay is," she said smugly.

"Good for you," Angel said. "How old is your great-grandfather?"

"Umm, I think around eighty-eight."

"Wow. How old are your grandparents?"

"Like, sixty-something. My mother's forty-eight, so they're like maybe sixty-eight, sixty-nine. They're at my other uncle's in New York."

"Angel, how old is Pic?" Kathleen asked.

"Thirty-three. Sit back, Kathleen," Angel said, pushing her. "Is Vanessa home?" she asked Alex.

"Oh, yeah. She's cooking with my mother. You know, they're into all that stuff together. Cooking, baking. It's like Julia Child or something."

"Who?" Angel asked.

Alex smiled and shook her head. "Never mind."

"What's your mother making?" Angel asked.

"Everything. Some kind of squash soup, two kinds of cranberry, two kinds of potatoes, two kinds of vegetables, turkey, some stuffing with sausage in it, this pie, that pie."

Squash soup? I thought. *Oh God.*

"We don't have grandparents," Kathleen reported. "They're all dead."

I'D been in Alex's house before. It wasn't that big, but it was really nice. When you opened the door there was a little vestibule with old tile on the floor, and beautiful glass in the windows of the door that led into the living room.

"Oh my God it smells good in here!" Angel exclaimed as we walked in.

Alex's great-grandfather and her uncle were sitting on the sofa, watching football. Her uncle was reading the paper. They both stood up, and Joy immediately ducked behind Angel's legs.

"Pa Bill," Alex said loudly. "This is my friend Angel. And these are her sisters, Jeannine, Kathleen, and Joy." Alex looked at us and gestured to the other man. "And this is my uncle John. Talk loud."

Angel stepped forward, Joy stuck to her leg, and held out her hand to Pa Bill. He was stooped and balding, wearing thick glasses, but steady and alert. He grasped Angel's hand.

"It's nice to meet you," Angel said. She turned and shook hands with Uncle John.

"Angel swims with me, Pa," Alex explained.

"Ah." Pa Bill nodded and peered around Angel to wink at Joy.

Uncle John took our coats and we went into the kitchen for a minute. Claire had on an apron dusted with flour and her hands were sticky with something. She kissed Angel without touching her.

"Hi girls!" she said to us brightly. Vanessa was rolling out dough on the kitchen table.

"Can I help?" Angel asked.

"Can you chop celery?"

"Sure." Angel turned to me. "Take the girls into the living room." She looked at the girls. "Be good in there. They're watching the game. Don't make noise."

In the living room, I pulled Joy over to the fireplace to sit with me on the floor. She'd never seen a real fireplace with a fire in it before. The cat was curled up on the floor, sleeping. Joy reached for it. I held back her hand.

"Be gentle," I whispered to her. "Like this." I showed her how to pet the cat with just one finger.

On the coffee table there was a tray with cheese and crackers, vegetables and a dip, and some olives in a little dish. There were also nuts and a nutcracker in a wooden bowl. Kathleen had plopped herself right down between Pa Bill and Uncle John and was already eating a cracker. I left Joy for a minute and, without fully standing, scooted over to the coffee table. On a shelf beneath it were some big books. The one on top was an atlas.

I looked up at Pa Bill. "May I look at this?" I asked.

"Why certainly, young lady," he said.

I looked at Kathleen, who was stuffing food into her mouth. "That's enough," I said to her under my breath.

"What're these?" she asked, pointing to the nuts.

Clearly Pa Bill and Uncle John were surprised by the question.

"They're nuts!" Pa Bill exclaimed.

"They're like peanuts, but they still have their shell," I explained to Kathleen. "You have to use that thing to open them."

"Let me show you, young lady," Pa Bill said. "Now, what's your name again?"

I went back to Joy and the fire, and happily opened the atlas.

Joy was stretched out next to the cat, stroking it from time to time, her own eyes getting heavy. I turned to the maps of Europe and studied each country, cross-referencing to the page that had facts about each nation, like the population, the per-capita income, and the national resources.

"Jeannine, I'm thirsty," Kathleen said after a while.

Joy was sound asleep on the rug. I stood up and went to the kitchen and asked for something for Kathleen.

"What're they doing?" Angel asked, getting some apple juice.

"Joy's asleep. Kathleen's talking."

"Of course," Angel said. "I hope she's not bothering them."

"I'm sure she's not, Angel," Claire said. "Pa loves kids."

"She can be a pain."

Angel headed for the living room to deliver the juice and check on Kathleen for herself. "Wow, she's being really nice with him," she said, observing Kathleen and Pa Bill through the doorway, opening nuts together.

"Maybe it's the other way around," Claire said.

Angel cocked her head.

"Maybe she's being nice because he's being really nice with her."

"Hmm," Angel murmured, nodding.

I stayed in the kitchen to help with dinner. Claire put me to work with easy jobs like folding napkins and slicing apples for a pie that was about to go in the oven.

"This is for you, Jeannine," Angel said as Vanessa crisscrossed strips of dough across the mound of apples, cinnamon, and butter. "With whipped cream."

I smiled. No pumpkin pie for me. I thought it was disgusting—such a strange texture, like that weird tofu Angel once brought home from someone at the pool who told her she needed it for protein packing.

I looked at Vanessa working with the dough and Alex stirring something on the stove. They didn't look much alike. Vanessa looked like Claire—soft, wavy, light brown hair and green eyes—but her skin was darker, more like Angel's. Alex was darker still, and she had dark brown eyes. Her hair was brown, thick, and curly.

I thought Alex must look like her father. I knew from Angel that he lived in Baltimore with his new family and didn't visit very often. But, Alex told Angel, every two weeks money went right from his paycheck into Claire's bank account, so that was something.

I knew I looked like my father, too, because I certainly didn't look like Pic. But I also didn't look like Angel, because she looked like her father. I thought it would be nice to resemble someone I knew.

Finally, Claire had us all taking dishes to the table. Uncle John waited a minute before carving to let us all admire the turkey.

Angel went over to the fireplace to wake Joy. "C'mon, Joyful," she said, kneeling down and lifting Joy, who was getting heavy, her big kindergarten self.

Angel took Joy to pee and then sat her between the two of us.

"Who wants to say grace?" Claire asked, looking at her grandfather.

"I will," Angel said, totally surprising me—and everyone else, too, I think.

"Okay," said Claire, and we all bowed our heads, except for Joy, for whom this was a completely unknown ritual. She stared at Angel.

"Thank you, Lord, for making sure we have enough to eat," Angel began. "And please help the people who don't. And bless the people who aren't with us today, like my grandmother and Alex's great-grandmother. And thank you, Lord, for giving us good friends who really help us when we need it. Amen."

We raised our heads. Claire leaned sideways and kissed Angel's cheek.

BY Thanksgiving, it was dark before five o'clock. Every Wednesday and Friday that fall I went to the Franklin Institute sometime during the day—after school, or instead of school—and waited for it to get dark so I could look through the big telescope. There was a guy who worked there at the observatory, a college student from Penn named Eric. His job was to help people with the telescopes (and, probably, protect the telescopes from misuse and vandalism). There was rarely anyone there, and I usually found him playing his Game Boy or doing homework.

Eric and I became friends, as much as I understood how to be anyone's friend. Eric got me a membership card to the museum so I could get into the building for free whenever I wanted. He knew much more than I did about the operation of the telescope, and yet had little curiosity about what we could see with it. So we looked together, Eric in command of the mechanical device, me choosing our points of observation.

I remember vividly the first time I saw Saturn. Eric was maneuvering the telescope, and when he beckoned for me to look, he gave no indication of the beauty waiting for me through the eyepiece. And then there it was, huge, the rings looping out to the margins of my field of vision, as perfect as any photograph or drawing, the desert colors of the planet and its rings vivid against the blue-black of the sky. I jumped away, rushed out of the telescope cage, and peered up. Nothing. Then back to the eyepiece, and there it was again. I had a moment of mistrust—was it really there, had Eric somehow contrived this—and then I had a rush of reverence for the machine, and understood Eric's admiration of it.

Maybe seeing Saturn had left me vulnerable, or perhaps feeling grateful. In any case, that night, for the first time, I let Eric touch me as I leaned against the wall of the cage. It wasn't unpleasant, once the ground rules were set —I did nothing, he did everything. No kissing. He could touch my tiny breasts, unzip my jeans and grope inside my panties, and jerk off into a napkin. As time went by, he spent more and more time touching me, exploring, and I began to look forward to his hands, and eventually his mouth.

Eric called me the White Dwarf—very apt, because I was so small and so pale. He didn't know just how appropriate the nickname was. A white dwarf is a kind of star that has burned up and ejected a lot of its gases—its own fuel, its life blood—and is collapsing in on itself.

I couldn't sleep at night. I read and read, but sometimes, after two or three nights of barely sleeping, I took a lovely L pill. I had stopped going to school almost completely. Most days I wandered around Center City, looking in windows, ducking into stores, trying on clothes, and napping in dressing rooms. I spent a lot of time at Borders, and when I thought someone might recognize me and ask questions because I was there so much, I switched to the new Barnes & Noble. I avoided the library, where the librarians asked kids if they were cutting school.

It was at the bookstores that I began looking at art books. I especially liked the ones about the Renaissance. I sat on the carpeted floors, buried between the shelves, balancing large, heavy books on my knee. I studied the implacable virgins of rocks and annunciations, the women of Botticelli with their almond eyes and flowing golden hair, the enigmatic faces of saints and sinners, and saw my sister.

CHRISTMAS was coming. The streets and stores were full of decorations and Christmas music. It continued to be very cold, and we had crazy ice storms that knocked down electric wires but transformed the trees and the shrubs into glitter. I loved the snow and the cold. It made the world seem quieter.

Three days before Christmas, Angel and I dragged our little Christmas tree out of the closet and set it up. At first, we stuck the branches in wrong and the tree looked like it was having an electric shock treatment. Giggling almost to hysteria, we pulled them all out and turned them around so the tree had the right shape. We got Joy and Kathleen to help us put on the ornaments and a pack of tinsel I had swiped from the dollar store. I got my snow globe that played "The Skaters' Waltz" from our bedroom and kept winding it up while they play-skated and threw tinsel around everywhere.

My snow globe was one of the things I still had from when we lived with Nannie Lou. At Christmas, Nannie Lou had so many people to buy presents for it couldn't possibly be done in one trip. During the weeks before

Christmas, we went to the mall more times than I've been there since.

We went to a mall "across the bridge," as Pop put it, in New Jersey. Since Nannie Lou didn't drive, Pop would take us on the weekend or in the evening after dinner. It didn't matter how late it was, because the mall was open until midnight for Christmas.

The bridge alone was worth the trip. It was painted sky blue and had tiny white lights that outlined its sweeping frame, so at night I felt like we were driving into the stars. Every time we crossed during the day I got on my knees in the backseat and looked out the very top of the window so I could see the wide gray river far below, hugged by piers and boats and smokestacks.

"What's the holdup?" Pop fumed one day when we were stuck in traffic on the up side. "Looks like a car pulled over."

"Pic had a friend who jumped off the bridge," Angel said.

My eyes riveted on her.

"It's true. She pulled her car over and got out and jumped right into the river."

"Don't scare the girl, Angel," Nannie Lou said.

"Why?" I asked.

Angel shrugged. "She was high. It was, like, four o'clock in the morning. It was on Thanksgiving."

"This Thanksgiving?" I asked, wondering how I hadn't known.

"No, a long time ago."

"Did she die?" I whispered.

Angel gave me her "don't be stupid" look. *Of course she died.*

"The things you children talk about," Nannie Lou fretted.

The day before Christmas Eve, on our last shopping trip to the mall, Nannie Lou gave us twenty dollars and told us we could buy a present for Pic, who was coming to stay over on Christmas Eve. By this time, Nannie Lou had realized that Angel could find her way to California if necessary, so she let Angel take me around the mall for an hour while she shopped. Pop would be sitting on the bench by the big clock if we needed him.

I'd never seen so many people in one place as at the mall that night, but for some reason I didn't feel afraid. Usually I felt dizzy in big, crowded places like the schoolyard and the supermarket, but the mall seemed very friendly that night. They were playing Christmas music nonstop. Angel and I looked at a million things to buy Pic. We knew the music Pic liked, rap music and oldies, but Angel wasn't sure she could play music in the treatment program. We saw a white Christmas candle with holly and bright red berries melted inside it, but Angel thought they probably couldn't burn candles in treatment programs, either.

We finally wandered into the Christmas shop in one of the big department stores. They had so many Christmas trees, each one decorated differently. There were shelves and shelves of nutcrackers and Santa Clauses and sleighs and reindeer. On one large display shelf they had holiday music boxes and glass snow globes. I started winding them, one by one, listening to the pinging carols and watching the little figures move. There was one that I couldn't leave alone. It was a large glass globe with ice made of a mirror, so when it was wound and the graceful little skater whirled to the skater's waltz, she was reflected in the mirror. An old-fashioned lamp curved over the ice pond; its yellow light matched the yellow of the girl's hair.

"Let's get this," I said to Angel. "Pic will like this."

Angel picked it up and shook it, and snow floated onto the ice. She looked at me. "It's really nice, but Jeannine, Pic doesn't have any money. I think we should get her something she really needs. That's what Nannie Lou said. Like maybe gloves."

I nodded. I wound the key one more time and walked away to the accessories department as the skating song played.

We bought Pic a matching mittens, hat, and scarf set. It was blue, Pic's favorite color, and it was only $17.99. When we showed it to Nannie Lou she said we were smart shoppers and it was the perfect gift.

On Christmas morning, I had a pile of presents. Angel set one aside and said I had to open it last. I had about six things to open. I got two books, one of Bible stories; a calendar for my room; a doll; and an outfit, a turtleneck and matching corduroy overalls. When I opened the last present, it was the snow globe with the skating girl. I was so happy. I hugged Angel and she said Nannie Lou bought it, but Nannie Lou said, "It was your sister's idea, Jeannine. All credit to her."

JOY still believed in Santa Claus, and Kathleen did too when she wasn't trying to act grown up. So we also hung up the stockings we had, although we weren't sure if there were going to be any gifts. I didn't understand the world of our finances too clearly, but Angel said that Frank paid for the rent on the house and all the other house bills, like the electricity and the telephone. Pic gave Angel food stamps to go shopping, and sometimes Frank gave her grocery money too. Angel bought all her own clothes, and some of mine, as well as cosmetics and toiletries with the money she earned at the laundromat. But since the summer we hadn't been able to buy any clothes, and Pic wasn't giving us much money for food. Angel said that Pic was spending a lot of money going out to clubs with her girlfriends and buying weed and vodka and whatever else, so Angel was spending most of her money on food.

"I can buy a couple things, I have a little money," Angel said as we contemplated the stockings hanging on the back of the sofa. We didn't have a chimney. "I'll call Christine. She always has presents for us. Maybe she can bring them to me, and then I'll put them out like Santa Claus brought them. I hope she didn't mail them or something."

I silently resolved to go shoplifting the next day.

ANGEL had practice on Christmas Eve, but only once, in the morning, and not at the usual five but at eight. "CJ must have the Christmas spirit," she said that morning, rolling her eyes.

Pic was already gone when Angel got up. Because she'd missed a shift earlier in the week, and also had missed a day the week before, she had to work a double on Christmas Eve, from seven in the morning until eleven at night, which made her really mad. She didn't want to get up that morning, and she and Frank had a fight because he was pushing her out of bed. She told him he should worry about getting himself a job and stop relying on her to be the breadwinner.

"You think that chicken shit you make could support anyone? You know damn well what supports us," he said, laughing in her face. He left the house while Angel was at practice and told me that he wouldn't be back until after he got Pic from work at eleven.

When she got home from the pool, Angel had sticky buns that one of the mothers had brought for the swimmers.

"I grabbed a few extras," she said, grinning.

Six extras to be exact, and they were big and fat and covered with raisins. Angel heated them up and called Kathleen and Joy and we sat around by the Christmas tree, drinking all the milk that was left and eating the sticky buns.

"Pic said for you to go to the store," I said.

"Did she leave any money?"

I handed her the food stamps and twenty dollars Pic had given me.

"Mmm," said Angel, counting it out. "This'll go far."

"Are we having a Christmas Eve party?" Kathleen asked.

"No," Angel said. "Why would we?"

"Gigi said they have one at their house," she said, pouting.

"Well, why don't you go down the block to Gigi's and visit their party?" Angel said. "Jeannine, do you remember going to mass on Christmas Eve when we lived with Nannie Lou?"

I nodded. Some of the details were gone, but I remembered clearly the dark, cavernous church and in front of us the altar, bursting with light and brightened by white and red poinsettias. I remembered the banks of white candles flickering in the side aisles, the soaring organ, the congregation singing carols together. I remembered feeling comfort and safety nestled there in the pew between my grandmother and Angel.

"Maybe we should do that tonight," Angel said.

"But we don't belong to a church," I said.

"So what?"

Aunt Christine came with our presents, and she stayed a while and visited, and then she drove Angel to a supermarket and helped pay for some extra groceries, including a ham for Christmas dinner, and drove Angel back. All this was great because usually we had to either buy stuff from the corner store or take a bus to the supermarket. It was so cold and windy, I was glad to stay home with the girls while Angel and Christine went out.

There was a Catholic church two blocks away. Late in the afternoon, Angel made us get all dressed and we went to mass there. It was freezing cold, and the girls whined the entire way. But Angel was right; it didn't matter that we didn't belong to the church. No one asked us any questions, and a couple of our neighbors recognized us and smiled and said hello and Merry Christmas. And Angel knew something I didn't—that at Catholic churches that have schools, the kids usually put on a Christmas pageant at the early mass on Christmas Eve, and sure enough, that's what we found. It was like a play of the Christmas story, with costumes and scenery and Christmas carols. Kathleen and Joy loved it, and we ducked out before the real mass started.

ON Christmas morning, the girls got up really early and wouldn't go back to sleep. They wanted presents. They wanted to wake Pic up, but Angel said no, Pic and Frank had been out late, real late, and wouldn't be happy about being disturbed. We'd wait a while.

Angel made us hot chocolate and French toast, which sounded exotic to the girls when really it's just eggs and bread. Eventually Angel sent Kathleen, Pic's favorite, up to see if Pic would get up.

Kathleen came back shaking her head. "But she said we can open the gifts," she squealed, shaking her little fists with anticipation.

Christine had bought us clothes—thoughtful, since our wardrobes were pretty ratty. She gave matching blue parkas with hoods to Kathleen and Joy, and a maroon one to me, which was good, since we were freezing in our red windbreakers. She gave us all new snow boots, and Angel got sweats and underwear from the Gap.

However late they had come home, Pic and Frank had at least left us gifts. Under the tree there were baby dolls for the girls, wrapped. And they'd gotten a Barbie doll for me—a little weird, since I never really enjoyed playing with dolls and I was a little old for them at this point, a freshman in high school. But there were also new flannel nightgowns for each of us, even Angel.

And we had the stockings. On Christmas Eve, after the girls had gone to bed, I'd put a slinky in each of their stockings and nail polish in Angel's. Sometime after that, Angel had put new socks and barrettes and gum and candy in ours. Kathleen and Joy were really excited, more by the fun of emptying the stockings than by what was in them.

Late in the morning, Alex came over. We watched TV and ate popcorn Angel had gotten at the supermarket. Alex also brought us presents. Her mother had made a lot of different kinds of Christmas cookies and these were all stacked in a big tin that had an old-fashioned Christmas scene on it, people in a sleigh riding in the snow. There was a card with it that was to our whole family. Angel said to leave the card for Pic to open, but we could eat some of the cookies.

Alex gave Angel a gift certificate to this salon where Angel could get her hair and nails done, and she gave me a gift certificate to Border's. She even had gifts for Joy and Kathleen: a stuffed polar bear for Joy and a cute little pocketbook with play jewelry in it for Kathleen. Angel had a gift for Alex, too, a pair of earrings. All in all, we felt like we had gotten a lot of presents.

Alex watched a movie on TV with us, and then she and Angel tried to figure out how to cook the ham before finally calling Alex's mother for advice. By the time she left it was the middle of the afternoon, and Pic and Frank were still in bed.

THINGS in our house had been spiraling slowly out of control, the circle growing wider each day. Pic was still going to work but was missing time, getting there late, and coming home even later. She was drinking a lot, and more and more we could smell the marijuana smoke coming from her room. Her moods were wildly erratic—sometimes she was seething with anger, some days as normal as Pic ever was, other days morose and near tears. She frightened me most when she was manic, breezy and elated, chattering away about impossible things like getting a dishwasher or going on a vacation to Florida. Ever since Angel had gone to Florida, Pic had been obsessed with going there.

Frank was barely around and almost totally ignored us, except when he yelled at Angel because something he wanted wasn't in the refrigerator or his laundry wasn't done. He and Pic would collide in the house sometime late every night, either loud arguing or loud making up. In the aftermath of the shooting, Angel missed a lot of morning practices because I didn't want to walk the girls to school. Sometimes Pic got them from the after-school program, sometimes she didn't. The teachers would call Angel at the pool and ask her to come and get them, and CJ would get mad.

During the Christmas break, CJ had set up an intense practice schedule for the swimmers. They had two long practices each day, and had to stay at SportStars and sleep in between. That week was a nightmare for me, a crushing preview of what it would be like the following year when Angel went to college. I was hoping more and more that she would do what she'd been musing about, going to LaSalle and living at home. Every day I had Kathleen and Joy for hours and hours—except for one day, when Christine came and took them out for the day because I had to go work a shift for Angel at the laundromat.

Two days before New Year's Eve, Pic told Angel she had to stay home on New Year's Eve and babysit. She was very excited because Frank was actually going to take her out to some cheesy party at some hotel sports bar.

Angel stood in the doorway while Pic tried on various outfits. "No way!" she said. "I've been working my butt off and I'm going to this party. Jeannine can babysit."

Pic was wiggling into a short strapless dress with sequins that emphasized how gaunt she was.

"Oh, Angel," Pic responded, almost gaily, "You've been

working your butt off doing what you want. I've been working for all of us."

"Oh, please." Angel sighed, disgusted.

Pic slid out of that dress and tossed it on her bed. She stepped into a black one that had a gauzy train. "Zip me up," she said, backing up toward Angel. "What do you think of this? It's Linda's."

"It's okay," Angel said, rolling her eyes at me. "So Jeannine can babysit."

Pic studied herself in the mirror for a moment, scooping her hair up. "You push everything off on Jeannine," she said. "Why should she have to do it?"

"Why should I have to do it? They're your kids," Angel said, getting louder. "We already take care of them ten times more than you do. If you don't want Jeannine to do it, hire a babysitter. Jeannine can come with me. They'll be plenty of kids her age at the party."

"I wouldn't let her go to any party you go to," Pic huffed.

"Yeah, right. It's a swim team party. Parents'll be there —some parents, that is," Angel replied sarcastically.

As usual, she'd found the exposed nerve. "Oh, the perfect fucking parents, right? Shut up, Angel. I want you in this house by eight o'clock on New Year's Eve." Pic stomped her bare foot to make her point. "In fact, you can stay home all day, because I have to work before I go out."

"Forget it. No way." Angel turned to walk away.

Pic was standing in her bra and panties, flapping the black dress for emphasis. "If you're not here that night, don't come back. You can get the fuck out."

"No problem," Angel muttered, not even bothering to turn around. The door slammed at our backs.

In our room, Angel sat down on my bed. She was weary. They had been swimming hard, and she was headed for the laundromat.

"I'm not trying to push this off on you, Jeannine," she said. "Fuck her. You can come with me. Let her get a babysitter like everybody else."

"I don't mind," I said. "We'll just watch TV. It's fine." I didn't want to get in a confrontation with Pic. "But do you think she'll let you come back?" I was worried.

Angel dismissed the idea with a wave of her hand. "That's all bullshit. She just wants to pull my chain. As long as she gets to do what she wants to do, she'll forget all about that."

ON New Year's Eve, a Saturday, Angel had only one practice, from eight to eleven in the morning. I was up with Kathleen and Joy, who were whining about there not being any cereal for breakfast. I found a box of macaroni and cheese, which shut them right up.

Angel came home from the pool and crashed. Pic was supposed to work but had stayed out late the night before, payday, so she called work and told them her daughter was very sick with strep throat, and then she and Frank slept all morning. By the time she got up, Angel was sleeping.

Pic had never gotten a babysitter. She was going to go out and assumed that one of us was going to do what she wanted. This time, it was me.

Frank and Pic left the house at about eight o'clock in Frank's car, which had no heat. It was very cold, so Pic had to forego her skimpy dresses and instead wore a red satin pants outfit and stiletto-heeled black boots.

When they left, Angel emerged from the bedroom. She looked great—wild, but great. She was wearing black leather everything, and had rinsed her hair a cherry red and gelled it up high. She had on blue nail polish and sparkly blue eye shadow to match. She had half a dozen little silver hoops in her left ear, and a blue dangling earring in her right. She too had on black boots, but hers looked like they belonged to a Hell's Angel. She reminded me not to go out in the street at midnight because people in our neighborhood always shot their guns into the air at midnight and the year before a kid had gotten hit by accident and now he was paralyzed for life.

After Angel left, I dragged my blanket downstairs and Joy and Kathleen and I curled up under it to watch TV. I made some popcorn and promised them they could stay up to watch the ball drop. They had no idea what I meant but the idea made them happy. Joy fell asleep anyway, sucking loudly on her fingers, as she always did, but Kathleen stuck it out and we did the countdown with the TV announcer.

All night long there had been firecrackers and gunshots out on the street. At midnight, I opened our door and let Kathleen stand in the doorway and bang on a pot with a spatula. Half the neighbors on our block were doing the same thing.

"Why do people do this?" she asked.

"To celebrate a new year, dummy. Also, I read somewhere that it's supposed to chase away the evil spirits."

Her eyes widened. "What evil spirits?"

"The ones that get little girls who don't go to bed."

After that, I scooped Joy up and we went upstairs. Kathleen begged me to let them sleep with me. She liked to pretend that my bottom bunk was a cave. I pulled Angel's blanket down so it hung past my bunk and we all cuddled up. When Kathleen fell asleep, I pulled out a book and read.

Sometime later, the front door slammed. I could hear Pic's voice, the tone angry and complaining. I curled up against Joy's warm little body and tried to fall asleep, but Pic was too distracting. I climbed across the girls and peered through the floor into the living room. Pic was on the phone, ranting, sobbing.

"I know he was gonna meet that cunt," she cried. "Maybe he was going to Atlantic City with those guys but she was in the plans, I know it. No, I came home in the car, that piece of crap wouldn't make it down the shore. Where are you? Yeah, what time do they close? Yeah, I'm coming now."

She stumbled back out of the house and it was quiet again. I retreated behind the curtain that Angel's blanket made, snuggled with the little girls, and tried to sleep, but I couldn't. Every time I was close, another bang would happen outside. Finally, I slid out of bed, went to the shoebox, and took a pill.

The bottle, which had been full when Frank dropped it, was more than half empty now. I had been worrying about where I would get more when these were gone. I had seen him searching through his stash, looking for the lost bottle, so I didn't think I'd be able to take another one from there.

Kathleen woke up for a minute, looking dazed.

"Are you okay?" I asked, and she started to cry. "It's okay. Don't cry. I was just kidding about the evil spirits."

She shuddered, and I pulled her down and tucked the covers all around her. Then I grabbed Angel's walkman and put on this tape of Christmas carols I'd stolen from Kmart. It was instrumental—no singing—and it made me feel peaceful. Eventually I went to sleep, the fireworks exploding in my dreams.

PART TWO

chapter eight

JEANNINE

On New Year's Day, I woke up to Pic and Frank hollering at each other in their bedroom. Kathleen was sitting up in my bed, silent, tears streaming down her face.

"It's okay," I reassured her. "Don't pay attention to them. That's what I do."

I felt sorry for her. Two years earlier she'd been just like Joy, who was peacefully asleep, curled up at the other end of the bed.

I yanked down the cover that had made our tent the night before and leaned out of bed as far as I could, and saw that Angel wasn't up in her bunk.

"Come on," I said to Kathleen, trying to be comforting. "Just go back to sleep."

It looked so dark outside that I thought it must be very early in the morning. Again I leaned out of bed, this time to look at the clock, and saw that it was past noon. Our window was rattling in the wind.

"Do you want some candy?" I whispered to Kathleen.

She shook her head no, and wiggled down under the covers. It was cold.

When Pic wasn't sobbing, we could hear very clearly

what she and Frank were saying. Kathleen pressed her hands over her ears.

"Bitch, I told you to stop bugging me about that," he was yelling. "You're hallucinating!"

"Your life's your dick," she shot back. "But what a real man does, you don't do that."

"I gave you money to pay everything. The long distance is off because you spent the goddamn money for the phone bill on something else and you know it."

"And why you need to call long distance anyway? Because you want to talk to that Jersey whore," she roared.

"You better shut the fuck up," he threatened.

"You're a motherfucking liar," she screamed, and I heard her slamming the bathroom door.

A few minutes later he opened the door and confronted her. "Everything in my drawers is messed up. I had some money in there, and my papers are all mixed up."

"You mean your porn?"

"You're out of your fucking mind, you know that?" he yelled back. "Were you going through my stuff?"

"Fuck off," Pic yelled and slammed the door again.

"Yeah, fuck you too," he grunted.

A few minutes later she was vomiting loudly, moaning and crying. I wasn't sure whether she was really sick or whether it was an act to make Frank feel bad. Whatever, I knew I wasn't moving from the bed.

We heard Frank outside our door. Kathleen curled up against me and we didn't say a word. He must have changed his mind about opening it, because next thing I heard was him storming down the stairs. Then I heard the front door slam.

For quite a while I could hear Pic's sobs, mingled with

the wind that was whirling around our house—strangely comforting, like it was wrapping us in a cocoon. A storm was coming. I figured Angel had stayed at Alex's, or Jamal's, smart considering the cold weather, but I wished she was home.

Eventually, Pic retreated to her room and the house was quiet. Kathleen was asleep again. Snow was falling, thick and heavy, white against grey.

JOY was shaking my shoulder, calling my name, whining. It went on endlessly, forever. I just wanted to sleep, to float downwards to oblivion, where there weren't even any dreams.

But she was relentless, and I woke up. She was hungry. Her pajamas were wet; she had fallen asleep in front of the television and peed on the sofa. She was afraid that Pic would come downstairs and find that she had wet the sofa and beat her.

The clock said five thirty. It was dark. Day or night? Which day or night?

"Where's Angel?" I asked Joy.

She looked at me, wide-eyed. "I don't know." She put her fingers in her mouth.

I stripped Joy's clothes off and took her into the bathroom to wash off. On the way I peeked through the door and saw Pic in her bed, empty bottles of vodka and orange soda in a ring around her.

It was Tuesday evening. Kathleen was watching television, lying on the floor because Joy had peed on the sofa, eating her way through all the chips and cookies left in the house.

The phone rang. I ran to the kitchen and answered. I was hoping for Angel, but it was the lady who owned the laundromat. Where was Angel for her shift? She's stranded on the other side of the city in the snow, I said, making it up. Yes, by Friday night she would be home and come to work, or I would, in her place. I'm sorry, I said.

The street outside was deserted and snow-covered. The plows had come down and boxed in all the cars. Probably Angel couldn't get home, I thought.

I tried to remember. It was Tuesday. New Year's Eve was Sunday. Monday it was snowing. Then what? Kathleen wouldn't sleep, wouldn't stop crying, so I broke a pill and gave her half. I figured it would be okay since she weighed almost as much as me, even though she was only in second grade. At some point we got up and they had cereal with the last of the milk.

I went over to Kathleen. "Where's Angel?" I asked her. "Did she come home today?"

She flinched like I had pinched her, and then she was crying again.

"Where's Angel?" I insisted.

"I don't know," she sobbed. "I can't remember. Can't you find her, Jeannine?"

"She must be at Jamal's house," I said. "Oh God, this sofa stinks. Come on." I pulled at her. "Help me find something to clean it with."

WE stayed up late on Tuesday night watching movies, waiting for Angel to come home. Pic was still up in her room. I heard her go into the bathroom once, but I hadn't actually seen her awake since New Year's Eve. I made toast, and

instead of jelly, I sprinkled the butter with sugar and cinnamon, the way Angel often made it for me. Joy and Kathleen loved it, so I kept making more until we used up all
the bread. Every now and then I'd go to the window, hoping to see Angel coming up the steps. Our street looked
beautiful with the snow shimmering under the streetlamp,
but Angel didn't come home.

I realized I probably missed her call, since I had been
sleeping most of the past two days. I decided I would call
Alex and Jamal to see if she was at one of their houses. I
went upstairs and searched through piles of Angel's stuff
until I found a swim team list. But it was after two and I
thought I should wait until the next day to call. Somebody's mother would probably answer and get mad. I got
the girls to come upstairs to bed, and before we went in
the bedroom, I made Joy sit on the toilet and pee. Pic's
door was closed.

ON Wednesday when I woke up, I went to the window and
saw a bus. The windowpane was etched with frost and icy
to my touch. I knew there must be school but it was after
eleven, too late to try to go, and I didn't want to go anyway. Kathleen was still asleep, but Joy wasn't in bed with
us. I ran into the hallway, calling her name. She scampered
out of her bedroom where she had been playing, lost in
five-year-old fantasies. I noticed that Pic's door was open.

"Where's Pic?" I asked.

"She said take us to school."

"Did she go to work?"

Joy smiled and shrugged and disappeared back into her
room.

I went downstairs and got the team phone list I'd found the night before, but when I picked up the phone it was dead. So I went to Pic's room, looking for the portable phone. I threw the sheets and blankets on the floor and found it under one of the pillows. I couldn't get a dial tone, so I put it back in the cradle, hoping it was just the battery. I had just gotten up but I felt exhausted.

All of a sudden, I wanted to take a shower. I was filthy. I couldn't remember the last time I'd taken a shower, but it definitely hadn't been since New Year's Eve. When I went into the bathroom and turned the water on, Kathleen came in and asked if she could take a bath with me. The bathtub was dirty, grunge all around the sides with hair stuck in it. I wasn't about to clean it.

"No, but you can get in the shower with me," I said.

We got in together. I stood with my face turned up to the showerhead, letting the hot water beat against me. I put shampoo on my hair and started washing, but I was so tired I just sank to the floor of the tub.

"Wash my hair," Kathleen insisted, sitting down as well.

Her hair was like Angel's, thick and wavy, and it had grown pretty long, below her shoulders. Just as I was lathering it up, I heard someone calling through the house for Rita. Only one person called my mother Rita, and that was my aunt Christine.

Just then she came into the bathroom. "Rita?" she cried.

I pulled the shower curtain back a little. "It's me," I said. "And Kathleen."

"Where's your mother?" she asked frantically.

"I don't know," I said. "Rinse your hair," I said to my sister.

I stepped out of the tub and Christine handed me a towel that was draped over the sink. She gaped at me. I never felt like eating anymore, not even candy.

"Jeannine, the front door was unlocked. Where's your mother?" she asked me again. "And where's Angel, at school? Why aren't you and the girls at school?"

"I don't know," I answered. Because I really didn't know. I couldn't answer any of her questions and just thinking about them made me want to go back to bed. I sat down on the toilet.

"Where are the clean towels? This bathroom smells like vomit," she said. Kathleen had turned off the water and was whining loudly about being cold.

"I don't know," I said.

Christine went to Pic's door but pulled quickly back. She went down the hall to the girls' room and pulled a sheet off Kathleen's bunk.

"Dry off with this, honey," she said, wrapping Kathleen in it. "Jeannine, I called your mother's job and they said she doesn't work there anymore. Then I called here and they said the phone's disconnected. What's going on?"

"I don't know," I said.

She breathed deeply, exasperated with me and the situation. "When was the last time you saw your mother?"

"Last night. But Joy saw her this morning."

"Jeannine, you have to take a little responsibility here," she scolded me. "When Angel leaves for practice, you can't just go back to bed. I'm sure she woke you all up this morning."

"She wasn't here this morning."

That stopped Christine for a moment. "Where was she?"

"I don't know. Pic kicked her out on New Year's Eve and she didn't come back."

"You haven't seen her since New Year's Eve? Have you talked to her on the phone?" She stopped. "When did the phone get disconnected?"

"It worked yesterday. I was going to call Angel today, but now it doesn't work."

"So you know where she is?"

"No, not exactly, but she's probably at Jamal's or Alex's."

"All right. We'll go out and call them. Or I'll go out and call them. It's really cold out, I don't want you girls to go out wet. Give me the phone numbers. And is there any food here? You look like a skeleton."

CHRISTINE came back in less than an hour with a bag of groceries. She hadn't been able to reach anyone—of course not, she said, they're at school, where you should be! Meanwhile, she wanted to make us tuna fish sandwiches, which I had never eaten and wouldn't eat, so instead she made French toast and bacon and hot chocolate. We were all happy with that.

While we sat at the table eating, Christine looked slowly around the kitchen. I saw what she saw—an over-flowing garbage pail that hadn't been emptied, piles of trash around it, dishes in the sink and all over the counter-tops alongside empty bags of chips, boxes of cookies, and bread wrappers. Stuff on the floor crunched under your feet when you walked. The rest of the house wasn't much better, and with Angel missing her shift at the laundromat, we had run out of clean clothes. All the towels were dirty.

"Let's try to clean up a little," she said.

Christine said we had to clean the bathroom and the kitchen because that's where the germs were. She took Joy to the bathroom with her, and left me in the kitchen with Kathleen to wash and dry the dishes. But first we had to go around the house and pick up all the dirty ones that were scattered everywhere. Kathleen refused to pick up the glasses in Pic's room that had cigarette butts floating in the bottoms.

We were in the middle of the dishes when Pic came home. Christine heard the door and came down the steps immediately. She started asking a million questions, but Pic just took off her coat and sat down on the couch, her scarf still wrapped around her head and neck. Lately Pic would get into these moods where she reminded me of myself. She seemed shut off from everything, like she was looking out from behind a veil.

"Girls, go upstairs," Christine said.

I pulled Kathleen along, whisked Joy from her perch at the top of the steps, and took them to their room.

"Aunt Christine wants us to clean. So pick up all the junk on your floor and put your dirty stuff in the basket."

A few minutes later, I smelled coffee for the first time since Angel had made it on the morning of New Year's Eve. I went into my room, closed the door, and looked through the vent.

My mother was half sitting, half lying on the sofa. Christine had given her a cup of coffee, which she held but didn't drink.

"Rita, look at me."

Pic turned to her, but I wasn't sure she was focusing on Christine. I looked at the two of them, full sisters, and thought how much more different and distant they were from each other than I was from my half-sisters. Christine, practical and efficient, a bit overweight, always reassuring. And my mother, taller and underweight, sliding from edgy to shell-shocked, who even today had managed to apply thick black eyeliner.

"You can't do this again. Do you hear me? You can't do this again. You look awful. What's in that bag? Where were you?"

No response.

"Rita, do you hear me?" Christine repeated.

"I hear you," Pic replied, disinterested.

"Did you get fired?"

"No, I quit," Pic said, with a trace of defiance in her voice.

"What? Jesus Christ, Rita. Why?"

"I can't work right now. Who's going to take care of the kids?"

"Do you know where Angel is?"

Pic put her face in her hands.

"Rita, do you know where Angel went?" Christine repeated.

When Pic looked up, she was crying.

"Don't worry," Christine said, putting her hand on Pic's arm, which made Pic flinch. "You know how Angel can be, but I'm sure she'll be back very soon, today, probably. Meanwhile, you can't quit your job. You have to go ask for your job back. Frank isn't even working, is he?"

"Frank left. He has a girlfriend."

Christine sighed. "Oh, God. But good riddance. He isn't helping you."

"Get out of my fucking house, Christine," Pic said suddenly.

"No," Christine said firmly. "No. I'm not leaving until you're together enough to handle all this. They're going to take your kids away again, Rita, and this time you won't get them back."

"It's all Angel's fault!" Pic complained angrily.

"What are you talking about? If it weren't for Angel this place would have fallen apart a long time ago."

"Everybody loves Angel," Pic whined bitterly. "Really, she's a selfish little bitch. She's always out running the streets."

Christine sighed and shook her head. "Rita, that's just not true. Every time I'm over here she's taking care of these kids and going to work. Or swimming."

"That fucking stupid swimming. Who knows if she even goes swimming all the times she says? I saw a letter one day. She had an abortion, the little slut."

Christine was speechless.

"Yeah that's right, Godmother," Pic went on. "Your perfect niece is a baby killer."

"I never said she was perfect, Rita," Christine said after a pause. "Jeannine says you kicked Angel out."

Pic dismissed that with a wave of her hand. "Jeannine lives in a fantasy world," she said.

Christine hesitated, and then decided this was not worth pursuing. Maybe she knew that I really did live in a fantasy world, at least part of the time. "I'm trying to clean up a little with the girls. Want to help us?"

Pic leaned over, grasping her stomach. "I don't feel good."

"What's in the bag?" Christine asked again.

"I need to lie down," Pic said.

"Do you want me to make you some tea and toast?"

"I'm sick," Pic said irritably.

"Well, why don't you go upstairs and lie down. But first"—she held out her hand—"give me the bag."

"No!" Pic stood and started up the stairs.

"Fine." Christine sighed, disgusted. "I'm going to take Jeannine over to the laundromat with the dirty clothes and towels. I'll leave her there and come right back."

"I'm okay here," Pic yelled. Then she burst into tears.

"Rita, let me help you. Please."

CHRISTINE and I struggled over the snow banks to her car with pillowcases filled with laundry. Kathleen watched from the living room window. At the laundromat, I sorted clothes and towels while Christine called her husband, Uncle Tony, from the payphone.

She explained all about Angel not being home. "I can't come home, Tony. Frank isn't there, God knows where he is, and these kids are a mess. They aren't going to school, they don't have any food . . ."

She looked over at me. I concentrated on the laundry. "She's only fourteen, Tony. She needs as much help as the little ones. Maybe more."

She dropped more quarters in the phone. "Listen, I need for you to call the phone company and pay Rita's bill with your credit card. There's no phone in the house. It's not safe."

I had the washers going before she was off the phone. "Tell the kids I love them. Get them to school on time, Tony. I'll call you in the morning."

She left me there with the laundry. I was okay with that. I liked the laundromat. It was quiet and familiar and it smelled good.

When she picked me up later, Pic was sleeping and the little girls were in bed—in their own room. I had gotten used to them sleeping with me and I didn't want to be alone. As we were straightening out the beds, I said, "You can sleep in Angel's bed. Or, I'll sleep in Angel's bed and you can sleep on the bottom."

"Okay," she said. "Jeannine, everyone's going to school tomorrow."

I just looked at her. I knew I couldn't possibly go to school. The whole idea of all those people, and moving around from class to class—I couldn't even remember my schedule.

I started to climb to the top bunk.

"Don't you have a nightgown? What about brushing your teeth?"

I found some pajamas and brushed my teeth. She turned off the light and went to the bathroom. I just lay there quietly, and when she came back in, said good night, and got in bed, I snuggled deep down into Angel's covers and felt her form and smelled her scent, almost as if she was there with me.

IN the morning, Christine tried to get us all to go to school, but I had been awake all night, reading while she slept. I had been reading all the detective and spy novels I could steal. I found those were the best to keep me from thinking. I couldn't fall asleep, and I couldn't just lie there because I'd think about Angel, visions whirling around—that she met the guy she was always looking for and ran away to New York, no, not in the snow, to Hawaii, or that she was kidnapped, tied up or being kept in a closet, and the ransom call would come but not to us, not even a kidnapper could be that stupid, to the team, or that she was in hiding at Jamal's because she was pregnant and they were trying to figure out what to do, or they were secretly married, they got married on New Year's Eve, or she had a bad abortion and she died. She died. No, no, couldn't let my mind go that way, so I'd read. But no detective novels about dead girls.

In the morning, when Christine got stern about getting dressed, I felt like the world was spinning around me and I had to lie down. I couldn't catch my breath.

She made me tea and toast and brought it to me in bed. "Listen," she said, sitting on the side of my bed. "I need to talk to you." She pulled my chin gently up, making me look at her. "I know you're really upset about Angel."

I nodded.

"Do you know something? Is there somewhere that she would go that nobody knows about but you?"

She waited. I said nothing. I was trying, but I couldn't think of anything.

"Jeannine!" she finally said, exasperated. "You have to talk. Normal people talk. I'm upset, too. I need your help. You're not a little girl anymore. You have to start acting your age."

"I don't know where she is," I said.

"Do you think she got so angry at Pic that she went off somewhere?"

"Maybe. But I think she would try to contact me," I said, trying to imagine Angel somewhere not thinking about me.

She sighed and rubbed my head. "Eat. I'm walking the girls to school. You stay here."

No problem. I didn't want to do anything *except* stay in

bed. But as it turned out, she couldn't get Kathleen to school either. Kathleen threw one of her screaming and crying fits and refused to go. She climbed into bed with me. So only Joy went, happy to return to her kindergarten room full of toys and playmates.

When Christine returned, she marched into my room and commanded that Kathleen and I get out of bed.

"Right now, girls," she said firmly. "If you're not going to school, then you're helping me clean this house. And get dressed," she added as she left the room.

Next she got Pic up as well. When Pic whined and resisted, Christine got tough. "You have to take charge here, Rita. Soon enough the school's going to send someone over here to find out why these kids don't go to school, and when they see this place, they'll call DHS and these kids will be gone."

I knew that wouldn't happen; they'd never sent anyone to check up on me all the years I'd been ditching school. But it seemed like a good thing to say to Pic.

So we cleaned. I knew Christine had to be a good housekeeper, because she'd learned it from Nannie Lou. Angel and I were amazed at the cleaning rituals we'd learned when we lived with our grandmother. As soon as it got a bit warm in April, we had to do spring cleaning. Angel and I had never heard of such a thing, but Nannie Lou seemed to hold it as important and natural as going to mass on Sunday. She said it was like starting over fresh every year after being cooped up all winter. Everybody had jobs, but it seemed to me that the girls had more jobs and the boys had fewer.

One of the biggest jobs was the windows. I couldn't believe how much work went into cleaning windows. First,

Nannie Lou took down the curtains and put them in the wash. Then Pop and Uncle Jimmy took the storm windows out. When the windows came out, they got taken to the kitchen, where Angel sat on the floor cleaning them. She sprayed them and rubbed and rubbed with rags until they squeaked. When she found out that only one was going back in each window because a screen would now go in, she flipped. "Why am I cleaning something that's going in the basement? Won't they be dirty again when we have to put them back in?"

"Just do it," Pop warned her.

It got worse when Nannie Lou assigned Angel to wash the screens outside with a scrub brush and ammonia.

"Couldn't we have Mr. Clean? This stuff smells like piss!" she howled.

Christine had clearly learned all the cleaning tricks from Nannie Lou.

"Start by stripping all the beds," she ordered.

I had never heard that expression, but I understood when I saw her pull the corner of the sheet on Joy's bed and yank it off in one quick movement. When Christine realized that we didn't have any other sheets, I was back at the laundromat. When she couldn't find supplies that met her standards, she went to the store and returned with a bucket, along with mops and sponges and cleanser and Windex and bottles of stuff I'd never seen before. When she discovered that we didn't have a vacuum cleaner, she went to Sears and charged one. She plowed through the downstairs, pushing furniture around and throwing the wrappers and pieces of food she found into a trash bag, spraying, sweeping, vacuuming, and moving stuff to find every last bit of our disgusting dirt.

Kathleen and I worked on our rooms and cleaned the bathtub where we'd been showering together in the filth the day before.

It took Pic all day, with lots of breaks and a few crying jags, just to clean her own room. I went to her door at one point, and she was stuffing all of Frank's clothes into pillow cases.

"I'm giving these to Good Will," she said defiantly.

I just nodded. "Your room looks good," I said, and went back to my own work.

Christine ran up and down the stairs, checking on all of us.

THAT night, Christine ordered pizza. We sat in our sparkling kitchen, all together at the table, with paper napkins, not paper towels, and ate our pizza from plates. Just as we were finishing, there was knocking at the door.

"Angel!" Kathleen squealed and ran to answer it. But once there, she called to me.

Instead of Angel, two men were at the door. One held up a badge. By this time, we were all in the living room.

"Come in," Pic said quietly.

The detective looked from Pic to Christine and asked, "Is one of you Angela Ferente's mother?"

"Me," Pic answered, quietly, her voice cracking a bit.

"Girls, go upstairs," my aunt directed. "Now."

I didn't want to miss this. I had them in their room and was peering through the vent in less than a minute. I was hoping they had some news, but afraid if they had bad news. I held my breath.

"You can sit down," Christine told them.

"No thanks, miss," the older cop said. "We're only here for a minute. We have a report that your daughter is missing. I believe an officer stopped by to speak with you?"

"Well," Christine started, "she's not . . ."

To my surprise, Pic put her hand lightly on Christine's arm and interrupted. "We had a disagreement on New Year's Eve," she said calmly. "She's a difficult girl. She don't want to live by my rules."

"Have you heard from her, ma'am?"

Pic shook her head. "I was gonna call you if she didn't come home this weekend. She's done stuff like this before."

"The information we have is that she's eighteen," the cop said, checking a notebook.

"Nineteen in July," Pic said.

"Do you want to file a missing person's report?" the cop asked.

chapter nine

———

ALEX

After Angel was missing for five days, CJ called a team meeting at practice.

There had been articles in the newspapers and stories on TV, prompted when Aisha Greene's dad, a cop, got the door slammed in his face after a brief conversation with Angel's mother when he stopped by there to find out what was happening. He turned it over to detectives, who visited Angel's house, my house, and Jamal's house. The newspaper stories explained how Angel hadn't been seen since New Year's Eve, and about how she was at the party, then went to her boyfriend's house, and then took the bus to go home, according to her boyfriend.

The articles told all about Angel, about the team, and about how she was being recruited by all these colleges. There was a quote from the principal of our school, expressing concern and pledging help in finding her, and a quote from CJ saying that she was one of the most exciting athletes he had ever coached.

We were always trying to get publicity for the team, but we'd have given anything not to get it this way.

Plus there was something off-base about the article, like it didn't convey the real Angel, just like there was something off-base about the picture that was run in the paper and shown on TV, a head shot of Angel taken for the yearbook during our junior year. In that picture she had brown hair streaked with blonde, one length, cropped at the chin and covering her ears, and she was wearing the black robe they made all of us wear for the picture. It didn't even look like her.

"What's up with this picture?" Melanie asked me. "Was she wearing a wig that day?"

The day the article ran we all sat around at the pool, delaying the workout. We read the article out loud and speculated. People said things in front of Jamal that weren't very kind, like that Angel was probably holed up with some guy she met on the bus. CJ told us to shut up and get in the water.

After practice, he told us to sit on the bleachers. We were all huddling together with our warm-up hoods up and towels wrapped around us. It was freezing outside and freezing inside. CJ paced up and down in front of us, tapping his golf club on the floor.

Finally, he stopped and stared at us. "If you-all know anything about where she's at, you better tell me," he said. "You might feel you have to be loyal to something she told you, but we're past that point now."

He stopped in front of Jamal. "I'm talking to you."

"Coach, I'm straight with you. I put her on the bus. That's it."

CJ tugged on his hat. He always, always, always wore a baseball cap. He was very fussy about them, didn't like the ones that had a stiff front. It had become a tradition that any of us who went away anywhere brought him a cap and were proud when he wore it. You knew you had really made him mad when he took off his cap. He used to take it off all the time when he argued with Angel. He'd finger his gray, kinky hair and say, "See these gray hairs? Before I met you, they were all black!"

He started looking at us one by one, staring right into our eyes. He stopped at me. Despite the cold, his face was dewy with sweat. He looked tired.

"Williams?"

I shook my head and I had to press my lips together and take a deep breath to keep the knot that was now always in my throat from rising up. I was wishing so much that I had a secret, wishing I knew something to keep from him.

He paced some more. Then he turned and spoke to us all, to no one in particular. "So no one knows anything. That better be true." *Tap, tap* went the club. He thundered, "Do you hear me? Don't put me through this, don't put her mother through this, if you know something."

He waited. No one moved. No one spoke. "Okay then," he said softly, his deep voice just a decibel above the rumble of the very ineffective heating fans. "No one knows anything."

"Well," Aisha said, "it's Angel."

"Yeah," CJ agreed, nodding. "It's Angel. It's Angel. I'm going to think she's okay until I know something else. Right?"

We nodded and murmured, trying hard to be convinced.

"But we need to help figure out where she is, so everyone can stop this worrying. Then when she comes back or we find her, I'll personally handcuff her to these bleachers until she goes to college," he said, his voice rising. "Now, how can we find her? Who knows this Ramon everyone's talking about?"

"The police already talked to him, CJ," said Aisha. "He was in New York on New Year's. My father told me."

Jamal started to get up until CJ went over and helped him sit back down again.

"So what?" CJ said. "I want to talk to him."

"I don't know him," I said. "But I know he lives on her block. Her sister would know which house."

"Her sister," CJ mused. "Anybody talked to her?"

"I called on Tuesday and woke up her mother," I said, "but she told me Jeannine was sick. If anyone's heard from Angel, it would be Jeannine."

"I called there this morning," said Jamal. "The phone's cut off."

"Really? Well then, somebody needs to go over there and talk to Jeannine and see if she knows anything and also find out where this Ramon lives. Williams?"

"Okay. I can stop by."

THE next day, I drove to Angel's house after practice. It was Friday. Dinnertime. I knocked and knocked, and finally Kathleen answered the door.

"Hey," I said. "Is Jeannine home?"

She shook her head. She looked awful. Her skin was yellow and she had deep, dark rings under her eyes. But she didn't open the door to let me in.

"Can I come in?"

"Jeannine's not home," she whispered.

"That's okay," I said, figuring she was relying on the "no strangers" rule. "Can I come in?"

She nodded, and when I pushed just a little on the door she moved back, like a feather in the wind. Joy was curled up on the sofa inside a sleeping bag, watching TV.

I sat down on the sofa and wiggled Joy's foot. "Hey, remember me? I'm Alex."

She observed me for a minute and pulled her fingers out of her mouth. "Is Angel at your house?"

"No, baby," I said, and she replaced her fingers and turned back to the TV.

Kathleen sat down on the floor near my feet. I bent over.

"Where's Jeannine?"

"At the laundromat."

"Oh. When's she coming home?"

Kathleen shrugged.

"Is the laundromat down the street that way"—I pointed—"and then turn right, that way?"

Kathleen hesitated. "I think so. Could you tell Jeannine to come home?"

"Yes, okay. I'm going to find Jeannine at the laundromat. Alright? You guys okay?"

Kathleen nodded, and I left.

I drove the way I thought I should to get to the laundromat, and sure enough, there it was on the corner. It looked like about the friendliest place in the neighborhood: brightly lit, no graffiti, big soda and junk-food vending machines visible through the door. There were no real parking spaces because the plows had pushed the snow into little mountains lining the sides of the streets. I left the car as close as I could to the curb, but it was jutting out into the middle of the street. There weren't too many cars out on the street though, with the snow and cold, so I just went inside.

Jeannine was alone, standing by one of the built-in

tables, folding laundry. She turned as I opened the door.

"Do you know where Angel is?" she asked right away.

I shook my head. "No. No, I wanted to know if you had heard from her."

She turned away and stared out the window. The fluorescent lighting made her skin a translucent blue. Her strawberry hair grazed her shoulders.

"I was just at your house. Kathleen seemed a little upset. Can you go home?"

"I . . . this is Angel's shift."

"Okay," I said. "When is it finished?"

"It's seven to eleven. We close at eleven. The kids are okay. My mother's there. She was probably in her room. My aunt Christine will be there soon, too. She's staying with us."

"Oh. How come she's staying with you?"

"My mother's not doing too well." Jeannine finally turned away from the window and looked at me. "Especially since Angel's been gone."

"When was the last time you saw Angel?" I asked.

"New Year's Eve. I saw her right when she went out."

"And she never came home?"

She shook her head.

"Were you up late that night?"

"I don't know. I don't remember exactly when I went to sleep. Pic came home at night and then she went out again, I think. I don't know exactly what time it was. My stepfather came home, maybe in the morning? He and Pic had a huge fight. It woke me up." Her voice kept getting softer as she talked. I could barely hear her.

"I called you a few times this week and your mom answered once and the other times the phone just rang. And then your phone was disconnected. So maybe Angel called."

"Maybe."

"You don't seem hopeful," I said, choking a little because it was so hard to say.

"Are you?" she asked in a tone that didn't request an answer.

When I left, I decided to go find Wrench. My sister was still home from college and she and my mom were planning on having a VCR night, cuddling up together with microwave popcorn, and I just wasn't up for it. I could see what my mother was doing. She was trying to keep me calm by acting like things were normal. And she was trying to keep Vanessa happy—she was always trying to keep Vanessa happy—by not paying too much attention to me. I didn't want to deal with them. I just wanted to be with my friends.

I drove by Wrench's house and saw his broken-down car out front, so I parked down the street where there was a break in the snow bank. His parents weren't home, and he was sprawled on the sofa in the living room in sweats and a pair of heavy wool socks. He was drinking a beer and watching music videos.

"Want one?" he asked. I nodded and he pointed to the kitchen. "In the fridge."

"Where're your parents?"

"They walked over my uncle's to play cards or something."

I got a beer, and he curled up to make room for me. I sat at the end of the couch.

"I went to Angel's," I said.

"She there?"

"*No*, I wish. No, her sisters were there. Her little sisters. I found Jeannine at that laundromat where Angel works, and I asked her if she'd heard from Angel and she said no."

"That's it?"

"Pretty much. Jeannine was like, past depressed."

He lurched up and into the kitchen. The house was so small and he was so big that it seemed like one movement. He brought back two more beers and popped his open.

"What do you think?" he asked me. "I mean, really."

"I don't know." My throat felt tight from trying not to cry again. "I feel like she would have called me. Or her sister. But then, you know her . . ."

"I think something bad happened. I don't know what. But this shit is too strange."

I chugged my beer and opened the second can. Wrench stretched out and put his feet in my lap. I was cold and his sweat pants and his body heat were warming me up.

"What about Jamal?" I was barely able to get the words out.

"Fuck no, he loves her, man. Loves her! I think something happened on her way home."

"Like what? Like some guy grabbed her and took her somewhere?" I was arguing. I didn't want to believe that. "Angel would go crazy. She'd be screaming and hollering. She's strong."

Wrench put his beer down on the coffee table and with no warning, he sat up and pulled me around against him so that my back was against his chest. He had one hand cupped over my mouth and the other around my waist, both my arms pinned under his. I wiggled and tried to scream, tried to kick and throw my body around. I could barely move. I was feeling panicked and angry and I couldn't breathe right.

Finally, he let go. "She as strong as you?"

"Fuck you," I choked, and burst into tears.

"Hey, I'm sorry," he said. "Alex, really, I'm sorry. But if some guy surprised her, forget it. She didn't have a fucking chance." He put his arm around me, gently this time.

I curled into him and sobbed.

Wrench kissed my head and told me to calm down. Maybe everything would turn out okay. Maybe he was wrong. Then somehow, I think I initiated it, I was kissing him, really kissing him. The only thing I wanted was to not think, not talk. I didn't know what I was doing, and I don't think he did either. Pretty soon, he was inside me. When he first pushed in it was like the best thing I'd ever felt, but when he got going, it hurt. Good, bad, whatever, it wasn't about Angel, and I couldn't face any more about Angel.

The best part was afterwards, my skin against his, wrapped up under a blanket in his arms. Safe.

WHEN I got home that night I didn't tell my mother about going to see Wrench, but I did tell her about going to Angel's and to the laundromat.

"Her aunt called me today."

Christine told my mother that she thought the strain of Angel not being there and not knowing what was happening was too much for Pic. She said that Pic and Frank had been fighting and that Frank had barely been home since New Year's. She was worried that Pic was very stressed out. She asked my mother if she spent much time with Pic because of the swim team.

"No, very little," my mother said. "I don't know her well at all."

Christine said that Pic had some problems with depression. She said that she had either quit her job or gotten fired. Then she said she was going to stay with Pic and the girls for a while.

The two of them agreed to meet at Angel's house the next evening. Christine thought it would be good for Pic to be connected to other people, people who cared about Angel. My mother said she would bring dinner, and me. My mother also suggested that CJ come along. She told Christine that CJ was organizing prayer meetings and a search effort, and maybe it would help Pic to be involved.

THE next day there was another article in the paper. The police had questioned the bus driver, who said he remembered her getting on, even though it was New Year's Eve and a lot of people were out and about.

Angel wasn't someone you'd easily forget. In addition to her scar and her spiky cherry hair and her New Year's Eve biker look, complete with electric blue nail polish, she had a nose stud and about twelve tiny earrings pierced in her left ear. But in order to get home, she would have transferred from the bus to the El, and then walked home six blocks. The bus driver couldn't remember where she got off, or if she was alone. I felt good for Jamal, though, because it verified that he was telling the truth.

"Why are we doing this?" I asked my mother when she started hurrying me up to go over there that afternoon.

"Because that's what you do when someone you care about has a crisis," my mother said impatiently. "You help."

"But I don't think she wants our help."

"Well, we'll see. We won't know until we offer. But wherever Angel is, she needs our help, and she would want us to help her sisters."

She had stopped at the supermarket and bought some groceries and dinner—two rotisserie chickens, salad bar stuff, cornbread, and some juice. She also had an apple pie and vanilla ice cream.

When we arrived, Christine let us in. We followed her through the living room, which looked very tidy, and into the kitchen. Kathleen was washing dishes. She slid over and put her arm around my waist.

Pic was sitting at the kitchen table, brushing knots out of Joy's long hair. My mother bustled in and put the grocery bags on the table. She put her hand on Pic's shoulder.

"You must be beside yourself, Rita. I can't imagine."

Pic looked up at her. "You can call me Pic," was all she said.

They all looked sick. Pic looked exhausted, or hung over, or both. Her eyes were flat, dull, like she hadn't slept in days and days. As she lifted the brush to Joy's hair, her hand trembled. A cigarette burned in a saucer on the table. Joy's long blond hair was matted.

"I brought some dinner," my mother said, sounding inappropriately cheerful. "Shall I set it out here on the table?"

"Yeah, sure," Pic said.

"Where's Jeannine?" I asked Kathleen.

"She's upstairs."

Joy drifted away from the table, but Pic didn't move, so my mother set up dinner around her, getting plates and silverware from Christine.

"Can I go up and see Jeannine?" I asked no one in particular, not sure if I should be asking Pic, or Christine, or my mother.

"Yeah, sure," Pic said.

I went upstairs. Jeannine was buried in sheets and covers on the bottom bunk bed, reading *Sense and Sensibility*. It had been a summer reading book for us the previous summer.

"Oh God, I love that book," I said.

"I want to live in this book," Jeannine said.

Their room looked just the same as the last time I'd been there—it was eerie. It was like Angel would come walking in from the bathroom any minute. Her bathing suits were still hanging on the doorknob. Her swim bag was on the floor, in the corner. And her shoes were still tumbling out of the closet.

I sat down on the side of the bed. "You okay?" I hugged Jeannine. "My mother's here. She brought dinner." I knew that a regular dinner was probably not the most enticing thing to Jeannine. "And pie and ice cream."

"Okay," she said.

She got up slowly, unsteady on her feet, and put a sweatshirt over the T-shirt and sweat pants she had on. To me she seemed about as skinny as a person could be and still be alive. She was fourteen, but she looked like she was ten. She hardly had any breasts at all.

"I have to pee," she said. "Don't go downstairs without me. Wait for me."

"Okay."

While I waited, I looked around some more. The letters were still posted on the dresser mirror. There were five of them up there. I realized with a start that I needed to tell my mother about them, so I pulled them off.

CJ had arrived by the time Jeannine and I got downstairs. Kathleen and Joy were eating their dinner in front of the TV, and the adults were gathered around the kitchen table. There were only four chairs.

"Hello ladies," he said to Jeannine and me.

"Here girls," my mother said. "Let me make you a plate."

Jeannine silently took the plate heaped with food and went and sat with her sisters.

"So," CJ said, continuing the conversation they were having before we came in, "I say we do as much as we can to keep this thing in front of the press. If we start a search committee, it does double duty. The press'll cover what we're doing."

"Yeah, so maybe wherever she is, she'll hear about it and realize she needs to get in touch with us," I said.

"That's the idea." CJ nodded.

"So we need some recent pictures of her," CJ said to Pic.

Pic was pushing the food around on her plate. She didn't seem totally tuned in to the conversation.

"Ms. O'Neill, you have any pictures?" CJ pressed when Pic didn't answer.

"You can call me Pic."

"Do you have any pictures?"

"I have some," my mother said. "I have some from Juniors that are pretty good."

"Mom," I said, thrusting the letters at her. "Look at these. Angel was getting these weird letters."

Pic's head snapped up. I handed them over to my mother.

"Where were these?" my mother asked, incredulous.

"Upstairs, in her room."

"Did you know about these before?" she grilled me.

"Yeah," I said. I was starting to realize I had made a big mistake by not telling about them immediately.

"Why didn't you say anything?" she said angrily.

"I forgot. She's been getting them since Juniors. Actually, since Champs. They were on her mirror," I said, defending myself. "It wasn't a secret."

"Let me see them," Pic said, and took them from my mother. After a minute she yelled into the living room, "Jeannine! Get in here!"

Jeannine bolted in, looking terrified.

"Why didn't you tell me about these?" Pic hollered at her.

Jeannine shrugged. "I don't know," she whispered. "They've been on our mirror for months, Pic."

"You are so goddamn stupid," Pic said with disgust, and Jeannine retreated back to the sofa, her uneaten plate of food pushed to the side on the floor.

My mother cringed. She and Christine gathered up the dishes and they spread the letters out on the table.

"We need to call the detectives," Christine said.

"We sure do," said CJ, looking at each one closely. "I think I know who sent these."

Angel had received at least five letters. Several were just messages, but a few had pictures drawn by the sender, and that's what tipped CJ off. He recognized the drawings as similar to those done by Valentine, our custodian at the pool, who spent a lot of his down time reading and scribbling.

After some fist banging and cursing about Valentine ("I always knew there was something wrong with that son of a bitch!"), CJ called the detectives who had talked with all of us. After the initial interviews, the police had decided to treat Angel's disappearance as a missing person's case, since she was eighteen and Pic had told her to get out. CJ and my mother were puzzled and angry about that, and so was Christine when they explained it to her.

So at first the detectives were reluctant to come and look at the letters, since none of them were threatening.

"No, they're not threatening," CJ explained, exasperated. "But they're insinuating. Don't you think it's a little strange for someone to send suggestive, anonymous letters to a beautiful young girl? And then for that girl to be missing?"

The police finally agreed to look at the letters, and asked that Pic bring them to the police station.

My mother agreed to go with CJ and Pic. Pic didn't want to go alone, and CJ didn't want to be alone with her, so my trusty mother stepped in.

Afterward, my mother said that Pic showed up in nice clothes and acted very "appropriate"—one of my mother's favorite words.

But the police made it clear that there was no crime involved. The letters weren't threatening, and anyway, Angel was an adult who had made no complaints about the letters. They did agree to talk with Valentine.

When they did, Valentine admitted that he sent the letters. He told the police that indeed he was infatuated with Angel, but he was shy and afraid to approach her. He said that he had intended to eventually reveal that he was the letter writer, and make his feelings known.

Thinking about that made me want to throw up.

He claimed that on New Year's Eve he had visited his mother at the assisted living facility where she lived, and then went home. The staff at the facility confirmed that he had been there. But he had no way to confirm his story that he'd stayed home through the snowstorm the next day, and hadn't gone out again until Tuesday when he went to work at the pool.

CJ pressed the police to search his apartment.

"The guy's in love with guns!" he yelled. "He reads weapons magazines all the time."

The detectives explained that they had no evidence of a crime. There was no cause to search his apartment.

"He's probably holding her hostage in the damn apartment!"

CJ was steaming. He fired Valentine for fraternizing, which I had never even heard of.

So we were back to Angel getting on the bus. What happened after that was a mystery.

"Don't you think that if she took her mother seriously, she would have stayed all night at her boyfriend's?" CJ pestered the detectives. "She told him that she had to get home."

"From what we've learned, this young lady has a lot of boyfriends. Maybe she had two dates on New Year's Eve," the police responded.

MEANWHILE, everybody did things in their own way to deal with the ongoing anxiety about not knowing where Angel was.

CJ and some of the parents had these prayer sessions at the pool after practice. I stayed for them a couple times, but they actually made me feel worse. I couldn't plead with God to keep Angel safe; that wasn't enough for me. I wanted Angel to come walking into the pool right that minute and I wanted God to just make it happen.

CJ took charge, which was always his way. He kept meeting with the police, pressuring them, and he called a meeting to organize a search committee. Besides all the swimming parents, he invited the principal of our school, and the president of the Home and School Association, and people from his church. My mother persuaded Christine and Pic to come.

They prayed at the search committee meetings too. Melanie's dad, who was a deacon at his church, appealed to Jesus to guide us to Angel, and a few people chimed in, encouraging him, saying stuff like, "Yes, Jesus, Amen."

After the praying, CJ talked about what had been done so far to find Angel. He said the police were still treating the case like a missing person's case, meaning not much was being done, so we had to take charge of finding her. He had a large stack of bright pink flyers with a picture of Angel and phone numbers to call. He spoke directly to Pic in front of everyone.

"Angel's a very important person around here," he said. "If you go look on our bulletin board, you'll see her name everywhere. She's set a lot of records on this team. The younger swimmers look up to her. We know Angel has her . . . other side, but she has a good heart, and she's going somewhere. She's leading other kids somewhere. So we need to find her. We need you to work with us to find her. We have faith. We will find her."

Pic surprised everybody at the meeting. She stood up and thanked everyone for helping to find Angel. She talked about how difficult the past two weeks had been. She was almost passionate. She almost seemed like a normal person.

We all took the flyers with the picture of Angel on them at the end of the meeting and all of us—the swimmers, the kids, the parents—spent days and days knocking on doors and stapling posters to telephone poles. We walked the whole route, from Jamal's to Angel's house. Pic trudged along with us, usually with Jeannine in tow.

One day in Kinko's, Jeannine said to me, "We're not going to find her this way. Unless she's dead."

I was so flustered I didn't know what to say. We were doing what CJ had told us to do, like always. I hadn't even thought about whether it was the best thing to do. "What do you mean?"

"Why would she be around here? If she got off the El and walked six blocks, then either someone took her or killed her. But she's not hanging around here reading flyers."

"But other people are reading the flyers. Maybe someone saw something. What else can we do?"

Jeannine shook her head. "I don't know."

My voice trembling, I asked, "Do you think she's dead?"

Jeannine bit her lip. "I think she would contact me if she could. Or you. It's been two weeks."

I nodded and held her arm. "I can't think she's dead, Jeannine. I can't. We don't even know if she took the El. Maybe she met someone and he's got her somewhere."

"Maybe," she said, staring at the copy machine. "I saw a movie about a kid who walked to school and never came home. Someone grabbed him and took him to a house. There was no trace of him for months. Everybody thought he was dead."

"How did they find him?"

"Somebody recognized him and called the police."

"See!" I said loudly. "That's why we have the flyers."

MY mother became obsessed with cleaning our house. That was her way. I couldn't sleep, and she couldn't sleep. I would wake up with a start at 1:00 a.m. and find her surrounded by all the books in the living room, dusting off each one and rearranging them on the shelves. She emptied closets, dumped out drawers, washed and ironed all the curtains, mended clothes that had been lying in a basket for months.

Some of the kids ditched practice, sometimes because they were running around the city putting up the Angel posters, and sometimes because they just couldn't handle being at the pool and thinking about Angel not being there.

Melanie became more like herself. It was our senior year, and between her grades and her swimming she was choosing between Princeton and UVA, but she was working harder than ever in school. She wanted to be valedictorian.

Me, I swam and trained like never before. At first, I swam as hard as I could at practice, just to exhaust myself so I couldn't think anymore, so the physical sensations of hard training, the lactic acid burn, the nausea, the lightheadedness, would crowd out any thoughts. And so maybe I could sleep.

Sometimes it worked, sometimes not. So I started to try to concentrate on something specific each time I got in the water, to think only about that one thing. For a long time, it was the entry position of my left hand into the water. CJ had been telling me for years that it was wrong. But now I had a reason to think about that hand on every stroke, because thinking about that, visualizing that, kept me from thinking about Angel and visualizing where she might be and what might have happened to her.

But I still couldn't sleep. If I fell asleep, I always woke up after a few hours, Angel the first thing in my head. Sometimes I couldn't even fall asleep. I figured I had to tire myself out or take sleeping pills. I had no idea how to get sleeping pills and I knew my mother wouldn't get them for me, so I got her to pay for Wrench and me to join a gym, and we went every night after practice. At the pool we only had a raggedy set of free weights, but at the gym they had every machine known to man, and an elevated track around the ceiling. We paid a trainer to design workouts for us, and we lifted every night, working on different muscle groups, and then finished up with a mile or two around the track. Usually on the way home, despite the deep freeze we were in and all the snow, we stopped in the park and had sex in Wrench's car.

Turned out my mother was doing that too. One night when Wrench's car was broken, I got a ride home right after practice with Melanie's mom, and when I walked into the house I found Mr. Simmons on the living room couch with my mother.

chapter ten

———

JEANNINE

A few days after Pic filed the missing person's report, two reporters came to the door. It was only about nine o'clock, so the only person up and about and ready to answer the door was Christine. She had already walked Kathleen and Joy to school. She had given up on getting me there, at least for the moment.

But although she wasn't out of bed, Pic was awake. That week, Christine had gotten Pic to a couple of AA meetings at a church a few blocks away. The meetings were at lunchtime. Christine would walk Pic there and meet her again to walk home afterwards. But she didn't really think Pic needed AA as much as she needed therapy so she was trying to persuade Pic to agree and gave her some numbers of places that would give her a discount. She was making Pic eat, too, and it seemed to be helping. Pic wasn't in bed as much and she was helping Christine with the housework.

Pic heard Christine talking in the living room and called down, "Who's there?"

"Reporters from the *Daily News*," Christine said.

"I'll be right down."

Right down took about fifteen minutes; she got dressed

and even put on a little makeup before leaving her room. I took up my post at the peephole.

Pic sat down in our very clean living room and folded her hands in her lap. The reporters wanted to run through the sequence of events again, so Pic calmly repeated what by this time she had already related at least a dozen times.

"So the last time you saw her was when she left that night?"

Pic nodded. "Yeah. Well, she was getting ready to leave. I left first."

"Was anyone here that night?"

"My other children. And then I came home."

"What time was that?"

"I don't really remember," Pic said. "It was New Year's Eve."

"And you haven't heard from her at all?"

"No."

"You must be very worried," the reporter said.

"I wasn't worried at first," Pic said. "Angel's got a mind of her own. Always has. But now I'm a little worried."

"Do you believe what her boyfriend says?"

Pic shrugged. "I don't know."

"Your daughter seems to be quite an athlete. Sounds like she has a bright future. What can you tell us about that?"

Pic hesitated. "She's going to college," she said, suddenly choked up.

"We'd like to get a photo of your daughter. Do you have one you could loan us?"

"Um, give me a minute," Pic said, and she ran up the stairs. By the time she burst into my room, I was lying in bed.

"I need a picture of Angel," she panted, out of breath.

"Over there," I said, motioning toward the shelf with

Angel's trophies. Her team picture was leaning against one of them.

"Don't you have a picture where that stupid scar isn't showing?"

Why don't you have a damn picture? I thought.

"No, no, this is good," she said suddenly. "Here, grab some of these, Jeannine." She started picking up Angel's trophies. "Get the ribbons, too."

"I thought you might want to see her trophies," Pic said to the reporters, setting up the trophies on the coffee table. "My daughter Jeannine has some more. And some of her ribbons. Hurry up, Jeannine," she said to me impatiently as I straggled down the steps, my arms full of Angel memorabilia.

"Are you Angel's sister?" the reporter asked me.

I nodded.

"You haven't heard from your sister, right? Any idea where she might be?"

I shook my head.

"Mrs. O'Neill, how about a picture of you in front of the trophies?"

"Okay, just a minute," Pic said. She ran upstairs again, and a few minutes later came down with barrettes in her hair and fresh lipstick.

After the reporters left, Pic pushed that beat-up coffee table against the wall and covered it with a sheet. Then she arranged all of the trophies and ribbons on it, and got me to find a few more pictures to put there as well.

CHRISTINE tried to get Pic to work with CJ and the people at the pool, but as usual Pic was doing her own thing.

She showed up to some of CJ's meetings and went along sometimes with the group distributing flyers, but she was oddly disconnected from all the people who were trying to help. After the reporters came, Pic realized that the press was fascinated by a missing girl—especially a missing girl who was an athlete, and especially an athlete with a reputation for being unpredictable and unconventional and, according to her mother, "a little on the wild side." TV stations and the papers were calling and coming to our house and interviewing Pic every day. She started being very attentive to how we all looked and how the house looked. All of a sudden, we were taking showers all the time and she was calling Frank, whining that the kids had no decent clothes and to bring her some money. Sometimes in the middle of the night, when I was lying awake reading, I'd hear her vacuuming with our new vacuum cleaner.

She started calling into all these talk radio shows. As soon as the hosts realized she was the mother of the missing girl who'd been in the papers and on TV news, they let her talk. Some days she was more coherent than other days, but her message was always the same: *Angel ran off somewhere because we had a misunderstanding, and I'm trying to reach her to let her know it's okay to come home.*

I felt like I was a bit player in a soap opera, and Pic was the star. She was playing the distressed mother, regretful about the disagreement with her daughter about New Year's Eve. She was proud of Angel's accomplishments, proud that Angel was going to college. I was playing the sad sister. It felt like the reality behind the show had almost been forgotten—Angel was missing. Weeks had gone by without any contact. *Angel is missing*, I wanted to scream.

One day Pic came into my room and found me sitting by the window, silent, tears sliding down my face.

"What's the matter with you?" she asked irritably.

"I think Angel might be dead," I said.

"What makes you think that?" she snapped at me.

"I think she would call me."

"That's no reason. She's not dead! Don't say that to anyone."

Sometimes the real Pic seeped into the role that she was playing. Radio hosts asked her questions that infuriated her, like why she was out all night on New Year's Eve anyway since she had young children at home. She argued with them and hung up.

Finally a lady on one show said, "Isn't it true that you were once in drug and alcohol treatment and your children were in protective services?"

I was cuddled up on the sofa with Kathleen and Christine, listening to the show on the radio while Pic was in the kitchen on the phone. Pic wanted us to listen to all the shows she was on.

Pic snorted, and then said, "What the fuck difference does that make?" and was immediately cut off the air.

"Who the fuck do they think they are?" she cursed, then put on her coat and headed out the door.

"Where are you going?" Christine asked.

"None of your fucking business. In case you forgot, this is my fucking house, and these are my kids. So why don't you just get the fuck out."

"I don't want her to leave," Kathleen piped up. "She cooks good."

"You're starting to remind me of Angel," Pic yelled at her, and it was not a compliment.

"Are you going to kick me out, too?" Kathleen hollered back at her.

A few days later Frank came by. He had a key and he walked right in. Kathleen and I were back on the sofa, watching TV. He seemed a little shocked by how nice the house looked. "You having a party?" he said to Christine when she heard his voice and came out of the kitchen.

Pic came racing down the stairs. "Don't think you can just come back in here like nothing happened," she said defensively.

He gave her a disgusted look. "I have to get something." He walked around her in an exaggerated circle so as not to touch her.

"I told you on the phone that I need money for the kids," she said to his back.

He pulled a wad of bills out of his pocket, peeled some off, and gave them to Christine. "Here," he said pointedly.

"I need the rent," Pic whined. "You know I had to go get food stamps because you're spending money that should go to your kids and me on that cunt!"

"Rita!" Christine said, reacting to the word.

Frank whirled around and looked at Pic.

"I already paid the rent. You think I'm gonna give the money to you?" He laughed. Then, out of the corner of his eye, he saw Kathleen. "School closed?" he said to Pic.

"No, she threw a fit so I kept her home."

"So you're turning her into a nutcase like this one," he said, indicating me. "Kathleen! Come here."

"She don't have to come to you," Pic said, stepping in between Frank and the sofa. "You walked out, remember?"

"Shut up," Frank said. "I can talk to my own kid."

"Frank," Christine began.

"You shut up too," he said.

Christine shook her head emphatically. "Whoa! Don't speak to me that way, Frank. I'm here helping."

"Okay," he said, putting his hands up in a gesture of surrender. "But these kids should be in school." Turning to Pic, his voice rising, he said, "This is why Angel's out there in the street. You don't have no control. You need to take control of her," he said, waving his hand at Kathleen.

"Oh, now you're so concerned about her," Pic said. "You aren't here, haven't called or nothing, for two fucking weeks. You so interested in her? Why don't you take her—go ahead, take her. You and your girlfriend can take care of her." She put her hands on her hips and jutted her jaw at him.

"Maybe I will. Maybe I'll just come back and get the both of them!"

"Yeah, right!" Pic snorted.

He went upstairs and came back down almost immediately with a pair of shoes and a few shirts. He left without another word.

Frank was right that things were bad with Kathleen. She was becoming a scary hybrid of Angel and me. She had Angel's temper, and it had been exploding more and more frequently, at home and at school. She was having nightmares a lot, and waking up crying, sobbing, asking for Angel. Because of the nightmares she was afraid to go to sleep, so she was staying awake late into the night, like me. Christine was still sleeping in my bottom bunk, but Kathleen tiptoed in and climbed the ladder to crawl into bed with me almost every night.

Sometimes late at night we would sneak outside and sit on our steps. It was cold, very cold, so we'd bundle up together under coats and blankets. Kathleen just wanted to cuddle up against me. I looked up at the night sky, at the piece of the universe that I could glimpse from a stoop in Kensington, and felt better. Wherever Angel was, we shared this same sky, and whatever happened, our eternity was the same.

PIC started theorizing that Frank had something to do with Angel disappearing. That he had raped and killed her. She obsessed about it all the time.

"Why do you think he didn't stay here since New Year's? I know it! He was always, like, stalkin' her."

Christine tried to distract her with other things. Still, she kept returning to Frank, sometimes blaming him, sometimes blaming Angel.

"Angel tortured him, you know. One day she was making him look stupid, but the next day she was swinging her butt in his face."

Christine caught me alone in the bedroom and asked me what I thought. "I don't know," I said. I almost wanted to believe it, so there was some answer. He had temper explosions, but they usually sputtered out quickly. "Maybe if he felt really threatened or something."

Finally, Pic called the detectives. She told them that they should talk to Frank about Angel. She made it sound like Frank had been having sex with Angel.

"She had an abortion she didn't tell me about," Pic said. "I bet it was his baby!"

The detectives came to the house after interviewing

him. "He has an alibi, Mrs. O'Neill. We're checking it out."

"Yeah, what's that?" she asked angrily. She didn't like to be contradicted.

"A woman, Lisa Gleason, she said he was with her all night."

"Oh my God," Pic said, disgusted. "For detectives, you guys are pretty stupid! He's bangin' the girl! What do you think she's gonna say?"

STRANGE how one tiny, invisible thing—a germ, a virus—can change the course of things. Christine had been staying with us for a while when her son got the flu. She had been home to see Uncle Tony and her kids every few days, but she always slept at our house. But when my cousin Michael got sick, she had to leave. He was really sick, she said, and Uncle Tony couldn't stay home to take care of him. Owning a funeral home, work never let up.

Kathleen completely freaked out when Christine gathered us together and told us she had to leave. Christine had been trying hard to keep tabs on Pic, but sometimes she left, saying that she had appointments about Angel. When the call came about Michael, she wasn't home.

"Your cousin Michael is very sick," Christine told us. "He has a high fever. I need to be there. But I'll come back soon."

Kathleen started whining, then crying. "No, no! No, you have to stay here, you have to stay," she sobbed. "I want you to stay."

"Kathleen, Michael needs me."

But Kathleen was too upset, and too young, to listen to reason. She wanted what she wanted, and nothing else mattered. Pic walked in while Christine was trying to comfort her.

"Take me home with you," Kathleen wailed. "Take me with you."

"Honey, you need to stay here with your mom," Christine comforted her.

"You can take her," Pic said. "Take them both. I have so much to do."

Kathleen was sobbing so hard that she couldn't speak. When she tried, she just let out deep, wrenching breaths.

Christine looked at us all, and made a quick decision. "Okay," she said. "I'll take them."

Christine hugged us and promised she would be back within days. "I hope you hear something good," she said to us. "And Jeannine, keep cleaning."

And so I was left alone with Pic.

CHRISTINE said she'd be back soon, and I wanted her to be happy with me when she returned. Probably she would have been happiest if I went back to school, but the next best thing was to keep cleaning. So the next day, after Pic left to go to "appointments," whatever that meant, I began.

Our closets were all overflowing with stuff. None of the doors even closed. I didn't want to deal with the one in my room, because I wanted everything of Angel's to be the same as always, so I tackled the one in Kathleen and Joy's room. I pulled out everything that was on the floor —broken toys and peed-on clothes and barrettes and wads of dust. It was all so jumbled up and dirty that I didn't even try to save anything. I crammed it all into some empty supermarket bags left from one of Christine's shopping trips and put it all in the trash. Then I mopped the floor.

After that, I lay on the living room sofa for a while, just staring up at the ceiling, fixing my eye on the peephole I looked down from when I was in my room. All my thoughts, all the time, were singed with thoughts about Angel, so the peephole led to memories of looking down at Angel. I remembered looking through one time and seeing her hand, nails painted black, holding her swim bag. Her fingers were long and slim, and she had prominent, round bones on the outside of her wrists. And then I thought about Christine, and how I wanted her to be with us, and how I used to only feel comfortable with Angel and my little sisters but now I also felt comfortable with Christine. *But what is comfortable, if you are me?* I thought. I hadn't been outside for quite a while, maybe a week, and at the moment I felt totally fine with never going outside again. My eyes leaked tears all the time, although I didn't have the sensation of crying.

I wonder if I'm actually crazy, I thought. *I would like to go to sleep. There aren't many pills left. Maybe there are more pills. Maybe Frank made a mistake and forgot some.* So I got up off the sofa and went to the loose floorboard, and pulled it up.

No pills.

But there were Angel's boots—the motorcycle boots, the ones she'd worn on New Year's Eve. I took them out and put them way in the back of our closet and lay on my bed, deep in the covers.

chapter eleven

———

ALEX

Right before Valentine's Day, the weather broke. The temperature had barely been above freezing since Thanksgiving, and there was over a foot of snow on the ground. All of a sudden, it was forty-five, then sixty. Water was running everywhere, in the gutters and down the sides of houses. People acted like it was spring, guys outside in T-shirts and girls in skirts with no tights or stockings.

Dogs were happy too, because instead of the quick walk around the block in the frigid wind, their owners were taking them to the park.

One of those dogs, off the leash and running happily ahead of his owner, found Angel.

CJ tried to keep the details from us, but it was all over the TV.

Curtis Dixon, the dog's owner, said that he'd been walking on a trail bordering a creek in Fairmount Park. At one point, the creek bank widened considerably, allowing for picnic tables and a grassy play area. His let his dog off the leash and threw a stick for him. The grassy area blended into a marshy overgrown bog. His dog ran in there and was barking wildly. The dog wouldn't come when his owner called him, so finally the guy went tromping off the path and into the mushy snow to where the dog was rooting and barking.

Sticking out from a pile of frozen leaves and trash, covered by a large sheet of old kitchen linoleum, was a hand, a left hand, with bright blue polish on the nails.

When the police came and cleared the debris, she was lying on her back. She had been shot five times, all in the face and neck. They knew she had been holding her right hand up to her face to protect herself, palm facing out, because it was shattered and blown apart from the bullets.

She was fully dressed in the clothes that she had worn New Year's Eve, all black, the leather pants and jacket. But she was barefoot.

ONE time my mother told me that there were certain days in her life that were markers, like BC and AD. Before her brother got killed in Vietnam, and after. Before my father left, and after.

Now I understood that. There was before Angel died, and after.

I had heard about the stages of grief. I was having all of them at once. It made me sick to say, but in some ways there was relief. The weeks of wondering and anxiety were over. But at the same moment there was disbelief, and not just the typical oh-what-a-shock type. I found myself thinking stuff like—*Wow, wait until I get with Angel about this*—*this is like the craziest, most infuriating thing she's ever done* . . . and then I'd snap out of it, so disoriented.

I tried not to, but I kept thinking about what she'd

seen and felt. Was she awake for a second, a minute, longer, after the bullets hit her? Was she lying alone in the snow, under the leaves, knowing she was going to die there?

And did she have a chance, just a moment, when she could have changed things—run, screamed, fought back, begged, or pleaded—and she blew it?

The questions came and went like boomerangs.

CJ made us swim. He didn't try to explain anything to us. The first night, after they found her, we slept at the pool. Or didn't sleep. We swam until we couldn't cry, couldn't talk, could barely walk. We climbed into our sleeping bags and escaped. I think our parents were grateful to him because they truly didn't know how to help us.

But as usual, CJ was busy doing things. He protected us from the press, who were coming after us like we were in the ranks of Mark Spitz and Janet Evans. He made it clear we were not to speak to them, and he made it even more clear to them that they were to stay away from us. He reminded the detectives that they should take another look at Valentine Russo. Now that there was a crime, they did search his apartment, but they found nothing linking him to Angel.

"Why isn't it at a church?" I asked my mother and CJ when we were told about the funeral arrangements.

"Did you ever know her to go to church?" CJ said. "That crazy mother of hers, she never took those girls to church."

My mother and I stayed quiet. We never went to church either. Then she said to CJ, "I don't understand how this happened. How did she fall through the cracks? What didn't we do?"

The swim team parents were going to provide the food for the repast, a word I never heard until CJ started talking to them about it. It was going to be at Angel's house, because Pic wanted it to be there. The mothers got together and came up with a menu and divided up the dishes to be cooked.

"That's disgusting," I said to my mother. "It's like a party or something. Why would we do that, get together and eat? It's gross."

"That's what you do, Alex," my mother explained in her trying-to-be-patient voice. "The whole thing is set up to help people move on."

I realized that was the problem. I didn't want to move on.

CJ had some very firm ideas about how the team should behave at the funeral. We all had to enter together. We all had to wear the same thing, our team polo shirts with the team insignia, and black pants. No skirts. He began to say something about how *some people* would wear an inappropriate skirt, and then caught himself, because of course he meant Angel.

It was a lucky coincidence that Angel's uncle Tony was a mortician, because Pic had no money for the funeral costs. My mother said a funeral could cost ten thousand dollars.

Her uncle's funeral parlor was in the suburbs north of the city. It was weird to say good-bye to Angel in a place that I never knew Angel to be. It seemed like all this should be happening at the pool.

Melanie helped me around that one. She said that Angel

was with us everywhere, and always would be, wherever we all ended up. Melanie went to church.

We had to line the sides of the aisle to the front of the big viewing room, standing, so that when people made their way down the aisles to the coffin we would be a presence, like an honor guard. People were very quiet as they walked in single file past us, taking tissues from the boxes we offered. I knew a lot of them—parents of former swimmers, our teachers, and other kids from our school. Most of them walked by without looking up, but once in a while someone would make eye contact and for some reason that made me cry.

Our own parents hovered nearby, their worry now not about Angel but about us.

My mother told me that Christine told her Pic wanted an open casket, but they couldn't fix Angel enough; the bullets had torn apart her face, and then she had been outside for so long. The casket had to be closed. Pic had arranged pictures on top of the casket, and she'd created a display of Angel's medals and trophies between some flowers nearby.

Pic was sitting with Jeannine right in front of the casket. There were some other people sitting there too, and I figured out that they were Pic's brothers. One was very red-eyed and occasionally held his head in his hands; a slim blonde with a big diamond rubbed his shoulder. I knew it was Jimmy and the hated wife Angel had told me about. Angel would not have wanted her there.

I tried to talk to Jeannine but Pic butted in and then there were people behind me and I had to move on. I wasn't even sure that Jeannine realized I was there. She looked like a mannequin, waxy, posed, and still.

I had a hard time associating the shiny pink-gold casket with Angel. I couldn't believe she was actually in there, and that later that day they were going to put it in the ground and she would be trapped in there forever. I felt like I was choking. In a way it was better to be outside, lying under the linoleum. I knew if it was me, I would want to be cremated and my ashes thrown somewhere, free.

chapter twelve

_____

JEANNINE

My mother bought me a dress for the funeral, a black dress with sleeves that hung almost to my fingertips. And she bought me black patent leather shoes with a small heel, and black tights. I was floating in the dress. I was pale, I was bony, I looked like a corpse.

I wanted to be the corpse.

Pic argued with Uncle Tony before the funeral. She wanted the casket to be open. But he said the damage to the body was too great, that he couldn't make Angel look good enough for the casket to be open. Pic was angry, very angry.

When we got to the funeral home, Uncle Tony's funeral home, there were a lot of reporters. Pic wanted to talk to them but she didn't want me out of her sight. She let Joy and Kathleen stay with Christine, but she wanted me right beside her. One lady asked her how the family was doing, and Pic responded that we were all praying together, and she pulled me close. Someone else asked her if she had any ideas about what might have happened, and she said that it was very hard to be a mother of a headstrong girl. Very, very hard.

I saw the detectives outside with the reporters. They were watching everything.

Uncle Tony sat us down in some folding chairs close to the casket. Pic put some pictures of Angel on top of the casket. She had brought some of Angel's trophies in a box and she put them on the floor, in between the flower arrangements.

Lots of people who I didn't know came by where we were sitting and said how sorry they were. Pic spoke quietly to all of them, mostly composed, but crying a little when other people were crying. Christine was trying to control Kathleen, who was wailing and sobbing. She finally left with her to go to some other room. Joy wandered around, touching the flowers and sucking on her fingers, until Frank came and picked her up and carried her around.

Out of the corner of my eye I saw a stooped old man in a shabby suit quietly crossing the back of the room. Uncle Tony shook his hand. It was Pop. I wanted to get up and go to him but I knew Pic would pull me back, and if she saw him, her mood could quickly shift.

I thought I should talk to Christine, tell her about the boots. I knew what it meant—that at some point, Angel came home. Or that someone took the boots off of her and brought them home. I needed to tell her, or tell the detectives, or tell Alex and Claire. I wasn't going to tell Pic. Ever since the police came to the house to tell us about the body, she had been different, cool and clear and glued to me, not letting me out of her sight, when my whole life until now she'd barely known I was there.

The swim team and a lot of their parents and CJ all came in together. The swimmers all had on their parkas and uniform shirts, a blur of purple and gold. They gathered around my mother and me. A lot of people were talking to Pic but I couldn't concentrate on everything that was being said. I don't think anyone was talking to me, but my mother had her hand gripped on my leg. Alex pushed up to me and stooped down so she was on eye level with me as I sat in my chair. She hugged me and asked how I was doing.

"Her sister's dead. How do you think she's doing?" my mother responded.

When they moved away Pic said that there was something the matter with that girl, the one who hadn't told about the letters, and I should stay away from her.

No one came who looked like the picture I had seen of Angel's father.

People stopped and touched the casket and looked at the pictures. I felt pretty sure that Angel wasn't in the casket. I didn't ever see the body. Pic told me that Angel was dead, and I never believed anything Pic said.

SOME people were coming back to our house after the cemetery. Some of the swim team mothers went straight to our house from the funeral home to set up food. They took some of the flowers with them, and the pictures of Angel. Christine took Kathleen and her kids to her house. She didn't think they should go to the cemetery—Kathleen was hysterical already. Joy stayed with Frank.

I rode back to our house with my mother in Uncle Tony's funeral car. One of his men drove it. We sat in the back, like it was a limousine. Pic was dressed all in black, with this lacy shawl over her head. Some of the time she looked out the window, and some of the time she looked at me.

Finally she said, "You found a pair of boots, huh, Jeannine?"

I felt the breath pop out of me.

"It's okay," she said. "You can tell me. Where Frank kept his stash, right? I found them before you. You know what it means, right?"

I shook my head.

"Come on Jeannine," she pushed. "What does it mean? You're not as dumb as you act."

"Angel came home and took her boots off," I whispered.

Pic sighed at my stupidity. "Frank killed her, Jeannine. He killed her. He hid the stuff there."

"Did you tell the police?"

"No, those idiots. His whore says he was with her and they believe her."

"Shouldn't we tell them?"

"No, *we* shouldn't do anything. I'll tell them when I'm good and ready. There's a few things I have to take care of first," she said, nodding at me like she was telling me a big secret. "You just keep your mouth shut. Got it?"

I nodded. "You let him take Joy."

"What does Joy have to with it?" she asked, irritated. "And where did you put the boots, Jeannine?"

"In our closet."

"Why?"

"So Angel would have them."

She gave me an incredulous look. When we got to the house, she pulled at my arm on the front steps and said, "Remember what I told you."

OUR house was full of people. It was so strange. No one ever came to our house before Angel disappeared. Now it looked like a house in a TV commercial, flowers everywhere, spic-and-span, people walking around with plates of food.

They had rearranged the furniture to set up a food table, and I realized for the first time that the small space between the living room and the kitchen was supposed to be a dining room. We just used it like part of the living room, a passageway to the kitchen.

There were heaping bowls and platters of food, lots of different smells, and it immediately made me feel sick. I wanted to go upstairs and try to throw up, or make myself throw up, but people I didn't know were going up and down the stairs to the bathroom.

Pic pulled me to the sofa and people got up to let us sit down. The pictures that had been at the funeral home were now set up on the table near the sofa, in front of us. One picture of Angel as a baby. The graduation picture with the cap and gown where she had a wig on. I wondered if they would still put it in the yearbook. Her team picture, muscles bulging, standing tall and cocky in her team suit. The picture that had been in the paper. The table was all beat up, but someone had put a tablecloth on it.

People were eating and talking, but very quietly. Alex gave me a little wave from some folding chairs across the room. She and some of the swim team girls were looking at picture albums someone had brought.

Someone asked Pic if she wanted a plate of food or a glass of wine.

"I'll take the wine," she said.

People were still coming and CJ was standing by the door, answering it. At some point I realized that Frank had come in, because Joy climbed up on the sofa next to me and curled up in a ball. She was ready to fall asleep, I could tell. I looked for Frank and saw that he was in the kitchen, leaning against the counter, eating a plate of food and talking to one of our neighbors. I touched Pic's arm and leaned to whisper to her, but she silenced me by pulling away. I wondered if she had a plan to kill him.

Someone brought her a fresh glass of wine.

I was furious that Frank was there. I couldn't take my eyes off him, watching him load his plate a second time and talk to people like we were at a block party. A steady stream of people came and spoke to Pic, but I didn't hear words. The noise in my head drowned them out.

At some point Pic pulled me up from the sofa and we went upstairs to the bathroom together. We had to wait outside the door because someone was in there. She was holding her wineglass.

Of course you have to pee, I thought. *You just drank about five glasses of wine.*

When we came back down the steps, Christine was just coming in the door with Kathleen and her kids. CJ was taking their coats. My mother pulled me toward them and out of the corner of my eye I saw Frank moving toward Kathleen. We all stopped in front of them.

I turned to Frank. "You shouldn't be here," I said to him.

He looked shocked that I had spoken, but barely missed a beat. "It's my house," he said.

"You killed Angel," I said.

My mother started and pulled my shoulder. "Shut up, Jeannine."

Frank started to respond but CJ moved in quickly to calm things down.

"Come on, honey," he said, trying to lead me away.

"We found her boots," I said.

"I don't have to listen to this shit," Frank said, and started for the door.

Kathleen looked at Pic and said, "You shot the gun. You shot in the ceiling."

"Are you all crazy?" Pic shrieked. "These kids are crazy!"

Kathleen started crying and yelled, "I'm not crazy! I saw you through Jeannine's peephole. You were hollering at Angel and you shot the gun!"

"Come over here," Pic said, grabbing Kathleen by the arm.

Kathleen pulled away, screaming at the top of her lungs, "You shot the ceiling. Angel said you could kill us. Angel said go outside, let's go outside."

CJ picked up Kathleen and headed for the door. Both Pic and Frank moved toward him. Kathleen was screaming, "Get away from me, don't touch me, don't touch me."

CJ carried her outside, right to the detectives.

chapter thirteen

———

ALEX

All of a sudden it was the middle of March—three weeks out from our short course championships, and time to taper. An important meet every year, it was super important this year for me, for Melanie, and for a bunch of other seniors who hadn't yet signed. It was our last chance to show our stuff to college coaches who were watching us, shopping around to complete their rosters and spend the rest of their scholarship dollars. It would have been an important meet for Angel, too, and that's what made it so hard to get motivated. Her death made us confused. What difference did anything make if you were just going to die anyway?

CJ and some of the parents said stuff that was supposed to help us accept what had happened—that Angel was so special that God had wanted her early, that for some reason we couldn't know He needed her in heaven early, that we had to have faith in His judgment even if we couldn't understand it just now. I listened to CJ saying those things with his eyes flat, his whole face grim, and I wasn't sure even he believed them.

I couldn't. I had become convinced of something I had

never thought about before: that things just happen, for no reason at all.

CJ spent a lot of time trundling up and down the deck, tapping his club, stopping to consult his workout book, muttering about our taper. Every once in a while he'd explode.

"You have to taper *off* of something!" he'd say. "You can't taper when you haven't done the yardage in the first place!"

True. In a typical season we'd have been swimming eleven or even twelve grueling sessions a week by early March; we would have been close to 80,000 yards a week. We would have had a real high to come down from, to taper off of.

But not this year. Angel's disappearance had kept most of us out of the pool, first copying flyers and posters at Kinko's to hand out all over the city and put in all the rec centers and supermarkets and libraries, and then, worse, those freezing cold days stomping over packed snow looking for her in windowless abandoned houses and lots strewn with old refrigerators and tires along the route she would have taken home.

I was one of the only ones who had actually trained more, and harder.

CJ revised his strategy. He decided to start our taper later, and not to bring us down as far as he otherwise would, not down the last week to four and then three and even to two thousand yards a day. Instead he devised workouts where we focused on speed, dividing us up into groups to swim sprint relays against each other or pitting the slowest male freestyler against the fastest female, splitting us up boys vs. girls on either side of the pool, trying to get us psyched.

Some days it worked better than others. Some days we forgot about Angel for a minute or two—forgot that she was dead, killed by her own mother. I kept returning to Pic shooting her in the face. How could you look at your own child and shoot her in the face? I looked at my mother and tried to imagine it.

When she finally confessed, Pic blamed it on Angel. Angel came home in the middle of the night, her cocky self, straight out of Jamal's bed and telling Pic exactly that when Pic asked her where the hell she'd been. She took off her boots and headed for the stairs, smelling of sex. Pic had watched Frank slip away with a girl, and here was her daughter, flaunting her sexiness. When Pic started to lose it about Frank and the girl, Angel retorted that if she wasn't a whining loser maybe she could keep her man. That's when Pic pulled the gun, which she had taken with her when she went to meet her friend at an after-hours club, and, in a rage, shot it into the living room ceiling. Then Angel coaxed her outside.

But somehow they ended up in the park, and somehow Angel let Pic lead her far from the road, and somehow Pic shot her.

Pic retracted her confession. She said she couldn't remember that part of the night.

MIDDLE Atlantic Short Course Senior Championships were held that year at a new pool in New Jersey, part of a suburban county's community college, about a half hour over the bridge from Philly. Instead of booking a hotel for the team, we commuted. In a regular year we would have been unhappy about that, but this year it was okay. We weren't much in the mood for partying and most of us just wanted to be home at night, in our own, familiar beds, not troubled by memories of other meets and other hotels when Angel was with us, leading us into forbidden adventures.

In most ways, the meet was like all other regional championships: large, tense, and fast. The powerhouse teams in our district were there with their giant rosters and expensive matching Speedo everything: suits, caps, warm-ups, towels, bags, T-shirts, even goggles. They came on their luxurious chartered buses with their team trainers and their massage tables and were staying near the pool in real nice hotels.

On the other end there were the small teams that had one or two very fast swimmers who they built their relays around. There were also a few stars at the meet, swimmers who were already out of college and back swimming with their home teams, staying in shape until Olympic Trials rolled around again, and emerging stars, like Jamal—the best high school swimmers in our district, swimmers who already had Senior cuts and would be looking to qualify for Olympic Trials in the coming year.

The big teams had huge, glossy banners with their team logos that they hung up behind their bleacher area. We had our Angel banner that we'd been swimming under for the past two months.

When we started looking for Angel and were copying all those flyers and making all those posters, CJ took one of the pictures and had a banner made. It was our best picture of Angel, the truest likeness, taken on the side of a pool as she jumped in the air wearing her team suit, cheering one of us on, her arms flung high, biceps bulging, spiky hair wet from her own race, her smile wide and warm, her

whole being totally absorbed in this moment of triumph. In
a powerful font under her picture, CJ had printed "Sports-
Stars, Team of Champions."

In another time we would have groaned and scoffed that
the motto was pretentious and dorky and embarrassing. But
we put the banner on the dirty concrete wall at the Nest
and tried to make it our inspiration. And when we got to
the meet, we hoisted the banner above our team section.

On the first day of the meet I was entered in three
events: the 200 free, the 100 fly, and the 200 individual
medley. Since I wasn't that fast in anything, CJ always entered me in everything I had qualified for, usually eight
individual events total. He hoped I'd make finals in something. It was hard to know how well I was swimming,
since our training and our taper had been so off. One thing
we could tell from my meets all year, though, was that my
middle-distance events were coming around, while my
sprints were flat. Who knew why—maybe, finally, the
years of training were kicking in, maybe the couple pounds
I'd lost in the past few months were making the difference,
maybe my recent hard swimming had actually helped. In
any case, I had a tiny bit of hope for my 200 free.

I was seeded in the tenth of twelve heats, not bad, and
although I wasn't right in the center of the pool, in Lane 6
I wasn't on the outside, either. When we got up to the
blocks, I saw that Lane 4 was empty. A very lucky break.
The fastest girl in the heat had scratched—one fewer for
me to have to beat to be in the top eight, and thus in the
championship heat of the three heats swum at night. Although I had often swum in the consolation and bonus
heats, I had never made it to the championship heat in a
championship meet.

Instead of his usual fierce pep talk, CJ just gave me a hug when I left the bleachers for the blocks.

Jamal walked up with me. "I'll swim this fast if you swim fast," he joked, although that was a big promise from him, because Jamal hated every event longer than 100 yards. CJ always put him in the 200 free anyway because Jamal was so fast that he could finish fifth or sixth and score points for the team without really trying.

I stood in the line at my block, watching the heat before me swim. I wasn't nervous. In another time I would have been standing at the block with my mind racing, trying to remember all the things I knew about how I should swim the 200 free, all the race strategy CJ had drummed into me, all the swim talk I'd had with my teammates about how they attacked the 200 free, whether they tried to build speed throughout the race or took it out in the first fifty and tried to stay ahead, or "negative split" it, swimming the second half faster than the first.

But I was thinking about nothing as my heat climbed the blocks and dove in. I felt the same way I'd felt every moment since February 14 when I wasn't crying—dazed, distanced from my feelings, like I was a cool observer watching a girl trying to cope with the unthinkable.

And by the 150 of my 200 free, I knew I was watching a girl have a very good swim. At the 100 yard turn I had passed the girl next to me in Lane 5, who had gone into the race with an entry time a second faster than mine. She was at a disadvantage, because the fastest girl in the race, the missing girl from Lane 4, would have been the one to beat, the one to pace against. The girl in Lane 5 was now in that position, and probably wasn't used to being there, and it was playing with her head. I, however, had nothing to lose.

I felt the endorphin rush as I made my last turn, my head peaceful, the world dropping away, my rhythm automatic, the pain in my legs numbing, and got a surge of energy near the end that I had so rarely experienced before. I finished first, with a three second drop in my time—from 1:58 to 1:55. That time changed me from a girl with a decent 200 free to a girl with very good 200 free, a girl only a second and a half away from a Junior National cut.

It was the first time I had felt anything like happy in what seemed like forever.

Then came the slow monitoring of the last two heats, the quick counting as the times flashed to see who had beaten me and who hadn't, to see whether I'd make it into the top 8.

In the end I was seventh.

"Williams!" CJ smiled. "Way to start the meet! You'll scratch the IM," he said—wisely, since I was seeded way low and had no chance of making finals.

"How about the fly?" I asked hopefully.

He shook his head. "You'll swim the fly. Go warm down."

Since we weren't staying in a hotel, CJ had made arrangements for us to rest in our sleeping bags in a gym on the campus in between trials and finals. At first I wasn't sleepy, but I was tight. I moved my sleeping bag over near Wrench and needled him into rubbing my back and neck. At some point I dozed off for a while. Later, my mother brought me a bagel and a banana, and I drank a bottle of Gatorade.

After the warm-up for finals, the pool was cleared and we stood on the deck for the singing of the national anthem. One of the officials sang it—pretty well, too. Typically the first event, a relay, would take off immediately after that, but instead, the meet director came on the mic and announced, "We'd like to observe a moment of silence for Angel Ferente, a SportsStars swimmer who recently passed away. Angel competed in the Middle Atlantic region for seven years and was headed for a Division I scholarship. We'll miss her."

The natatorium was immediately silent. Everyone who had competed at this level knew Angel; everyone in the swimming community knew she had been missing, many parents and coaches and officials had helped to look for her, had donated money, had called CJ because they didn't know what else to do. I looked up to the stands, searching for Jeannine, who was sitting with my mother. Her face was the mask of sorrow it had been since Valentine's Day.

Those days, I was always on the verge of tears. It didn't take much for me to start, so by thirty seconds into the minute of silence the tears were spilling down my face. When sixty seconds passed and the first heat of the relay was called, I bolted for the locker room.

Even from the stands my mother could read my frame of mind. She followed me.

She sat me down on a bench in the warm, wet air of the locker room. I was hiding inside my roomy, flannel-lined warm-up, the hood pulled out as far as possible so I could see little and no one could see me. She pulled the hood back. She looked directly into my eyes, my eyes sad, her eyes sad, the way our eyes had been since Valentine's Day.

"The only way for this to make sense is for you to make it make sense," she said.

I stared back, dumb.

She tried again. "The only way anything makes sense is for you to give it meaning."

I knew where we were going, but I didn't feel strong enough to scramble around for a purpose, something that would make me want to swim fast, even faster than I had in the morning. College didn't seem very interesting anymore; nor did the Division I scholarship I'd been fantasizing about for so many years. When I thought about college I thought about Angel and me going to Rutgers together, rooming together, getting up in the dark before dawn and stumbling out to morning practice together.

"Swim this meet for Angel," she said. "Make the banner come to life."

One of the glories that comes with being in the championship final heat is that you and the other seven finalists parade out to the blocks, accompanied by music that you have all chosen, and once you are standing behind the blocks, the announcer reads a short biography that you submit in the morning after making the night swim.

I ran up to the speaker's stand and asked if I could change my bio. The father volunteering behind the mic sighed, but handed it back to me. I made my changes and scurried to the ready room, where we were lining up to parade out to the blocks. I hadn't been there early enough to help choose the music, but it was good enough: "We Are the Champions," by Queen. We marched out, me in my SportsStars warm-up jacket and my team and our parents cheering loudly for me, shaking the cow bells and rattles we brought to every meet. As we rounded the turn for the blocks I could hear CJ's low booming voice saying, "Williiiaaams . . ."

We stood behind the blocks, stripping out of our warmups, shaking ourselves loose, stretching. The stands quieted as the bios were read ". . . a senior at Council Rock High

School . . . a participant in last season's Junior Nationals in this event . . . headed for Syracuse University . . ." And then it was time for me. "In Lane Seven, Alex Williamson, a senior at Kennedy Academic High School. Alex dedicates this race to her teammate, Angel Ferente." First there was a hush, and then a huge cheer from our section, and then everyone in the natatorium stood and clapped. I felt sorry for the girl in Lane 8, whose bio was barely heard.

My swim that night set the tone for the meet for us. I dropped two more seconds, swimming 1:53:11, and just qualifying for Juniors. I was third in the event and scored 16 points for the team. What I knew about how to swim had become intuitive; in some mysterious way, what my mind knew about how to swim had shifted from thought to impulse. I just got in and did it. I'd heard CJ and other coaches talk about "muscle memory"—that when it came time to swim the race, everything you had learned from thousands of hours of practice needed to kick in, you couldn't possibly think through the race in the under two minutes you had to swim it. All that strategy and planning and the endless repeated practice of small things like not turning your head too far to breathe or holding your hand at a slightly different angle so it would pull more water— all those things needed to become automatic. Suddenly, in a moment of epiphany, I understood, as if I had been blessed with a revelation.

Race by race, over the next three days, we swam better than we ever had before—consistent, fast, surprising. Everyone on our team wanted the opportunity to get up in a final and hear that bio: Jamal Joyner, Kim Simmons, Aisha Green, Melanie Johnson dedicates this race to her teammate, Angel Ferente.

On Sunday night, the score of the meet was so close that the winner was going to be determined by the final relay, the boys' 400-yard freestyle, a winner-take-all event. You only scored points for first place.

Sometimes when one team is so far ahead that the results of the relay don't matter, the pool empties out on a Sunday night after a long meet. But not that night. The stands were packed.

"I'd never say it to them," Melanie whispered to me, nodding at our guys, "but better that it's them and not us."

I nodded. She was so right. Our boys had a much better chance of winning than our girls would have, without Angel. Our boys freestyle relay team was made up of Wrench, Damon, Tyree, and Jamal as anchor. They were very fast, but they had strong competition from several other teams, and not just the ones who could also win the meet. There were several that were in this relay to make a Senior cut, even if they couldn't win the meet.

As he often did, CJ had entered the boys with a very fast time so they had a center lane. The rest of us lined up along the side of the pool, getting ready to watch and cheer, while the relay teams assembled behind the blocks. I watched our boys saunter up; God forbid they should look nervous and uncool. They were laughing and joking, as always. CJ quickly followed them and said something we couldn't hear that sobered them right up.

CJ's strategy in a 400 free relay was always to "frontload" it—put two fast swimmers in the race to get a lead, giving the third, slowest swimmer calm water and preventing him from having to "swim in traffic." Then put the fastest swimmer at the end. Wrench led off for us, followed by Tyree. Our third swimmer, Damon, although fast

enough to have a Junior cut, wasn't as fast as some from
other teams, so by the anchor leg, Jamal dove almost simultaneously with three other guys. He looked beautiful in
the water, dark, dark brown against the sparkling blue water, his heavily muscled arms rising and falling in a way
that seemed effortless, looking unhurried but so very fast
at the same time. He went into the last turn at least a body
length ahead and came out more than that, all the lower-
body work he'd been doing giving him tremendous propul-
sion off the wall. The cheering of the other teams began to
subside as they realized that their chances were dying, and
our cheering swelled as we realized that we were going to
win not just the race but also the meet.

Jamal touched two body lengths before the next swimmer; the relay had beaten their own best time, a Senior National time to begin with, and had won the meet—the first
time ever that SportsStars had won a championship.

Our boys who weren't already in the pool grabbed CJ
and, whooping, pushed him into the water and then can-
nonballed in themselves. The girls followed, shrieking and
laughing. I held on to Melanie's hand and we jumped high
off the side, creating a huge splash. Purple and gold caps
popped up and down all around me. And then through the
sprays of water, in the rainbows created by the bright
lights overhead, I saw Angel, bouncing up and down with
us, her arms waving, smiling wide, joyful, cheering. I
moved toward her, then got pulled under by someone. I
bobbed to the surface and twirled left and right, looking
for her in the frenzy of bodies.

But I'd lost her. She was gone.

chapter fourteen

———

JEANNINE

I t didn't take long for Pic to confess. She seemed to think that people would understand that Angel was impossible, that Frank was impossible, that I was impossible, that Kathleen was impossible, that her life was impossible, and that she was a victim driven by a lifetime of loss and disappointment and an alcohol-fueled fury. When they didn't, she retracted the confession, and pled not guilty.

No one who knew her well doubted the first version.

There was in fact a bullet lodged between the wall and the metal of my peephole. Kathleen had been awake when I was sleeping, self-medicated. At the end of a long chain of carelessness and neglect, I had left her vulnerable.

But no one could account for what happened after that bullet was fired and Pic and Angel left the house. Why did Angel get into the car? Why did she march way off the road, in bare feet on a freezing night, into a deserted part of the park? Was Pic stable enough that she could actually overcome Angel with the threat of the gun? How had Pic, weak and woozy, managed to cover Angel's body with leaves and sticks and a huge sheet of linoleum?

The gun was never found, but the bullet in our house matched those that killed Angel. Pic stuck to her claim that she remembered nothing, and the jury returned a verdict of manslaughter, twelve to twenty years.

I torment myself wondering what would have happened had I been awake. Would I have done anything? Would I have had the courage to race down the steps and shock Pic so she came to her senses? What would have happened if Angel had come home earlier and climbed into bed with us, just like other nights? Where would we be if everything had just gone on? Would she have gone to college? Would I have made it through high school? Would Kathleen have turned into a version of Pic? My therapist cautions me about the futility and destructiveness of the what-ifs.

After Pic was arrested, Frank tried for a minute to get custody of Kathleen and Joy. Later on, Alex said he wanted them because he could get cash welfare and food stamps by having them. That's what her mother told her.

Kathleen insisted that she wanted to live with Christine. The judge looked at Frank's criminal record, his work history, his parenting history, and then at Christine, and the choice was obvious. My aunt was willing to take me too.

I loved my sisters and my aunt, but I couldn't fathom living with Uncle Tony and two boy cousins in the suburbs. Angel wasn't there to speak for me, so I had to speak for myself. I asked Claire if I could live with her. I preferred a household that would include just Claire and me— the quiet home of an English teacher who loved books, with Alex close by in her dorm at LaSalle.

Claire got me into Kennedy as a sophomore. No one wanted to turn down the girl whose mother killed her sister. During that first year, I wasn't able to make it to school every day, and then I had to take months off for inpatient treatment for what was diagnosed as anorexia. But little by little, with medication and therapy and support from Claire and Alex, and CJ and Christine, I began to respond, to eat, to talk, to emerge.

I know that I will never see my mother again. I think about what Angel would think about that, and I know she wouldn't do the same. She would, without thinking, be compassionate and, as she did so many times, make an overture toward reconciliation. But that would be sacrificing myself, the bit of sanity and peace I've got, and I won't do it. I do not forgive her for taking my sister from me, for robbing my sister of the life she should have had. I'll also urge Kathleen not to reconnect with her. Kathleen already refuses to visit her in prison, or see Frank, and the court has allowed it. She is healing, but like me, she'll spend her life trying to make sense of what happened that night.

I go to Penn now. I'm majoring in physics, with a minor in art history. I still live at home with Claire; a dorm, dining halls, and noisy, partying students would not be possible for me. I look forward, not too many years from now, to long, silent nights in a lab or a mountaintop observatory.

Every single thing that had been in mine and Angel's room ended up with me in my new room at Claire's—all of Angel's clothes, her suits and towels, her medals and ribbons, her jewelry, her hair brush, her many pairs of shoes. I set up a large dresser that holds it all, the medals and trophies displayed on top, with pictures and news clippings. Alex asked me if it was a little weird, like a shrine. So? I answered. From time to time I pull out a sweatshirt and sleep in it, run her jewelry through my fingers, feel the hair in her brush.

She is my watermark, hovering sometimes on the surface, sometimes just below, indelible, always with me.

acknowledgments

Thanks so much to friends and family who have encouraged me and provided feedback on this manuscript. I also want to thank the staff at SparkPress and SparkPoint Studio for helping me to understand how much I didn't know about how to publish and market a book. What an education!

About the Author

Photo credit: Jermaine Parker

ELISE SCHILLER has been writing fiction, memoir, and nonfiction and actively participating in writing groups since adolescence. She has published several short stories and a number of articles and essays. In August of 2019, SparkPress published her memoir, *Even If Your Heart Would Listen: Losing My Daughter to Heroin.* She is now working on the second book of her Broken Bell series. Schiller also blogs about the opioid epidemic, books, and family history on her website.

After a thirty-year career in education and family services in Philadelphia, Schiller retired in 2015 to write full time. She is an active volunteer and served on the Philadelphia Mayor's Task Force to Combat the Opioid Epidemic. She currently serves on the advisory board of the Philadelphia Department of Behavioral Health and disAbility Services and is an active member of the Friends of Safehouse.

When not writing, reading, or volunteering, Schiller enjoys visiting museums and historical sites, often with one of her seven grandchildren or various nieces and nephews in tow.

SELECTED TITLES FROM SPARKPRESS

SparkPress is an independent boutique publisher delivering high-quality, entertaining, and engaging content that enhances readers' lives, with a special focus on female-driven work.
www.gosparkpress.com

Child Bride: A Novel, Jennifer Smith Turner, $16.95, 978-1-68463-038-7. The coming-of-age journey of a young girl from the South who joins the African American great migration to the North—and finds her way through challenges and unforeseen obstacles to womanhood.

Enemy Queen: A Novel, Robert Steven Goldstein, $16.95, 978-1-68463-026-4. A woman initiates passionate sexual encounters with two articulate but bumbling and crass middle-aged men, but what she demands in return soon becomes untenable. A short time later she goes missing, prompting the county sheriff to open a murder investigation.

Firewall: A Novel, Eugenia Lovett West. $16.95, 978-1-68463-010-3. When Emma Streat's rich, socialite godmother is threatened with blackmail, Emma becomes immersed in the dark world of cybercrime—and mounting dangers take her to exclusive places in Europe and contacts with the elite in financial and art collecting circles. Through passion and heartbreak, Emma must fight to save herself and bring a vicious criminal to justice.

Seventh Flag: A Novel, Sid Balman, Jr. $16.95, 978-1-68463-014-1. A sweeping work of historical fiction, *Seventh Flag* is a Micheneresque parable that traces the arc of radicalization in modern Western Civilization—reaffirming what it means to be an American in a dangerously divided nation.